Tales From Grimlock Cove

Volume 1

Oscar Whiting

Whiting Publishing LLC

Edited by Brett Savoy.

Cover design by Coverkitchen.

Copyright © 2023 by Whiting Publishing LLC

All rights reserved.

No part of this book may be reproduced in any form or by any electronic or mechanical means, including information storage and retrieval systems, without written permission from the author, except for the use of brief quotations in a book review.

This is a work of fiction. Unless otherwise indicated, all the names, characters, businesses, places, events and incidents in this book are either the product of the author's imagination or used in a fictitious manner. Any resemblance to actual persons, living or dead, or actual events is purely coincidental.

To Kara, who supports as generously as she loves.

To my mother, who taught me to question the norm and peer into the unknown.

To Marty and Lilly, who know nothing about books but everything about companionship.

In loving memory of my father, who framed my first poem and convinced a quiet child he was worth hearing.

Contents

1. The Sacrifice at St. Julian's	1
2. The Red-Eye to Nowhere	22
3. The Stranger In My Phone	40
4. The Forgotten Fairgrounds	60
5. The Many-Eyed Motel	85
6. The Touch of Broken Glass	104
7. The Investigation at St. Julian's	122
8. The Halloween Miracle	141
9. The Provenance (part one)	154
10. The Provenance (part two)	177
11. The Wolves and the Sheep (part one)	200
12. The Wolves and the Sheep (part two)	227

The Sacrifice at St. Julian's

Grimlock Cove, 1887

———

The moon hung heavy over St. Julian's Catholic Church. Blustery October winds ripped dying leaves from nearby trees and rattled the windows. In the church's attic, Renata Cordero and her daughter, Bella, lie tucked in their straw beds. Renata's bed was situated at one side of the attic by the stairs, while Bella's was pushed against the far wall opposite Renata's. It had been hours since the two had settled in, but Bella did not sleep. As a girl of twelve years, Bella hardly considered herself a child, and yet she lie awake afraid. It wasn't the autumn winds or the ghostly moans of an old church that concerned her. It was the voice calling her name from the shadows.

"Bella?"

Thinking it might be her mother, Bella brushed thick curls of auburn hair from her face and looked to Mother's side of the room. A shaft of moonlight came through the circular attic window, pushing back against the darkness that otherwise filled the room. Mother's bed lay hidden from the moonlight—where the darkness gathered.

"Bella?" the voice came again.

This time Bella heard it more clearly. It was feminine, but this was not her mother's voice. Though it's tone had been kind, a stranger's voice is still a stranger's voice. Glancing around, she saw no one, and the voice called again. Bella retreated beneath her blanket, lifting the edge just enough to peek out. She looked to the dark corner where her mother slept but saw only a wall of shadows. Bella thought to call for her mother, but Mother hated to be woken up, and her temper left bruises, so Bella remained as still and quiet as the dead. It was peculiar, though. Bella held that a moth beating its wings could wake Mother, so if Mother could sleep through the sound of this voice, then perhaps she, Bella, had imagined it.

"Time is short," the voice said.

At this, Bella snapped the blanket down over her head. Her instinct was to scream, but she did not scream, and she did not cry. Instead, she offered up a hushed, rote prayer to a dead saint just as Mother had taught her, hoping to soothe her overactive imagination. But her prayer was cut short when slow, steady footsteps approached. The boards creaked beside her bed as someone or something came to a stop, and that voice came again—inches from her ear.

"There must always be a sacrifice."

Bella's eyes pooled with tears. Be it fear or her own stubbornness, she did not move. Though the stranger lingered, she kept herself tucked in as though her blanket were a fortress, until the stranger's steps trailed off through the attic. After a long while, her racing heart slowed, her eyes grew heavy, and Bella slipped into a fitful, shallow sleep.

When Bella was only three, her birth mother had taken violently ill. Shortly thereafter, her father had buried her mother in a soft patch between their garden and the sea. Shortly after Bella's sixth birthday, she'd awoken to the sound of her father moving about their humble shack of a home. Despite the black clouds shrouding the horizon, he'd intended to head for the cove to retrieve his traps, promising to return with a bounty of Dungeness crabs—enough for a few meals and more than a few dollars at the market. After a kiss on her forehead and a great big bear hug, her father had stepped out into a dark morning that, as God willed it, had left Bella an orphan.

Renata Cordero was also well-acquainted with loss. After her husband's persistent cough had fallen silent, Renata had found herself a widow with an infant boy. The church had noted the widow's situation and had made her an offer. So long as Renata maintained the church, the church would provide her and her child food and shelter. She'd agreed to the church's terms and had made her home in the drafty attic of St. Julian's Catholic Church, but only six years after having moved in, tragedy had found Renata once again. Her son had gone missing.

It had been at this time when the church had met to discuss the future of the late fisherman's daughter, the orphan Bella. The tall, svelte Renata stepped forward without hesitance and declared in a quiet yet determined voice that she would take the child in as her own. Mindful of Renata's recent loss, the church had been unanimous in their decision to place the orphan in the widow's care. Six years later, Renata and Bella continued their service to the church they still called home.

Young Bella spent her days caring for St. Julian's and her

evenings perched at the attic window, reading books from the church library. Some of the books she kept indefinitely, knowing the town of Grimlock Cove had little appreciation for the written word. She had books on the sacraments, church history of the 16th and 17th centuries, and even a few books in Italian, which she kept even though she couldn't read them. Bella had even managed to sneak a rather scandalous book into her collection. A carpenter, who'd been replacing some flooring for the church, had found the book hidden in the floorboards. The priest had intended to burn the forbidden tome, but the ever curious Bella had rescued the book and kept it hidden amongst her things.

As evening approached, Bella found it impossible to concentrate on her reading. The voice from the night before lingered, persistently echoing, *There must always be a sacrifice.* The priest at St. Julian's, Father Riley, had once said hearing voices was a telltale sign of witchcraft. The matter had arisen when Mrs. Crow had claimed to have heard Father Riley engaged in unrequited intimate relations with one of her daughters. Tragically, Father Riley's severe tests proved both Mrs. Crow and her daughter were suffering hallucinations due to their own involvement in witchcraft. With that revelation, the will and fire of godly men purged Grimlock Cove of the Crows' wickedness. Bella considered Father Riley's wisdom with a heavy heart. If she had suffered delusions—imagined voices and such—it would explain why her mother hadn't heard the voice, but this explanation didn't sit well with Bella. After all, she hadn't any experience with witches, witchcraft, or any such thing. She'd been born in a salt-worn fishing shack and raised in St. Julian's. Sure, she'd hidden away one forbidden book, but it was just a book.

The hour grew late, and having found no comfort in her thoughts, Bella turned her attention to the world outside the attic window to watch the dusk sun melt into the horizon. As the sun set, the forest that wrapped around the town became a jagged silhouette against the darkening sky. Flickers of firelight lit the windows of Grimlock Manor, which sat far and high on a hill overlooking the town. Horse-drawn buggies cast long shadows as they left along the main road. The lazy clip-clop of hooves grew faint as the last horse turned off the road and onto a dirt path that led out of town. Once the town's main street had settled for the night, Bella knew it was time to lock the church doors and set about her evening chores.

"Come along, Bella. Don't drag your feet," Mother said, waiting at the top of the stairs. She pointed to the attic floor, where olive green paint had cracked and peeled, revealing stained wood. "I'm picking up a can of paint tomorrow to touch up the floor, but I don't want you making it any worse than it already is, and mind yourself on the stairs. The church hasn't the funds for the carpenter to repair the loose boards."

Bella gave a terse nod. Mother started down the stairs to the nave, and Bella followed after, annoyed. It's not her fault the floors were peeling. It's not as though she were the only one walking around the attic.

After the pair had dusted, swept, and mopped the nave from one end to the other, Bella set about extinguishing the altar candles. She puckered and blew out each votive one by one, and when the last flame died, she watched as a single wisp of smoke rose from the ashy wick. The thin, gray band slithered up, vanishing into the shadows that filled the church. Bella had always found it curious how strangely grim the church became in the absence of light. Stained glass windows that had shone so vibrant in the daylight became dull, gray, and lifeless. The crucified Christ above the high altar—a symbol of love and sacrifice—became a shadowy, corporeal wraith in the dark. All of St. Julian's became an inverse image of itself—a baleful tomb rather than a holy temple.

Mother stood by the attic stairs at the back of the nave,

where she struck a match, and lit her candlestick so Bella could find her way to the stairs. As Bella crossed from the altar to her mother, she noticed the portraits of mournful saints and angels along the walls. Father Riley had said the saints looked down with love, and angels' eyes were always on God's children. But these saints seemed to hide their eyes from Bella, and the angels regarded her with pity. Bella turned her attention back to her mother's light, dismissing what she'd seen as the shadows playing tricks on her eyes. When Bella arrived at the foot of the stairs, Mother handed her the candlestick.

"Mind your steps, Bella," Mother said as the pair started up the stairs.

Bella climbed the stairs carefully and said, "Are we alone here?"

"What do you mean?"

When Bella reached the attic, she placed the candlestick on her mother's nightstand and crossed over to her own bed. "I mean, are we alone in St. Julian's?"

"Father Riley says we are never alone in the house of God," Mother answered cooly.

Bella climbed onto her straw mattress. "Yes, but is there someone else besides God?"

Mother's knees popped, as she lowered herself to the edge of her bed. Her tall, lean frame appeared haggard, and she sighed, seeming to resent her aging body. "There is no one else," she said, letting down her salt and pepper hair. "Only the angels."

Bella noted how quickly her mother's hair—once black as a burnt wick—had grayed.

Mother leaned forward to blow out her candle but stopped when Bella asked, "How old are you?"

Her mother straightened up, raised a brow. "How old do you *think* I am?"

Bella paused and gave her mother an appraising look.

"Sixty years, but not a year more than that," she added, intending to be polite.

Mother scoffed.

"Older than the town?" Bella said, surprised that her mother could be so old.

"No," Mother said, leaning in again to blow out the candle.

"Older than St. Julian's?"

Mother gave up on putting out the candle and straightened up again. "What's this about, Bella?"

Bella didn't want to admit she feared the dark, but the words leapt out of her all the same. "I'm afraid."

"Of what?"

Feeling childish at the prospect of admitting she was afraid of the dark, Bella replied, "Well, not so much afraid. I just— I don't feel safe here."

"You don't feel safe? Here in the church?"

Bella's eyes fell.

"Where is your faith?" Mother asked.

Bella said nothing as guilt welled up.

Her mother continued, "Well, the way you mumble your prayers and drag your feet to your chores, I should've known your faith had faltered."

"It's not that, I just—"

"If your faith hasn't faltered, what have you to fear?"

"I fear we're not truly safe in this church."

Mother raised a brow and leveled a sharp eye at Bella. The longer the two sat in silence, the more uncomfortable Bella grew. She thought perhaps she should apologize or walk back what she'd said. *I've misspoken*, she could say, but before Bella could diffuse, her mother shifted her focus to their surroundings and said, "But who could fault you? Suffer the children, so say the scriptures. To the meek belong the kingdom of God, isn't that what they say?"

Bella held her tongue, unsure of how to answer.

"It must be difficult for you to believe when impoverished servitude is your lot in this 'kingdom'," Mother continued. "When all the power is reserved for those of means."

Bella thought of the Grimlocks. Through the attic window, she could see their moonlit manor on a far hill. "Like the Grimlocks?"

"The Grimlocks," her mother said, groaning. "This town calls the Grimlocks pioneers. They claim we owe our founding family for braving the wilderness with nothing but faith and the favor of the Lord."

As her mother continued, Bella's mind wandered back to the strange voice she'd heard. Mother had said there was no one else here but the angels. Could the voice she'd heard been some kind of warning from an angel?

"Are you listening?" her mother said, snapping Bella to attention.

Bella hadn't heard a word but knew to nod quickly.

Though clearly skeptical, Mother continued, "As I was saying, they built this town on the backs of people like me, but that's not how history tells it. As the story is told," her mother paused, clearing her throat importantly, "as a terrible storm raged all around, our founding family sought shelter in a small cove. As they clung to their last fraying threads of hope," she paused again and folded her hands with mock reverence, "John and Mary Grimlock were visited by an angel of the Lord."

"An angel?"

"Indeed," her mother said, returning to her usual tone. "The angel told the Grimlocks they were fulfilling God's will."

"So, they weren't afraid?"

"I suspect the truth is they arrived with a wagon full of supplies and paid laborers, but of course, that's not how legends are made. With miles of lumber, fields of fertile soil, and rivers of fresh water, this was the Grimlocks' promised land. The town believes the Lord promised this land to the Grimlocks, but alas," her mother swept a hand across their humble surroundings, "it would appear all that wealth had been promised *only* to the Grimlocks."

"The true test of our soul is how we treat the weak in *our* time of need," Bella said, quoting a devotional Mother had given her. "Isn't that right, Mother?"

Mother said nothing. She sat rigid, appearing agitated. Bella couldn't imagine how a devotional could've troubled Mother. Wishing to avoid any discord, Bella returned the conversation to Mother's story. "So, what did the angel look like?"

"I doubt there was an angel, Bella, but if there had been, it would've—"

"How did they *know* it was an angel?"

"It is poor manners to interrupt," her mother snapped.

"I'm sorry," Bella said in a small voice. Mother's sharp tone normally preceded a rod across Bella's legs. Though even the priest preached mercy, Mother seemed to think mercy was too permissive and preferred the rod of correction instead.

"As I was saying," Mother continued, "the angel blessed the town, and now you and I play *very* important roles. *We* are blessed to shiver in the house of the Lord while the Grimlocks grow fat in their furs before a roaring fire."

Bella shifted uncomfortably. Her mother's once faith-filled disposition had darkened since the church had declined her request for improved living conditions. Mother had reassured Father Riley that she didn't expect luxury, but had insisted there must be some middle ground between her straw mattress in the drafty attic and his feather bed and furs.

"What if you married, Mother?"

Mother stiffened, her face growing hard. "The priest isn't told to marry for provision. Why should I be any different?"

Bella braced herself as though she were about to be struck.

Her mother sighed her disapproval. "You read all these books and yet you understand so little."

Bella's countenance fell. She looked at the books on the floor beside her bed and felt foolish under her mother's gaze. The scriptures had said a kind word could dissuade the wrathful, so Bella attempted a kind word. "But I have you to teach me, Mother. I won't disappoint you. I'll marry well."

Mother softened with a bitter smile. "A vocal woman is destined to be alone, with only herself to talk to. She must either be quiet or accept her lonely lot in life."

"I don't wish to be alone."

"Then be quiet and mind what is expected of you."

"I could marry a Grimlock," Bella said. "Then we'd have furs and fires to keep us warm."

"Truly," her mother said, her words dripping venom. "But I'd rather see the Grimlocks hung by the neck with their opulent furs and laid to rest in their own damned fires." Mother leaned forward, her brown eyes glinting in the candlelight. "Understand this, Bella. Power *always* requires sacrifice, but it is *never* the powerful who pay the price." With that, Mother snuffed the candle's flame, and the attic fell dark, save for the moonlight coming through the window.

Bella's conversation with Mother had done little to comfort her. She dreaded sleep despite the prior night's encounter having left her exhausted, but not long after Mother had put out the light did Bella's eyes grow heavy, and she drifted off into a dream. She did not dream of far off places or wondrous things. Instead, she found herself standing at the attic window, looking down on the main street.

The town was closing as the sun vanished in the horizon. It was just another evening until she saw it—something like smoke, black as pitch and about three feet deep, spilling out onto the street beneath her window. Her stomach sank. Something wicked had infested the town, and it was coming from St. Julian's. Bella's pulse quickened, her fists pounding on the window. She shouted to warn the people in the street, but no one noticed her or the encroaching smoke. Across the street, her mother stepped out of the general store with a can of paint, a hammer, and a small box of nails. Bella's shouts turned to frantic screams as the smoke slithered up, serpentine and predatory, winding itself around her mother's pale, gaunt frame. Mother stopped, and her mouth fell open. The smoke moved up and slithered into her mouth. After a deep, gasping inhale, Mother's eyes glazed over, and she stood there, vacant as a marionette. Bella's head split with the screams of a young boy. Clutching the sides of her head, she struggled to stay on her feet, keeping her eyes on her mother. Mother's hands went red with blood. It ran from her fingertips, pooling in the dirt at her feet. Then blood spilled from her mouth, pouring over her teeth and down her chin. Bella shrieked, slapping her hands against the windowpane, but Mother stood perfectly still, unmoved. Despite the sight of her, the townspeople carried on—either unaware or unconcerned. When the blood ceased to run, Mother's pale skin blushed with color, and her gaunt frame filled out, appearing stronger, nourished, and well-rested. Mother's eyes once again found focus, and after a moment, she started forward as though nothing unusual had happened.

A dry heat swelled behind Bella. She reeled around to find black smoke—that same as she'd seen in the street—had crept into the attic. The air soured, and Bella struggled for a full breath. With what little breath she had, Bella issued a throat-rending cry for help. Undeterred, the smoke slithered up to Bella, coiled around her legs, and climbed up her belly to her neck. She struggled against it, but the will of the wicked thing proved too strong. The smoke smothered Bella, drowning her voice in a cacophony of loathsome voices. The voices were aged and frightened, yet angry and demanding. Louder and louder the voices shouted, mocking Bella's will, casting blame and curses. Bella ached, weeping in silence, herself growing angry, yet powerless under the full weight of it all. Suffocating, burning, breaking, she collapsed, swallowed up by this darkness.

Bella awoke in her bed, breathing fast and damp with sweat. She sat up and looked around, but saw no smoke, no creeping darkness—only the usual shadows broken by the single shaft of moonlight coming through the attic window. Though it had all been a dream, Bella pulled her arms and legs in tight under her blanket and let very real tears fall. She had been so helpless—so alone in her dream. She'd hoped, as she'd cried out, that her mother, the priest, or anyone willing to help would hear her cries, but no one answered. Could they not hear her, or did they simply not care?

As Bella lie curled up in her bed, the stranger's voice returned. "Bella?"

She pulled her blanket over her head and hid, trembling.

"Do not be afraid. I am an angel of your Lord."

Bella took a shuddering breath and wiped the tears from her eyes, remaining hidden.

"You are a chosen vessel of your Lord," the voice said. "It takes a brave soul to fight the darkness, but an even braver soul to stand their ground when the darkness fights back."

A hand came to rest on Bella's head, the fingers lightly tapping a broken rhythm. Bella's heart beat in her throat, her every breath shallow.

The voice spoke in a close whisper, "The sun will rise again and warm you once more. Wait for nightfall, and upon the midnight hour, meet me at the altar of your Lord."

With that, the floorboards creaked as footfalls trailed off. Bella remained tucked in beneath her blanket. The angel had called her brave, but she certainly didn't feel brave. She did, however, understand why everyone who had ever met an angel in the Bible had been so afraid, but it did leave her to wonder, indignant, *Why don't angels visit at a more reasonable hour or properly introduce themselves? Did no one teach them manners?*

The following day, the angel's voice held Bella's thoughts captive, as she wondered why the Lord would send an angel to visit her, much less why the Lord should choose *her*. After a long day of chores and study, Bella's tired mind struggled under the weight of it all. Forgetting to mind her step, Bella slipped and nearly tumbled down the stairs when one of the loose boards slid under foot. Mother scolded Bella for her thoughtlessness and blamed St. Julian's for not providing any means of repair.

"Out of my own pocket," Mother said bitterly, adding a hammer and nails to her shopping list. "I'll be back shortly."

Bella nodded and waited at the attic window to see her mother crossing the street from the church to the general store. Once she saw her mother enter the store, she rushed to her bed and retrieved that very special book she'd hidden amongst her things—the book she'd rescued from being burned by swapping it with another book that had, ironically, claimed literacy to be a spiritual danger. Unlike the books she'd borrowed from the church's library, this one had a presence about it. Just touching the thing sent goosebumps running up the back of her neck. Father Riley had called the book a forbidden education in witchcraft. Granted, it'd been youthful curiosity mixed with a healthy dose of mischief that had inspired Bella to save and hide the book away, but she'd never had the courage to actually read it. She'd feared it, but she recalled nothing in the scriptures addressing the smoke-like darkness she'd seen. So, perhaps a dark book might better explain dark things.

Bella sat at the attic window with the musty, red leather book resting heavy on her lap. She moved her mother's candlestick closer, so that the light fell across the cracked cover, and the title shimmered in gold filigree: *The Shadows Grimoire*. She cast a nervous glance out of the window to the general store, not wanting to be caught by her mother. Seeing no sign of Mother, she turned her attention back to the book on her lap. Despite her trembling limbs and churning belly, Bella opened the book and found an illustration of a woman bound to a burning stake. Flames, crudely sketched in blank ink on the yellowed page, seemed to lick up the woman's boney legs. A distant gang of voices issued a guttural, droning hum. As candlelight danced over the page, and the thrum grew louder, the burning woman's faded, black eyes glared up at Bella. Startled, she quickly turned the page. The hum fell silent. On this page were six children kneeling around a small body. One child held up a curved dagger with both hands while the others cradled burning candles beneath their bowed heads.

Bella squirmed, sickened. She flipped through the book, finding nothing of angels or the dark smoke she'd seen in her dream. She began to think she'd made a terrible mistake, and Father Riley had been right in wanting to burn this hideous book, but then she found a chapter that caught her attention —a chapter entitled, "The Eternal Nature of Witches: Like Smoke From the Flames, Our Souls Ascend."

"Like smoke," she muttered and began to read.

We are eternal, outliving the flames that would consume lesser souls. Though mortals may attempt to burn you alive, fire alone only vanquishes the body, freeing the witch's soul like smoke from the embers—

She stopped. For a moment, that sulfurous smell and chorus of voices from her dream played back. That feeling, being silenced, suffocated in the darkness, returned. "No!" Bella shouted, shaking her head. Fearing she might've been heard, she looked out the window to the general store. Mother was at the front speaking with the clerk. Relieved, but feeling short on time, Bella pressed on.

Though mortals will seek to burn you alive, fire alone only vanquishes the body, freeing the witch's soul like smoke from the embers. However, without a body, the soul is incapable of interacting with the physical world. Therefore, it is imperative that the witch's soul find a willing vessel wherein the soul may remain hidden. Magic notwithstanding, the vessel's mortal capabilities will limit the soul accordingly, thus the witch should seek capable vessels in the interest of self-preservation.

Regarding possession, a vessel must open itself up in order to be possessed. Possession is then accomplished by the vessel committing an evil act. Such an act will fracture the host's soul, creating an opening through which the occupying soul may enter. However, if a willing vessel cannot be found, it is possible to coerce or bargain with a weary vessel. In a moment of weakness or desperation, a mortal is unlikely to discern the witch's true nature and intention, but the witch must be wary of the wise, for the wise may see through such manipulations.

After obtaining a vessel, maintaining power will require ongoing sacrifices—

Bella stopped again. "Sacrifices," she said under her breath, remembering the voice had said, *There must always be a sacrifice.*

After obtaining a vessel, maintaining power will require ongoing sacrifices be made every six years to sustain the witch's soul, lest it grow weak and succumb to death. The following shall provide examples and illustrations of acceptable rituals for revivifying the soul.

Bella read fast, hanging on every word, but to her dismay, the chapter ended prematurely, with the next page being the start of the next chapter. Bella looked between the two pages to see a page had been torn out. She ran a finger down the frayed edge left behind and wondered who would've taken it and why.

The attic stairs creaked, announcing Mother's return. Bella slammed the book shut, bolted for her bed, and tucked *The Shadows Grimoire* in between her blankets.

"Bella?" Mother said.

Bella spun around to find her mother leaving a can of paint, a hammer, and a box of nails beside her bed.

"It's time to lock up. Don't forget my candle," Mother said with a nod to the window sill.

Bella nodded, retrieved her mother's candlestick, and followed after. As the pair descended, Bella's thoughts of witches and smoke were overtaken by the words of the angel. *"Wait for nightfall, and upon the midnight hour, meet me at the altar of your Lord."* Bella repeated the words under her breath all the way down the stairs and across the nave until she reached the high altar, where Christ hung crucified. He looked down on her, anguished, dying, but somehow she found comfort.

"The angel said you chose me," Bella said, pausing, wishing to reach out—to feel the arms of her Lord, but instead she closed with a quiet, "Thank you." And with that, Bella folded her hands, bowed her head, and recited a prayer she'd learned in mass. "Hide us this night in the shadow of your wings. Visit this house and drive from it your enemies. May your holy angels dwell here, and may your blessings be ever upon us, through Christ our Lord. Amen." Bella looked up to find Christ still anguished. "Oh," she said, clasping her hands together and bowing her head again, "And please help Mother. Though her weeping endures for a night, may her joy come in the morning."

After the night's work was done, Bella and her mother retired to the attic. Mother settled on the edge of her bed and said, "Go right to sleep tonight, Bella. I'll be up early to nail down the loose boards and paint the floor. I won't have you keeping me up till the witching hour with your prattling."

Bella's ears perked up. "What's the witching hour?" The question had leapt out of her before she could catch it.

"Midnight," Mother said cooly and snuffed out her candle.

The shadows swallowed Mother, and Bella laid back on her mattress. In the hours that followed, she tossed and turned and drifted in and out of sleep until the angel called for her. "Bella?"

Bella's eye's shot open. She tensed up, fearing the angel might wake Mother.

"Bella?" the angel called again.

The voice wasn't close as it had been before.

"The hour is upon us," the angel said, her voice carrying from the nave below.

Remembering the angel's invitation to meet at the altar, Bella slipped out of bed and stepped lightly to the stairs. The descent proved slow as unsteady boards threatened to shift underfoot. Upon reaching the floor, she looked to the altar and beheld a resplendent, angelic form. The angel's appearance was exactly as Bella would've imagined. A heavenly light illuminated the angel and only the angel, giving her a radiant, ethereal glow. The angel's hair shimmered like polished silver and undulated as though she were adrift underwater. Her green eyes shone unlike any Bella had seen before, though the rest of the angel's face hid in a lustrous, white light.

Flooded with relief, Bella rushed forward.

"Bella," the angel said, her tone proud and affirming as Bella arrived at the altar. "You answered the call."

"You said I was chosen," Bella said, getting right to it. "What did you mean?"

"You've seen the darkness."

Bella spoke with hushed urgency, "I have. Can you help us?"

The angel looked left and right as a smoke-like darkness manifested in dark corners of the church. The sulfury black started toward them, rolling over pews and billowing up walls, obscuring the saints and the crucified Christ. The darkness swelled until it filled the nave, enshrouding Bella and the angel.

Bella took a step closer to the angel, seeking safety. "This is what I saw in my dream last night."

The angel spoke in a soothing tone. "I know you're frightened, but this is the burden of having eyes that see."

"Please," Bella said more urgently as the voices began, low, and the smoke swirled around them. "You *have* to help us."

"Help you?" the angel said, incredulous. "This darkness *belongs* in Grimlock Cove. The founders welcomed it."

Bella stepped back. "They what?"

"It's true."

"I don't believe you," Bella said, faltering. "If they could see the darkness for what it truly is—if they could only see—"

"They don't care to see it, so long as *they* are comfortable."

"But if they *knew*—"

"Bella," the angel said more earnestly. "Do you truly believe they don't know?"

Bella's mouth opened to press the argument, but she remembered her dream. She remembered her mother standing idly in the street, and the people passing by as though not a thing in the world was wrong.

"They know," the angel said. "They *all* know, but it is easy to ignore so long as you're comfortable."

Bella jabbed a finger at the darkness. "How could anybody be comfortable with *this*?"

"What can be done?" the angel said. "This evil has survived souls much older and much wiser." The angel cocked her head, considering Bella. "What hope have *you*?"

Bella looked at the angel, remembering the Christ hidden behind the smoke. "But I do have hope."

The angel looked down on Bella. "I could give you power—power to stand against that which threatens you—against those who don't understand the truth like you do."

Bella continued, "But this is not just about me. Everyone in this town is in danger. I need to tell them the truth of it."

"You are but a child," the angel said, pitying Bella. "They don't listen to your mother now. They certainly won't listen to you."

Bella drew back. "Did you call me only to be cruel?"

The angel sighed. "I thought you might have an open heart."

Bella's insides turned and her legs nearly failed her. "You were hoping for a willing vessel."

The angel's mouth twitched.

"You're not an angel," Bella said, her hands balling into fists. "You're a *witch*."

At this, the angel's radiant glow fell dark, giving way to a presence most frightful and grim. Billowing black robes unfurled around the witch. Her silvery hair fell limp as she drew the robe's black hood over her head. Though the hood cast a shadow over the witch, Bella could see green, hateful eyes glaring back.

Despite the tremble in her voice, Bella stood firm. "I know your secrets. You need a body to possess, but I swear you will *die* for want of a body."

"I have all I need, child."

"Liar," Bella snapped.

The witch drew herself up, her robes whipping like sheets in the wind. "I stand before you, both beautiful and dreadful, and yet you bark like a fool-headed dog."

"You forget where you are, witch. You're in the house of God, and in God's house, you cannot stand."

The witch erupted with laugher. "There is nothing divine in wood and glass. Who do you think built these four walls?" The witch threw her arms wide. "I built *all* of this. There has been no better place for me to 'stand' than in this sepulcher—this tomb—" the witch paused as the surrounding smoke parted, and she pointed at the crucified Christ, "—this memorial to *death*."

"The power of Christ compels you to go," Bella said, shaking yet standing her ground.

The witch's voice strained with subdued violence. "I survived the injustice of Ipswich and the bloodlust of Salem by hiding in the houses of *your* Lord."

"I'll tell *everyone* about you," Bella said.

"I've already told you, child," the witch said, reaching a hand into her robe. She withdrew a folded piece of old, yellowed paper and held it out. "I have all I need."

As Bella drew a breath to call for help, the witch vanished, leaving the air crackling in her absence. The smoke withdrew at once, and the folded-up paper fell to the floor. Bella's heart hammered. She turned on the spot, surveying the empty room. Her hand trembled as she knelt to retrieve the fallen paper. Not wanting to spend another moment where the witch had been, Bella hurtled up the creaky stairs, giving no thought to the loose steps or any noise she might make. She crossed the attic in a few long strides and leapt into her bed. Her heart thundered and dread churned inside her, leaving her weak, swallowing so as not to vomit. She rolled onto her side, unfolded the paper the witch had left behind, and held it up to inspect, but the room was far too dark to make out what was on the page. Everything in her wanted to hide under the covers and let the sunrise dispel the dreadful night, but she remembered the missing page from *The Shadows Grimoire*, and she had to know.

Quickly yet quietly, she crawled out of bed and knelt on the floor in the moonlight pooling beneath the attic window. Around her spread patches of cracked, green paint, revealing crimson stains beneath. The old page crinkled in Bella's hand, but she could make it out by the light of the moon. The page bore a crude sketch of a woman kneeling in a small room beneath a single window. On the floor before the kneeling woman lie the pulpy remains of a smaller body. Bella's stomach sank as she remembered the instructions from *The Shadows Grimoire*.

. . . a sacrifice . . . an evil act.

Bella felt cold.

Without a body, the witch will be incapable of interacting with the physical world.

"Without a body," she breathed as the page trembled in her hand. *The witch has a vessel*, she thought, and Mother's voice resounded within her. *Power always requires sacrifice.*

A shadow crept up the moonlit page.

"Bella," Mother said.

"No," Bella breathed. She twisted around to see her mother towering over her. Dull moonlight outlined Mother in silver. Gray and black hair veiled Mother's face, but her eyes—her brown eyes—glinted green. Mother held her right hand behind her back while her left hand hung limp at her side.

"Please," Bella said as tears swam. "Not you."

Mother's head tilted to one side, and her right hand fell from behind her back to reveal a hammer. "There must *always* be a sacrifice."

The Red-Eye to Nowhere

Grimlock Cove, 2016

———

Bands of deepest violet stretched through an endless void. No city lights twinkled below, and no silver moon bore witness to the night. Yet in this endless expanse, a single twin engine passenger jet drifted like a lost soul wandering through cosmic space. Kagome "Mei" Ito sat alone in the empty red-eye. She had booked a flight to visit her sister, Nori, in Grimlock Cove, but this was not that flight.

———

The drone of the jet's engines played on like a dirge. *Ding!* The chime rang through the cabin when the fasten seatbelt sign switched off. Mei squinted into the white glow of her laptop, clicking through unchecked emails. There were several rejection letters, thanking her for her interest in their company, as she was deemed either overqualified or not experienced enough. An email from her Krav Maga class requested payment, as her autopay had been declined. Finally, her alma mater was requesting donations. Mei sighed and mashed the delete key until her inbox was empty. *Out of sight, out of mind*, she thought, but the relief of an empty inbox was short-lived as another email arrived. Mei lifted a finger for the delete key until she saw the sender. Nudging her glasses up, she opened the email and leaned in closer to read.

Hey, sis! I can't believe you actually have time off. The motels in Grimlock are crap, but my couch pulls out. It's a small bed, but it should fit your tight ass.

<3 Nori

Mei smirked and composed her reply.

Oh! That sounds perfect for YOUR flat butt. Big sister gets the big bed. That's the rule.

See you soon,

Mei

The sisters hadn't known their father, and a month before Nori's high school graduation, they had held each other, watching their mother's casket being lowered into the ground. After high school, Nori had left home to attend a no-name college in a nowhere town, but she hadn't gone alone. Mei had been there to help with the move. When Nori walked to receive her Bachelor of Journalism, Mei had been in the crowd shedding proud tears. And when a small newspaper in Grimlock Cove had offered Nori her first job, Mei had booked the first available flight to celebrate.

Nori's email reply arrived.

Mei,

If you can hear me, it's Nori. Do you remember what mom said to us right before she passed?

Mei sat back. *That's so odd*, she thought, considering the message until the captain's voice came over the intercom.

"Eh, this is Captain Vogel speaking. We've turned on the

fasten seatbelt sign as it looks like we've got some turbulence up ahead. Shouldn't take too long to get through it, but we'd like to ask everyone to remain seated."

"Everyone?" Mei said, glancing around the empty cabin before returning to Nori's peculiar email. "Do you remember what mom said to us right before she passed?"

The tonal shift from Nori's first email to the second worried Mei. Her hands hovered over the keyboard, not sure of how to respond. As she did, the laptop rose from the tray table, levitating for a moment as the plane dropped in a bout of turbulence. Mei pressed her back against the seat, feet against the floor, and gripped both armrests. The cabin rattled, lights flickering as the plane rose and fell. Something surged through Mei. She clenched her teeth as the rest of her convulsed. After a final, jarring drop, the plane leveled and the cabin settled. Mei, breathing hard, relaxed and opened her eyes. The cabin lights had died. The only remaining light came from the exit signs on either side of her.

The intercom switched on with a static click. "Eh, this is your captain speaking. Seems she's not responding as we'd hoped. So, we're going to try another approach."

"What?" Mei said. "Who's not responding?" She leaned into the aisle to find a flight attendant. "Hello?" Seeing no one, she unbuckled her seatbelt and pushed herself up to her feet. Empty seats and black porthole windows ran along the length of the cabin, while both the front and rear ends of the cabin hid in darkness. Mei looked around for her laptop and found it on the floor at her feet. The freshly cracked screen shone as a fractured rainbow. "Perfect," she said, retrieving the laptop and tossing it into the seat beside her.

Maybe it was the stress, or maybe it was the altitude, but her head began to throb. Mei reached up and pressed the flight attendant call button, but it failed to light up. "Also perfect," she said, and with a slow turn, she stepped into the aisle to find an attendant when a tall, broad-shouldered man appeared at her side. "Sh– shit!" she said, jerking away and falling back into her seat. The man stepped into the red glow of the exit row. He wore a plaid shirt, dark jeans, and sunglasses. The man lingered for a moment before passing her row. "Sorry," she said, embarrassed at her outburst, but the man didn't acknowledge her outburst or apology and took a seat in the next row up.

Mei paused a moment to calm her nerves. She'd thought the flight had been empty, and she knew for certain the next row had been empty. More than that, something about the man unsettled her. She felt connected to the man, and the feeling left her queasy. Her head still ached, so she craned her neck, hoping to see a flight attendant. "Excuse me?" she called. "Can I get some water, please?" She paused for a moment. "Sir?" she said to the man seated in front of her. "Sir?" The man ignored Mei, but she continued, "Did you see a flight attendant while you were up?"

The man sat perfectly still and silent.

Feeling invisible, Mei gave up on finding help and determined to help herself, but as she braced to stand, she stopped, distracted. Something had appeared in the window to her right. Mei watched the window, waiting. For a moment, she forgot her aching head. Her hand drifted toward the window, certain she'd just seen her mother's face.

"Ma'am?" a voice said from over Mei's left shoulder.

Mei jumped and twisted in her seat to find a flight attendant standing in the aisle. The attendant was lovely, with sharp features that belied her apparent age. Her eyes shone green despite the dark, and her silvery hair flashed copper in the red glow of the exit lights.

"Are you alright?" the flight attendant asked.

"No," Mei answered, quickly turning back to the window.

"Can you see—" but she stopped herself when she looked back to find the window empty—devoid of any face.

"Can I see what, ma'am?"

Mei's mouth hung open as she searched the void beyond the window.

"Ma'am?" the flight attendant said.

"Water," Mei said, turning back to the attendant. "Could I have a cup of water?"

"Of course."

Mei forced a smile. "Thank you."

"I'll just need one thing first."

Mei gave a compliant nod, though she couldn't imagine what this person could possibly need before providing a simple cup of water.

The flight attendant gestured to the seat in front of Mei and asked, "Do you recognize this man?"

Though the question struck Mei as odd, she shook her head, hoping to conceal the sickened knot in her stomach.

"Are you sure?" the flight attendant pressed. "If you would just take a moment to—"

"No," Mei snapped. "I mean, yes. I'm sure. I don't know him. I just need some water." She forced another smile. "Please."

The flight attendant straightened up and smiled congenially. "Let me get that water for you."

Mei thanked the attendant under her breath, but the uneasy feeling swelled as she found herself alone with the man. She didn't know him, yet the connection felt strangely intimate, in the way violence is intimate with trauma.

Mei's unease turned to fear when the man raised his fist, clutching a pocket knife. The blade was already stained red. Her breath caught at the sight of it. Frozen, she watched the man bring the knife down hard in a stabbing motion. Though she couldn't see what he'd struck, the hammer blow from his fist caused his whole seat to shake. His hand rose up again and fell with another seat-shaking blow. Mei recoiled, shielding herself until she somehow heard Nori cry out.

Fear gave way to Mei's protective, elder sister instincts, and she shot out of her seat after the man only to stumble, lightheaded. Her arms and legs betrayed her, unresponsive. Her eyes rolled back, Nori's scream cut off, and all fell silent, save for the drone of the plane's engines.

Ding!

The fasten seatbelt sign switched off. Mei found herself seated aboard a red-eye flight, though the joyful prospect of seeing her sister darkened under a looming sense of doom. The plane's engines hummed through the cabin like a droning incantation. Mei sat alone with her laptop, her fingers lightly resting atop the keyboard. Much to her surprise, an unread email from Nori waited in her inbox.

Mei,

It's Nori. Do you remember what mom said to us right before she passed?

Though the question was strange, Mei thought back and drafted her reply.

Hey. I do. She said we only had each other, but that was all we needed. Do you remember what I told you after she passed?

The intercom crackled and Captain Vogel's voice filled the cabin. "Eh, this is your captain speaking. We've turned on the fasten seatbelt sign as it looks like we've got some turbulence up ahead. Shouldn't take too long to get through it, but if you can hear me, Mei, your sister is—" The captain's voice turned to garbled static as the plane dropped and shuddered. Mei pressed back against the seat and gripped both armrests as her laptop slid off the tray table and crashed to the floor. The plane shook until the flickering cabin lights died, leaving Mei alone in the dark, save for the red glow of the exit row lights.

"Eh, this is your captain speaking. Looks like we've stabilized."

"Well, that's a relief," Mei said, still tensed and breathing fast.

The captain continued, "We've ruled out intracerebral hemorrhaging and confirmed there is no bleeding in the brain. However—"

"What?" Mei said, leaning into the aisle, but as she looked ahead for the cockpit, a great white light swelled, flooding the cabin. Mei shrank back and threw a hand up to block the light, but even with her eyes closed tight, the light was blinding. "What the *hell* is this?" Mei shouted, head throbbing as she pressed both hands over her eyes and held them there until the light switched off. She slowly lowered her hands and looked around the cabin. The unstoppable light had left no imprint on her eyes, but it had left her head aching.

"This the *last* time I fly economy," she said, looking around for her laptop. The thing sat open, screen cracked from the fall. Mei sighed, knowing she couldn't afford to replace the laptop much less fly first class. "Perfect," she said, but as she made to retrieve her laptop, an image appeared in the window. Mei shrieked, pulling back. A spectral face took shape in the window, and the words fell out of her at once, "Mom?" It was impossible, and yet the face was unmistakable.

Mei reached a slow hand out for her mother. "It can't be," she breathed. As her fingertips found the windowpane, her mother's face faded from view and the window became a black void once again. "Mom?" Mei's voice cracked, and she pressed both hands flat against the window and held them there. What she wouldn't give to feel her mother's arms holding her now. Her heart ached for even the briefest moment of comfort that only her mother could give. Mei sat, her hands pressed against the window, until she grew self-conscious and withdrew back into her seat. "I need a drink."

Mei pressed the flight attendant call button. Nothing. Frustrated, she smacked it three more times, but still it failed to light up or make a sound. "Also perfect," she said and unbuckled her seatbelt, stood up, and turned to start down the aisle, but as she did, she collided with someone tall and solidly built. She stumbled and fell back into her row. The person stepped into the red glow of the exit lights, causing Mei to tense up with a sharp inhale. The plaid shirt, the dark jeans, the sunglasses—she recognized it all. And sunglasses? Why would anyone wear sunglasses at night? The man said nothing as he took a seat in the next row up from Mei.

She slunk down into her seat, cradling her throbbing head in her hands. She needed a sedative, but decided she'd settle for a drink. "Where is the *goddamned* staff on this flight?" she said to herself.

"Ma'am?" a voice said from Mei's left.

Mei jerked away.

"Are you alright?" the flight attendant said, her green eyes glinting despite the dark.

"No," Mei answered firmly. "I am not okay. Can I *please* have a drink? I'll take whatever you have."

"Ma'am," the flight attendant said with a note of hesitance.

"Water. Can I just get some *water*?"

"I'll give you whatever you need," the flight attendant said. "I just need one thing from you first."

Mei threw up her hands. "What could you *possibly* need? It's just water, for God's sake."

The flight attendant pointed to the seat in front of Mei. "Do you recognize this man?"

Mei's stomach sank, and her face fell.

"You do, don't you?" the attendant said.

Mei twitched her head and said in a much smaller voice, "No."

"Ms. Ito. You've been very brave tonight, and I know you've been through a lot, but I need you to look at this man one last time."

Mei screwed up her face, turning away from the flight attendant.

"Do you recognize him?" the flight attendant pressed.

"No," Mei said. Her heart beat harder, causing her head to throb all the more. She didn't want to acknowledge the man even existed, much less that she recognized him.

"This man vexes you," the flight attendant said.

"Vexes?" Mei said. "Who says *vexes*? Who *are* you?"

The attendant jabbed a finger at the man. "Who is *he*?" And as she said this, the man's fist rose into the air, a three-inch steel blade protruding from his hand.

Mei pressed back against her seat and looked away as the man brought his fist down hard. The sound of the knife piercing soft flesh, and his fist landing with a thump, sickened Mei.

"Who is he?" the flight attendant asked, leaning in.

"I don't know," Mei said, truly not knowing the man but knowing she despised him.

"But you *do* recognize him?"

"I—"

"Do you?" the flight attendant pressed harder, leaning over Mei.

Mei withdrew into herself as the almost pitiless violence continued in the seat before her. Blow after thudding blow, his seat rocked, and Mei shrank.

"Don't!" the flight attendant said, snatching Mei by the wrist. "Don't hide."

Mei's eyes snapped to the flight attendant's hand. Blood dripped from Mei's fingertips, running down over both of their hands. Mei wrenched her hand free when Nori's scream rose from where the man sat. "NORI!" Mei shouted and shot up, but a sudden, sharp pain split her head, her eyes rolled back, and she fell into her seat. Then Nori's voice, the attendant, the knifing—at once it all fell silent, save for the drone of the plane's engines.

Ding!

The fasten seatbelt sign switched off. The plane's engines sounded strangely like muffled conversation. Mei sat alone with her tray table down and her fingers irritably tapping on her keyboard until an email arrived from Nori.

I remember Mom putting my hand in yours the night she passed away. You promised you wouldn't leave me, and to prove it, you held my hand all night until morning. In a way, you've been holding my hand ever since. Now, I'm holding yours, and Mei... I promise. I'm not letting go.

Oh, Nori, Mei thought, finding the email comforting. The intercom clicked on and Captain Vogel addressed the empty cabin. "Eh, this is your captain speaking. We've turned on the fasten seatbelt sign, as it looks like we've got some turbulence up ahead. Shouldn't take too long to get through it, but if you can hear me, Mei, your sister is here, and—" The captain's voice turned to static as the plane shook and fell in a sharp descent. The force of the drop lifted Mei up and out of her seat. Breathless, she took hold of both armrests. The plane shuddered and caught, slamming Mei back into her seat. The cabin lights flickered, and voices murmured indistinctly until the plane leveled off. Every cabin light had died, save for the exit row.

The intercom clicked on. "Eh, this is your captain speaking. Mei, if you can hear me, I need you to wiggle a finger."

"What?" Mei loosened her grip, chest still heaving. "You can't be serious." She leaned into the aisle. "Are you *serious*?"

The intercom cut on again. "Just a little wiggle."

"Perfect," Mei said . "I'm trapped thirty-five thousand feet in the air with Captain Pervert."

"Come on, Mei," the captain insisted.

"Fine." Mei raised her left hand into the aisle, made a fist, and wiggled her middle finger at the cockpit. "Satisfied?" She held it there for a moment until someone brushed against her hand. Mei pulled back, apologizing, but her apology cut off when she saw *him*. The man wore a red plaid shirt and dark jeans with sunglasses. He passed by without a word, taking a seat in the row ahead of her. Mei stayed perfectly still, save for the shiver moving through her. Her chin trembled as words sat trapped in her mouth.

"Excuse me?" a voice said from the aisle.

Mei glanced over to find a flight attendant standing in the aisle beside her. The attendant's silver hair shimmered while her green eyes cut through the dark.

"Kagome Ito? Can you hear me?" the flight attendant said.

Mei twitched her head in a quick nod.

"Good," the attendant said. "I need you to be strong one more time."

Tears swam in Mei's eyes as she watched the man's fist rise into the air.

"Mei," the flight attendant said as Mei shut her eyes tight. "You've got to look at him—look him in the eye."

"No," Mei said in a small voice. The seat in front of her shook as his fist fell and rose and fell again. The thumping sound of a fist bludgeoning a body played like a sickening drum. She winced every time the knife broke flesh and the seat rocked.

"Please," the flight attendant pressed.

"I— I can't," Mei said, burying her face in her hands, but

her hands were warm and slick. She pulled her hands back to find blood covering her palms, trickling down her wrists. Mei shrieked in horror, trying to wipe away the blood, but it seemed to keep coming as the thumping and squishing sounds continued from the seat ahead of her.

"Stop!" a voice—Nori's voice—plead from where the man sat.

Not another heartbeat passed before Mei forgot her fear and shot up to her feet. "Don't touch her!" The words erupted, feral and full of fire. The man's hand rose into the air again. Mei lunged forward, catching the man's wrist. Her rage rose like an inferno. The man in plaid appeared unfazed. His left hand gripped his armrest while his right hand still held the knife. "Nori?" Mei called, searching the row, but Nori wasn't there. Mei's eyes moved to the man, finding him unharmed. There was no blood or sign of injury, and yet Nori's screams continued to ring.

"Stop!" Mei said through gritted teeth.

Visions of Nori's anguished face flashed before her. The man's head snapped to face Mei, triggering her rage, and she bore down on him with a roar. With one swift motion, she twisted his wrist, slipped the knife from his grip, and plunged it into his chest. Blood spurt, sending a spray of red over her hand. "Bastard!" Her voice cracked as she withdrew the knife and hammered it again into the man's chest. She could feel the knife grazing bone. Waves of blood flowed from every wound, spilling over her hand as she brought the knife down again and again and again. Finally, Mei stopped, chest heaving, and took in the sight. Specks of blood had peppered the seat backs before them. The man's chest was a mess of lacerated plaid and pierced flesh. Mei swayed on the spot before retching at the sight. Despite all the damage, the man remained seated, facing forward. His arms hung limp as his heart pumped blood from every wound.

"Mei?" the flight attendant said, unmoved by the horrific scene.

Mei looked up, dripping red and shaking. "What have I done?"

"What you *had* to do," the flight attendant said.

The knife weighed heavy in Mei's hand, and she dropped it as though it were something indecent.

"I believe it is safe to say, this is the man who attacked your sister?"

Mei's chest rose and fell in labored breaths. "Yes."

"Good," the flight attendant said with a wicked smile. She raised a hand toward the emergency exit door. "You may go now."

"What?" Mei said.

The flight attendant twisted her hand in the air as if turning a knob, and a series of solid clicks followed by a loud *chunk* sounded behind Mei. She turned in time to watch the emergency exit door fall away from the plane and into the void. A roar of wind wound up and churned in the cabin.

Mei, buffeted by the wind, gripped the nearest seats. "Are you crazy?" she called over the rushing wind.

"You don't want to stay here, do you?" the flight attendant said.

"You're going to kill us!" Mei struggled to move away from the door, but she was determined. She would have climbed over the man in plaid's body, but he had vanished. There was no knife, no blood, no sign anything had happened. It was in that moment, Mei's reality shifted. She looked around the plane as though seeing it for the first time. "This isn't a plane," she muttered. The drone of the engines turned into vocal murmurs. "I'm not on my way to see Nori. I— I was with her. We were together." Then row after row vanished. "What is this place?" She looked at the flight attendant. "Where are we?"

The attendant held a smile. "Your mother helped me find you. Even in death, she still watches over you and your sister."

And like smoke carried away on a breeze, the silver-haired flight attendant also vanished. Mei's heart hammered. She thought herself lost in a fever dream—trapped in some kind of limbo, until a familiar voice cut through the confusion like a ringing bell.

"You made a promise," the voice said.

Mei's hair whipped around her face, her eyes watering in the rush of wind. *Impossible*, Mei thought. *Unless I'm dead*. Mei turned toward the voice. Her feet inched up to the open exit where she braced herself and stared into the unknown expanse beyond the plane, and there, just outside the door, her mother approached. Her mother's form was incorporeal—a misty body afloat in the expanse.

"You made a promise to your sister," her mother said in a firm tone Mei knew all too well.

"I did all I could," Mei said. "I—"

"You haven't done *all* you can. Not if you stay here," her mother said.

"I don't know where *here* is, and I—" the admission stuck in her throat. Taking a moment, she steadied her voice. "I don't know my way back."

Her mother reached out a hand and beckoned Mei forward. "It's easy, Kagome. Just follow your heart to the ones you love."

Mei looked around at the plane.

"There is nothing left for you here," her mother said.

"I'm scared," Mei said, turning back to her mother, whose face softened.

"I would be, too."

Mei's chin quivered.

Her mother kept her hand out for Mei, unwavering. "Come, Kagome. It's time."

Mei reached out and took hold of her mother's hand. Her hand was warm to the touch, and Mei felt something she hadn't felt since her mother had passed away. She felt safe. Mei inched her feet just over the edge of the plane. Below her, an endless expanse swirled in black and violet. Her legs nearly gave out at the sight, but her mother's strength held her steady.

"Keep your eyes up, and your heart on the ones you love," her mother said.

Mei straightened up atop unsteady legs and gave a firm nod. Her mother's face wrinkled with a smile, and Mei stepped out of the plane. Weightless, but not like flying, she drifted forward, buoyant as though she were floating in a stream. Mei's eyes stayed on her mother while her mother's smile changed from proud to bittersweet as a flood of white light enveloped the two. Mei felt her mother's hand slip free. The blinding swell of light drove Mei to cover her eyes, but as she tried to do so, she found her arms unresponsive. The whole of her became heavy and her thoughts indistinct. She tried to call out for her mother, but the words wouldn't come. Her mother's voice rose but was buried in the rumble of voices.

Mei's eyes—the only part of her she could move—twitched beneath eyelids that wouldn't open. So, she drifted alone, disconnected from anything tangible. Dread weighed heavy. The terror of having no control paralyzed her until a hand took hers and gently squeezed. Everything in her made to squeeze back, but her own hands hung limp. The other hand squeezed hers again. The touch was familiar, safe. It was a connection to something real. Mei willed again to squeeze back, and with great effort, her fingers twitched, and the weight of her body returned in full. An excited voice rang out as Mei's eyes fluttered open.

The blinding, white light turned cold and fluorescent, and

an old hospital room came into focus. The smell of aftershave and antiseptic flooded her nostrils. The blurred form of a man in white loomed from her left. Another form—a woman— stood to her right, gripping her hand. The familiar drone of the plane's engines that had sounded more and more like muffled voices became clear words. Mei had never seen the man before, but she recognized his voice.

The man smiled and said, "Hello, Mei. I'm Dr. Vogel. You're at Grimlock Memorial."

The woman on her right leaned in and kissed Mei's forehead.

Mei exhaled, "Nori?"

Nori's flush, tear-kissed face hovered over Mei's.

"Are you okay?" Mei asked between breaths, surveying her sister.

Nori nodded and reaffirmed her grip on Mei's hand. "I told you I wasn't letting go."

"Now," Dr. Vogel said, cutting in, "we're all thrilled to have you back with us, but the police—"

Nori twisted to look back at him, and judging by the manner in which he flinched, it was clear to Mei exactly what look Nori had given the doctor.

Dr. Vogel lowered his voice as if Mei wouldn't hear him and said to Nori, "The police said they needed to question her as soon as she—"

Nori cut him off, "Not now."

The door to Mei's room opened. Standing in the doorway was a nurse with a face Mei recognized. Silvery hair framed unmistakable green eyes that passed from Mei to Dr. Vogel. "Doctor?"

"Yes?" the doctor replied, turning.

"May I speak with you in the hall?" the nurse said.

The doctor looked uncertainly between Nori and Mei and said, "Please, excuse me for a moment."

After the doctor left, Nori gushed, but Mei shushed her and looked to the cracked door. "They're talking about *him*."

"Dead?" Dr. Vogel said more loudly than he had intended, as he seemed to catch himself and continued more quietly. "How? He was stable and recovering."

"The coroner will have his official findings, but it appears the man suffered a fatal pulmonary edema. All of his stab wounds reopened, and his lungs filled with fluid. He drowned in his own blood. It is dreadfully strange, doctor."

"I'll say," Dr. Vogel said, sounding genuinely perplexed. "Well, the police will still want a statement from Ms. Ito, if you could finish up with the patient."

The nurse nodded, and Dr. Vogel turned and started down the hall, continuing to mutter to himself, "So very strange."

His footsteps faded from earshot as the nurse stepped in and closed the door behind her.

I've never seen her before in my life, Mei thought, watching the silver-haired nurse approach. *How could I have seen her in my dream?*

"That was quite a hit you took, Ms. Ito," the nurse said, reaching Mei's bedside.

"She knows Krav Maga," Nori said, beaming at her sister. "That asshole was lucky to even make it to the hospital."

Mei's eyes stayed on the nurse. "What happened to me?"

"You don't remember?" Nori said. "We were leaving the bar, but you forgot to close out your tab. When you came back outside, this guy was coming at me with a knife. You ran at him, shouting. He took a swipe, but he must've had trouble seeing you—which is what he gets for wearing sunglasses at night. Anyway, you somehow took his knife and . . ." Nori broke off, hesitant to finish the story.

"And you acted in self-defense," the nurse said.

"Yeah," Nori said, wide-eyed. "You 'acted' again and again and again. I had to pull you off of the guy."

"But he lived?" Mei said. "You stabilized him. How could his wounds reopen?"

Nori looked confused, but the nurse kept her eyes fixed on Mei's. "Just before you woke up, it was as though—" she paused, considering her words carefully. "It was as though someone had yet again stabbed the man again and again and again."

Mei swallowed hard, and for a heartbeat she was back on the airplane, hammering the knife into the man's chest. The sound of the blade sinking in, followed by the thump of her fist on his chest. She tried to soothe herself. *It was just a dream*, she repeated until her pulse slowed. "Nurse?"

"Yes, Ms. Ito?"

"May I please have a cup of water?"

The nurse answered with a pitying smile, opened her mouth to speak and—

Ding!

THE STRANGER IN MY PHONE

Grimlock Cove, 2017

———

There are many spirits in this demon-haunted world. Some of them are helpful, meaning no harm. They may nudge when the stove's been left on or draw attention to a hapless child crawling toward danger. But not all spirits are kind. Some, like the living, are exceedingly wicked. Some such vile spirits keep to the shadows, disinterested in mortals or themselves afraid. Then there are the more transgressive spirits who harbor an unquenchable thirst—a need to torment—to satiate a lust for violence. Like the worst of humanity, they relish the suffering of others. These are the demented ones, the worst of the dead come to torment the living. Indeed, they, too, were once content to hide in the shadows, but in the quiet town of Grimlock Cove, these malevolent spirits come out of the shadows to rip, to cut, and to tear what the living hold dear.

Mr. and Mrs. Davis had tucked in for the night, resting easy while their son, D'Andre "The D-Train" Davis, lie awake in his bed. He was lean, athletic, and exhausted, but like many, he found it hard to put his phone down and call it a night. The phone was new—a long overdue upgrade and early high school graduation gift from his parents. It was their none-too-subtle hint to stay in touch, as he'd be leaving for college after the summer. In the cold light of his new phone, D'Andre watched "Mecho-x-milly," a teal-haired streamer in a unicorn hoodie, playing what would likely be the game of the year. With a wink and heart hands, she took a break to acknowledge her top donations and welcome new subscribers. After responding to a few of the many messages in the chat, she reminded viewers to subscribe and turned her attention back to the game.

D'Andre watched the streamer cut down a wave of monsters with a shimmering broadsword until a figure, very out of place, stepped into view of the camera and waited behind the streamer. The figure wore a hooded, scarlet robe. D'Andre held his phone up closer, trying to make out the face that hid in the shadow of the hood. The streamer, focused entirely on the game, missed the flood of messages in chat telling her to turn around. The stranger raised an arm, letting a long, scarlet sleeve slip back, revealing a pallid, withered hand. The stranger held a finger up to its shadow-veiled face, playfully signaling to the viewers to keep quiet. Emotes and messages flooded the chat window, but despite tip after tip rolling in with messages warning her, she didn't check the chat. She didn't see the robed figure lean over her shoulder, and she didn't see the figure withdraw a long, thin, silver blade.

So weird, D'Andre thought. *Must be desperate for subs.* A notification popped up on his phone, pulling his attention from the stream. It was a message from his friend, Charles "Chonks" McMoony.

Chonks was a pale kid with curly brown hair, chipmunk cheeks, and a presence that brightened every room he entered. The two had become fast friends after making the football team at Grimlock High. On the field, they were known as the D-Train and Chonks. The D-Train for his relentless speed as a running back, and Chonks for being an immovable wall on the offensive line. Off the field, they were just D'Andre and, well, Chonks was still Chonks.

D'Andre ignored the chat notification as Chonks had recently made a hobby of sending filter pics of his dog, Mr. Barkly, wearing a variety of fake mustaches. There'd been a handlebar mustache, a bushy, walrus-looking one, and a thin pencil mustache complete with a bowler hat. It was sort of funny the first couple times, but for D'Andre, the charm had worn off, so he swiped the notification away, only for another to pop up in its place. D'Andre moved to ignore that one, as well, until he saw the name. Forgetting all about the streamer's weird stunt with the creepy, costumed person, he tapped the notification. This wasn't Chonks sending pics of his admittedly dapper, mustachioed dog. This was a private message from Amber Stone.

@ASinkingStone: Hey Pookie! Whatcha doin?

He'd die if his teammates ever knew she called him "Pookie," but when it was just the two of them, he loved it.

@TheDTrain: Nothing. U?
@ASinkingStone: I'm in bed. Thinking of you.
@TheDTrain: Same.
@ASinkingStone: You're in bed thinking of yourself? ;)
@TheDTrain: Lol. No. Thinking of u.
@ASinkingStone: I'm making a collage of our senior year,

but I don't have any good pics of you and Chonks outside of school. Can you send me some pics from our camping trip?

@TheDTrain: Sure.

@ASinkingStone: Oh, and the collage will NOT include any creative dicks. Got it?

D'Andre laughed and sent prayer hands. After a full season of editing penises into his teammate's selfies for a laugh, it'd become an expectation, bordering on tradition. And these had not been lazy, low-effort memes. One highlight had been turning his coach's whistle into a silver-clad penis, which had even managed to draw a smirk from the coach. But if he had to pick, D'Andre's favorite was a pic of the quarterback. The self-aggrandizing QB had demanded Chonks take a pic. The QB then straddled a weight bench, flexing for the camera. But in D'Andre's version, the QB straddled a flaccid unicorn penis—complete with feathered, alabaster wings and a raging erection for a horn. Infantile? Absolutely, but this was D'Andre's art, and his art teacher had taught him two things—to never stifle creativity, and how to edit photos.

@TheDTrain: Ok. Nothing crazy. I promise.

He switched over to his photos app and scrolled through to find the pics from their spring camping trip, stopping at a picture of Amber. In the pic, she was seated beside him in the glow of birthday candles. It'd been his seventeenth birthday. Her smile had been for the camera, but her eyes had been on him. D'Andre didn't mind when the crowd chanted, "D-TRAIN! D-TRAIN! D-TRAIN!" from the stands, but when Amber's eyes were on him, he would freeze up like someone had switched off his brain and his personality.

Amber shone bright in so many ways. Her kindness had, without directly saying a word, taught D'Andre to be kinder to himself. She was strong because she was always willing to ask for help, and brilliant because to Amber, admitting she didn't know something was an easy first step to learning something new. If Amber Stone could see something good in him, he'd be damn sure to not disappoint.

Looking at the birthday picture, he remembered trying to hide his feelings for Amber. He'd spread his attention evenly across everyone at the party, so as to hide that his every thought and heartbeat had been for her. When the cake had come out, she'd kept her eyes on him. He'd glanced around the table before fixing his eyes on the little, flickering candles. And though he'd missed the look she'd given him, the camera hadn't missed a thing. It hadn't been a look of a friend or well-wisher. Her look had said she wanted the same thing he wanted, and Chonks had come through by sending the pic to D'Andre. A month later, Amber and D'Andre spent an entire Friday night laughing over slice after slice of pie until the Broken Mug cafe closed, and the wait staff ran them out.

D'Andre scrolled further until he found the selfies Amber had asked for. It'd been only a few weeks ago. In one of the pics, a small campfire lit three smiling faces. Behind them rose a wall of evergreens with moonlit edges. Amber hung on D'Andre's arm, beaming. Chonks filled most of the shot behind them with his arms around the other two. The moon gave Chonks a kind of angelic glow, like a six-foot, 295-pound cherub. This had been the first time Amber and Chonks had spent any real time together, and by the end of the night, the three nursed headaches from laughing.

D'Andre swiped between a few different pics, trying to choose the best one for Amber. Her eyes were half-closed in one, and D'Andre looked like he was about to sneeze in another, so he settled on the third and sent it.

@ASinkingStone: Thanks! <3
@TheDTrain: Miss u
@ASinkingStone: Same. Goodnight, Pookie bear!
@TheDTrain: Goodnight
He wished she was lying beside him, but he knew there

was no chance under his parents' roof. Sure, he and Amber would spend the weekend together, and they'd be seeing each other nearly every day over the summer, but that wasn't enough. The closer it got to his birthday—their one-year anniversary—the more he felt this new aching as though he might burst. D'Andre sighed, silenced his phone, and set it on his nightstand, but not a minute later, the phone lit up.

@ASinkingStone: *Not funny. Send me the REAL pics.*
@TheDTrain: *Huh?*
@ASinkingStone: *I asked you not to add weird stuff. Send originals plz.*

D'Andre shook his head, knowing he hadn't edited the pic. With a flick, he scrolled up to find the picture in question. At first glance, the selfie looked just as it had before. Amber hung on his arm with moonlit Chonks standing behind them, but then he saw it. The silhouette of a fourth figure stood over Chonks' right shoulder. The figure wore scarlet robes lined in silver moonlight, the figure's face hidden beneath a scarlet hood. At first, he had to admit it was more than a little creepy, but then he remembered the same hooded figure standing behind the streamer. *This must be a new meme. She's messing with me*, he thought.

@TheDTrain: *Lol okay. Ngl. U got me.*
@ASinkingStone: *Got you???*
@TheDTrain: *Yeah. Looks real.*
@ASinkingStone: *I'm lost. Can you just send me the real pic plz?*
@TheDTrain: *Stop playing. U got me. Game over. Going to bed.*

D'Andre shook his head, returned his phone to his nightstand, and curled up in his blankets, too tired for jokes.

The next morning, D'Andre grabbed his phone and dragged himself into the kitchen. His father had already left for work, and his mother, who worked as a nurse at Grimlock Memorial, was still in bed after another night shift. D'Andre grabbed the sugary cereal his father hid on the top shelf of the pantry, poured a bowl, and stretched out on the sofa in the family room, remote in hand.

The TV clicked on and an urgent blast signaled breaking news. It was all so obscenely loud first thing on a Saturday morning. D'Andre scrambled to turn it down, hoping not to wake his mother. The news anchor led in with a breaking story of murder, but D'Andre didn't want to hear a breaking story of murder. He didn't want to hear about this disaster or that disease or another war and the inevitable end of the world. In other words, he didn't want the news. He wanted to enjoy his cereal and wake up slow—very slow—from the safety of his couch without a window to the world's insanity. So, he changed the channel and kept changing until he found something that made sense.

Finally, having found a suitable escape—a cartoon cat and mouse pummeling each other—D'Andre nodded his approval and tossed the remote aside. "Oh, Tom," he said through a mouthful of crunching berries. "How are you always letting Jerry beat your ass?" D'Andre's phone lit up, demanding his attention. It was his coach, but D'Andre's Saturday morning agenda was fully booked with cereal and cartoons, so he ignored it and drained the milk from his bowl.

After a second bowl, D'Andre noticed his phone still lighting up. "Why, though?" he grumbled. "Why on a Saturday morning?" He scrolled through his notifications to find seventeen missed messages and nine missed calls—most of which were from Amber. His stomach sank. "She's gonna be pissed."

The first few messages were from friends. *Man had a*

knife and disappeared! I saw it live bro! Another had messaged, *Did you see mechoxmilly's stream?*

Confused, D'Andre muted the TV and read through his messages.

It's too early for this energy, he thought, and opened Amber's messages.

@ASinkingStone: *OMG. PLZ CALL.*

D'Andre's pulse quickened. The phone rang once, then Amber answered.

"Are you okay?" she said, panicked.

"Yeah. What's going on?" he said.

There was no reply.

D'Andre continued, "Look. I'm a little freaked out. I got a million messages, and—"

"D'Andre," Amber said.

Her burdened tone stopped him cold.

"It's Chonks," she continued, struggling to stay composed.

"What about him?"

"He's dead."

D'Andre's head went light, and his chest tightened. The room around him turned. His heart beat in his throat. Amber said something else, but it failed to register.

"Wait," he said, shaking himself. "Wait. What are you talking about?"

"It happened last night."

"What happened?"

"I— I don't know."

D'Andre shook his head, waving a dismissive hand at whatever foolish things Amber was saying. "He's not dead. He's—"

"His mom found him this morning," she paused, "in his bed."

"No, she didn't," D'Andre said, shaking his head hard, eyes watering.

Amber continued, "They rushed him to Grimlock Memorial."

"So he's alive?"

"D'Andre. I'm so sorry, but—"

"No. My boy's good. He just messaged me last night," he said and pulled the phone away from his ear to find the last message he'd received from Chonks. As expected, Chonks had sent a picture of Mr. Barkly. This time the dog had a full beard and wore a flannel shirt. D'Andre imagined Chonks was far more amused than Mr. Barkly. "See?" he said as though Amber were beside him. "He was just playing with Mr. Barkly." Ignoring Amber's small voice coming over the phone, D'Andre switched over to his messaging app to see the photo of them all together before the campfire—the photo he'd sent Amber.

"Shit!" D'Andre said, dropping his phone as though it were on fire. The phone tumbled to the floor, Amber's voice calling out, "Hello?" from the earpiece. He rubbed his eyes, telling himself, "That's not real. *That* is not real."

Amber repeated, "Pookie? Baby? Talk to me."

D'Andre picked up the phone, keeping the screen facing away from him. After taking a moment to calm himself, he turned the phone around. In the picture, the three stood gathered around the campfire as expected. Amber hung on his arm, and Chonks stood behind them, but to the right of Chonks stood the stranger in the scarlet robe. The bloody tip of a knife jutted out from Chonks's throat, a wash of red blood staining his front.

Amber had hung up and was calling back, but D'Andre ignored her call and swiped to another pic. It was another selfie where he and Chonks toasted cans of cheap beer, and once again, the faceless, robed stranger posed with them. The stranger's pale, skeletal hand held up a bloody knife in a mock toast. Chonks was still smiling, frozen in the moment. The robed figure, however, moved, taking the knife and resting the tip on Chonks's forehead. D'Andre watched as the figure drew the blade down Chonks's face, making one clean cut down the middle. The boy's flesh split open, red spilling out.

A message from Amber popped up.
@ASinkingStone: I'm coming over!

D'Andre ignored her message and swiped through his pictures, hoping to escape the robed stranger like someone frantically shutting doors to keep a monster out. "Pictures are *just* pictures. They can't hurt us," he said between quick breaths. After swiping through twenty or more pictures, he stopped on a photo taken in front of the school's trophy case. In the picture, D'Andre was pointing to an empty space on the shelf with a caption that read, "Reserved for The D-Train." He watched the photo for a moment, even checking the reflection in the glass for the stranger, but he saw nothing unusual. His breathing slowed as he continued to swipe through his photos, stopping on a selfie in front of the bathroom mirror. He checked every corner, but saw no sign of the stranger, causing him to question what he'd seen.

D'Andre, fearing losing his grip, reasoned with himself. Pictures capture a moment in time. They are snapshots of the past that have no effect on the present. Whatever he'd thought he'd seen must've been the effects of having received horrible, shocking news. He reasoned his mind must've slipped. The trauma had made him desperate, driving him outside his own mind. The sudden shock of hearing his best friend had died had been too much in the moment, but he could see that now. After taking a moment to let the news sink in, D'Andre felt confident he'd reaffirmed his grip on reality. There was no bogeyman in his phone, no murderous stranger stalking his photos. D'Andre shook his head, embarrassed at having lost himself.

@TheDTrain: Sorry I freaked out. Glad you're coming over.

After hitting send, he collapsed back onto the couch. *Chonks*, he thought in disbelief. It didn't feel real. A part of him expected Chonks to message at any moment, saying they should go to the movies or grab a pizza.

@ASinkingStone: It's ok. On my way. Stopping at the Broken Mug first.

@TheDTrain: Cinnamon rolls plz

@ASinkingStone: of course <3

As D'Andre sat alone on the couch, with every passing moment, the news of his friend dying sank in. It was hard to believe this was actually happening in his life. Until this morning, death had always been something other people dealt with. Death had been a stranger—one that had only affected people in the news. It had never hit this close to home, and yet here he was staring at the last message Chonks had sent him. He opened it again to see Mr. Barkly. D'Andre ached, and his aching drove him back to his photo album to look for more pictures of Chonks. He found pictures from a house party, where he and Chonks had woken up on the front lawn smelling of cheap vodka and vomit. The party had marked the end of their junior year. The morning after the party, they were supposed to serve as camp counselors at the Whispering Woods Summer Camp for St. Julian's Catholic Church. That'd been, by the decisive and unanimous judgment of the camp's leadership, the first and last time D'Andre and Chonks served as camp counselors.

D'Andre lingered on the photo, focusing on Chonks and fighting the urge to look for the robed stranger. *The stranger isn't real*, he reminded himself as he swiped through to the pics from his seventeenth birthday party. He, Amber, and Chonks were supposed to road trip for his eighteenth birthday in just a few weeks. They'd hit the SoCal beaches, get high in Hollywood for a day, and catch a music festival on the way back. D'Andre choked back the lump in his throat and focused on better days.

In the birthday pics, Chonks was hamming it up. D'Andre couldn't keep the tears back as acceptance crept in, bringing with it questions as to how Chonks had died.

"I'm glad somebody's having a relaxing morning," his mother said as though she'd simply appeared in the kitchen.

D'Andre jerked in place, startled by his mother's surprising ability to move through the house unnoticed. After a moment, he spoke up. "Mom. I need to talk—"

"I'm on four hours of sleep," she said, cutting him off, "but Nurse Crow isn't feeling well enough to do her damned job. Now I have to go back in to cover her shift."

"Isn't that the lady you're always calling a bi—"

"Witch," she said, cutting him off. "We don't use that other word in this house."

"You do," he muttered, but not so she could hear, and returned to his phone.

His mother emptied what remained of the hours-old coffee into a tumbler and started for the door. "Dr. Vogel better be on his *best* behavior," she said, snatching up her keys, "because I am in no mood."

"Mom—" he began again, hoping she might take a moment.

"You're a grown man, D'Andre, so whatever it is—handle it. I don't have the time or energy," she said, slamming the door behind her.

D'Andre cursed and sank back into the couch. He swiped to the birthday pic of him and Amber. The candles cast them both in a magical, warm light while the background fell away into shadow. It was a perfect moment. He still remembered the wish he'd made before blowing out the candles. *I wish we could be together forever.*

As D'Andre reminisced, a flicker of movement snapped him back to the present. He blinked, focusing on the picture. Had he seen it, or had it been another trick of his mind? Had the shadows behind Amber moved, or had it been the stress breaking him again? D'Andre closed his eyes tight and took a moment to breathe—to settle his thoughts and center himself. He'd never lost someone close to him, and though he'd always heard it'd be hard, he'd never thought he'd lose his mind over it.

As self-doubt mounted, he remembered the streamer from the night before. She'd pulled some creepy stunt for subscribers by having someone come on stream wearing a robe. Could that be it? Could that image have stuck somewhere in his memory banks and become what his overwhelmed mind was using to embody his fear?

There had been times when his mother had claimed to have seen some strange things at Grimlock Memorial on her late shifts—and by strange, she'd meant bordering on the paranormal. D'Andre had always dismissed it as his mother being overtired and overdramatic, but maybe this was a family flaw. Maybe the Davis family couldn't handle stress. Perhaps he *was* more like his mother than he'd care to admit, and with that, he'd found another thing to dread.

Refusing to accept weakness, D'Andre forced himself to look at the photo of him and Amber again. There he sat with Amber, her face lit by the candles, and just behind her, emerging from the shadows, appeared the robed stranger. A chill moved over D'Andre as the hooded figure glared up at him. The stranger moved to Amber's side, raised a thin, bloody blade, and brought the knife's point to Amber's neck. D'Andre's heart leapt into his throat. The stranger traced the knife up the side of Amber's neck, past her cheek, and came to a stop at her temple. D'Andre's reasoning crumbled under the weight of fear, the phone trembling in his hand.

"Don't," he said. "Don't do this."

The stranger turned and looked at Amber, then back up at D'Andre.

D'Andre shook his head, his voice solemn, pleading. "Not her. Please."

The stranger shook its head in mock imitation, slowly lowering its pale hand.

D'Andre exhaled his relief all too soon. The knife's silvery point nearly grazed Amber's ear as it descended from her temple and down to her shoulder, where it then drifted in front of her neck, the edge playing at her throat.

"No!" D'Andre shouted, gripping his phone with both hands.

The stranger slowly nodded *yes*.

D'Andre's pleading turned to impotent rage. "It's just a fucking picture! You can't do shit to someone in a picture!"

The stranger nodded faster, thrilling at D'Andre's fear, seeming to relish the moment.

"You can't—" D'Andre started again but stopped as an idea struck him. "Wait. You *can* do shit to pictures." And with that, he exited out of his photos app, and in a few heartbeats, he had the birthday picture loaded into his editing app. The stranger remained next to Amber, knife drawn, but the figure searched its surroundings, seeming confused.

"That's right, Tom," D'Andre said. "Call me *Jerry* 'cause I'm about to beat that ass."

The stranger shrugged at D'Andre's threat and flipped the knife around, reversing its grip and raising the knife high over Amber's head, preparing to hammer the blade into her chest.

"Perfect," D'Andre muttered, tapping the icon resembling a magic wand and effortlessly selecting Amber. A dotted line appeared around her, and with another tap, he hit *CUT* and Amber vanished from the picture.

The stranger recoiled, twisting in place, looking for Amber, but only an Amber-shaped void existed where she'd sat.

"You can't hurt her if she's not there, stupid ass," D'Andre said.

The stranger kept the knife aloft, appearing perplexed.

D'Andre shook his middle finger at the stranger, hurling insults. Amber was safe, and he had the stranger trapped. Then, from inside the picture, the stranger turned and faced the smiling image of D'Andre seated next to where Amber had been.

"Oh, sh—" D'Andre began, his words choked as the stranger brought the knife down into D'Andre. Searing pain shot through D'Andre's right shoulder. The phone tumbled out of his hands, his knees buckled, and he hit the floor. The phone landed a few feet away from where he lie crumpled, clutching his bleeding shoulder. He couldn't move his right arm without blinding pain, and as he reached out to his left for the phone, a cut opened across his chest. His shirt and bare skin split, bloody. D'Andre cried out, wincing as another cut opened on his left arm. The stranger continued to cut and slice from within the photo. D'Andre's feet slipped along the floor as he tried to move close enough to reach the phone. Another cut opened on the side of his neck, causing him to clench his jaw in pain. With a roar, D'Andre embraced the pain, pushed with everything he had, and launched himself forward toward his phone.

Grabbing the phone with his left hand, he rolled onto his back to see the picture of himself awkwardly staring down at his cake as though nothing had happened, yet blood spilled from multiple wounds in both the picture and his very real, tortured body. The stranger once again held its knife aloft, preparing to deal another stabbing blow, but with a deft tap of his thumb, D'Andre switched to an eraser and quickly swiped across the screen, causing the stranger's knife and hand to vanish. The stranger writhed in place, facing the stump that the eraser had left behind. With another quick gesture, D'Andre erased the stranger's bottom half, leaving a disembodied, hooded head. The hood turned slowly and looked up at D'Andre, appearing defeated.

Between ragged breaths, D'Andre said, "You like hurting people? Well, I hope this hurts like hell." He zoomed in on the head and swept a finger over the stranger's image with slow, deliberate strokes. The stranger's head writhed in place until D'Andre erased every last pixel.

All that remained of the birthday picture was an Amber shaped hole, the erasure marks where the stranger had been, and D'Andre hunched over his birthday cake, bleeding. Sweat covered D'Andre, mixing with blood and tears. The room spun one way, his head another. The warm creep of his own blood pooled beneath him as he triggered the emergency call function on his phone. A calm yet urgent voice answered, but D'Andre gave no reply. The voice came again, calm and attentive. After a few labored breaths, D'Andre answered with his address and requested an ambulance. The voice on the phone responded, but whatever was said was missed as D'Andre lost consciousness.

One week had passed since D'Andre erased the stranger in his phone. Police were still investigating the death of Charles "Chonks" McMoony, but every question had led to a dead end, and D'Andre knew they'd never believe the truth. The day of the attack, Amber's locked car had been found empty in the parking lot of the Broken Mug with the engine running.

Amber had become a missing persons case, and much like Chonks's murder, the police had only found dead ends, but again, D'Andre knew the unbelievable truth.

D'Andre's mother had thought an early birthday might cheer him up, as if he hadn't lost his two best friends only a week ago. The smell of sizzling burgers drifted up the hall from the kitchen. The aroma slipped under D'Andre's locked bedroom door, but he wasn't hungry. He hadn't been hungry since he'd lost Amber. D'Andre had excused himself over an hour ago, claiming nausea. Now, he laid still on his bed, watching the ceiling fan turn. The salt from dried tears marked the corners of his eyes, while his thoughts stayed on Amber. He pictured himself seated at the kitchen table, moments from now, waiting to blow out the candles on his birthday cake, but this time he'd be seated alone. Chonks wouldn't be taking pics and making jokes. The seat beside him would be a void where Amber should be—a void he, D'Andre, had created in his haste to save her.

The sound of friends and family mingling remained a constant rumble down the hall.

"Baby?" his mother's voice came from the other side of the bedroom door.

As usual, he hadn't heard her coming.

"I know," he answered before she could say more.

She lingered silently for a moment. "I know it's hard, but your friends would want you to have a happy birthday."

D'Andre stayed silent and watched the ceiling fan turn until his mother's footsteps faded down the hall. As he sat up on the edge of his bed, he could hear his mother making excuses for him. "He's not feeling well," she said. There was comfort in hearing her cover for him. He was surprised to hear it, but then she said, even louder, "But I'm sure he'll suck it up and get out here to see his guests."

Groaning with resentment, he got up and started for the

bathroom. If he looked half as bad as he felt, he'd need to freshen up. On his way to the door, he stopped at his closet and eyed it for a moment, unable to move past it. That was where he'd left his phone. Over the last week, he'd fought the urge to turn on the phone and bring up the picture from his seventeenth birthday. The picture where he'd sat with Amber at his side, and she'd sat closer than a friend, giving him a look he'd forever erased. A decision in the heat of the moment that had felt right, but a decision that haunted him.

He'd deleted her.

Deleted? he thought, lingering at the closet door. In the time since the attack, his mind and emotions had been a constant storm—chaos and turmoil churning. It'd taken time to gain a modicum of perspective. As he stood thinking, he wondered aloud, "Did I delete her, though?"

A nervous chill swept over D'Andre as he opened the closet door. At the bottom of the closet sat a bright orange shoebox. He took the shoebox to his bed, set it down, and stared at it for a moment. He wondered what powering on the phone might do. Maybe the stranger hadn't been erased. What if another stranger waited to torment, to cut, to kill? He raised the lid with an unsteady hand, and there at the bottom of the shoebox waited his phone. The black screen, marked with fingerprints, reflected his face. He'd been right. He did look as bad as he felt, but in his reflection he also saw hope, or maybe it was desperation—either would be enough to drive him to turn on the phone.

D'Andre picked up the phone and ran his thumb over the power button. *What if I could undo it? Could I bring her back?* With a forced, dry swallow, he pressed and held the slender power button. For a moment, nothing happened, and he feared the battery may have died during the three weeks it sat in the closet, but then the screen flickered and lit up. The persisting, internal debate over whether the stranger might reappear ended when the phone unlocked, having recognized his face. The battery was red, sitting at one percent. His thumb ran ahead of him, as though it had a will of its own, and launched the editing app. The app opened, picking up right where he'd left off, and he saw it. He saw himself sitting alone by the candlelight, but he wasn't bloody anymore, and beside him was the void where Amber had been.

Facing off with the stranger had been chaotic, and the finer details of what had happened were hazy at best. D'Andre remembered manually erasing the stranger, but when he'd selected Amber, he struggled to recall if he'd opted to *delete* or *cut*. If he'd deleted her, he'd done so before erasing the stranger. To undo deleting her, he'd have to undo erasing the stranger first. But if he had cut her out of the photo, what he'd cut would be stored like copied text waiting to be pasted. An anxious tremor moved through him. His finger hovered over the screen. The next touch would be the difference between her coming back or truly being lost forever. With his stomach in knots, he tapped the screen, and a little text bubble appeared that read *PASTE*.

D'Andre's knees faltered. In that moment, all the world came to a stop. His breath caught, and he said aloud, as if in a prayer, "Please, come back to me," and tapped *PASTE*. In an instant, Amber reappeared in the photo as she'd always been—beaming and beautiful. D'Andre caught himself on the side of his bed. His eyes stung with fresh tears, his pulse racing. He laughed and cried and pounded his fist on his bed, victorious. After a moment, he got to his feet, still holding his phone and staring at Amber's glowing image. But he didn't know what to expect, or how any of this worked. Thinking to message her, he tapped on his messaging app, selected her name, and started composing a message when the screen went black. D'Andre cursed and checked the shoebox for his charger. Empty. A knock sounded at his bedroom door.

"D'Andre?" his mother said.

"Busy!" D'Andre called back, searching under his bed for the charger. She knocked again, harder. "I'm busy!" he said, moving to his dresser to check the drawers.

"Boy, don't tell me you're busy. You've got guests here waiting on you, and you've got a phone call."

D'Andre threw up his hands, frustrated before answering the door to find his mother holding her phone.

"This is why we got *you* a phone," she said, handing him hers.

"Who is it?" he asked.

"I didn't ask, baby. I've got a house full of guests, the food's getting cold, and the birthday boy is still hiding."

"Okay," he said, soothing his mother. "I get it, Mom. I'll be right there."

She gave him a look that said he'd better be, handed him the phone, and left down the hall.

D'Andre took the phone, expecting the birthday wishes of an auntie or uncle. "Hello?"

There was no reply. Only the ambient sounds of clinking glasses and muffled conversation—like that of a cafe.

"Hello?" he said again.

A shuddering breath came over the phone followed by a confused, familiar voice. "Pookie?"

The Forgotten Fairgrounds

Grimlock Cove, 1988

———

Just off a two-lane road, hidden among the evergreens, sat the venerable Broken Mug. The decades-old little diner, untouched by trends and changing tastes, was a monument to another time. It served as a reminder: Though time presses on, the past remains, hidden among us, untouched by the years.

As the evening approached, the June sun kissed the horizon, throwing over the diner long shadows broken by beams of gold. Inside, a haggard server braced herself on the bar, watching the clock on the wall tick closer to closing time. A cook hid in the back, the squawk of a portable AM radio providing the Dodgers play-by-play. The only other souls in the diner were a pair of sweethearts seated in a window booth.

Elizabeth "Elly" Eaton sat opposite Josh Janowski. Josh moved the straw around in an empty to-go cup, chasing the last drops of soda, while Elly eyed the last bite of the Mug's "world famous" cinnamon roll that waited on a plate between them. Josh had blue-hazel eyes like Elly's, but he'd held that his eyes couldn't melt a heart like hers. Elly hadn't disagreed. When she'd met Josh at last year's Halloween party, it hadn't been his eyes, his thick, chestnut hair, or his wide, bright smile that had won her over. The two had spent most of the party standing off to the side, holding red cups and easy conversation. When she'd met Josh, she hadn't just met a new guy—she'd found the other half of her heart.

Elly hid her nerves almost as well as her desire for the last bite of cinnamon roll. She had plans for tonight—plans she hadn't yet shared with Josh. Hoping to persuade him, she pulled her stray locks of strawberry blonde hair behind her ear so that the sunlight fell across her face. Then she wrinkled up her nose and put on a sweet voice. "So, I have a *tiny* favor to ask."

"Totally," Josh said, nudging the plate toward her. "It's all yours."

Surprised, Elly snatched up the last of the cinnamon roll. After savoring it, she said, "Thank you, sir, but that wasn't the favor."

Josh's look of casual chivalry gave way to regret.

"It's my parents' anniversary this weekend," Elly said.

Josh looked at Elly sideways. "But I thought your mom—you know."

"That she left us when I was a kid. She did, and no, there's no new mom in the picture."

Josh looked like he had questions but didn't know where to begin.

"My dad still celebrates their anniversary," Elly said. "Every year he pours a cup of coffee for her in the morning, sets flowers out on the dining room table, and leaves a sealed envelope with her name on it by the flowers."

Josh sat back with a somber and heartfelt, "*Dude*."

"I know," Elly said, nodding. "It's totally sad, but I want this year to be different."

"Sure. How can I help?"

Elly leaned in. "Do you remember the old Grimlock Family Fair?"

Josh nodded. "Used to happen every year. Then it got shut down because people kept going missing. Now, they say the people who went missing haunt the fairgrounds."

"Right. Well, after we moved to Grimlock Cove, our family's happiest times were at the fair."

Josh cocked an eyebrow. "Really?"

Elly had never opened up about the details. In fact, this was the first time she'd shared this part of her life with anybody. To her surprise, the prospect of sharing aloud with another person brought into sharp focus just how tender those old wounds were. It took a moment, but Elly kept any hint of pain or threat of tears well-hidden and said, "My family moved to Grimlock Cove for my dad's work, which meant Mom had to leave her family and hometown behind. Dad says she never adjusted. When he would ask her if she was okay, she'd say she must've forgotten to pack her smile and promised to find a new one."

"I guess she didn't find a new one?" Josh said.

"She found her smile once a year at the fair. Dad said when we were there, they forgot all about real life for a few hours. Said it was like they were young again—flirting, laughing, stealing kisses."

"Do you remember any of that?" Josh said.

"Bits and pieces, but my dad is pretty open about it. He said on our last trip to the fair, Mom insisted we all pile into this photo booth. She wanted something to remind her of how happy we were. Four flashes later, we had a photo strip of goofy faces and surprise kisses—a memory to cherish. According to my dad, he took me for a funnel cake, while

Mom went to a crafts tent to buy a picture frame." Elly sat back, pausing a moment. "Our time in the photo booth was the last time we were all together. After that, she abandoned us."

"Whoa," Josh said, his voice low. "Are you okay?"

This was something Elly loved about Josh: he was never smothering but always checked in. "I'm fine. It was a long time ago."

"And your dad still does all that for her on their anniversary, even though she left?"

Elly shook her head. "He's convinced she was taken like the others."

"What'd the police say?"

"They said she left on her own. Nobody saw a woman struggling, no screaming, or anything. They said there was nothing new about unhappy housewives leaving for another man or whatever."

"I'm sorry," Josh said.

Elly thanked him. "Look. I know my dad. He's never going to let go of Mom. He's going to celebrate his anniversary alone at a table set for two just like he does every year. So, I want him to have something special from the place they had their last date night. I think he'd love that."

"The fairgrounds have been closed for years, though. You think there's anything left?"

"I think it's worth a look."

Josh shifted in his seat. "I don't know. My old man made me swear not to go there."

"I know, but—"

"Dude. You know how much my dad *hates* weed, right?"

"And yet," Elly said, miming Josh puffing on a joint.

"That's not the point," he said and pointed to the tan '78 Chevy Silverado parked outside. "My dad has a *Just Say No* bumper sticker, gives money to the cops and everything. But when I told him a couple kids got caught getting high at the old fairgrounds, he didn't start in with a *only losers do drugs* lecture. He said, 'Boy. If you're gonna get high, do it *anywhere else*.'"

"I get it. Believe me. If *anyone's* dad is against us going there—"

"It's yours. I know," he said, sitting back. "But what are you going to tell your dad if you show up with something from the fairgrounds?"

"If we find something, I'll say we got it from an old junk shop. If we find nothing, we didn't go to the fairgrounds at all. We were at a movie or something."

Josh continued to wrestle with Elly's proposal.

"So, are you in?" she said.

Josh glanced at the server behind the bar and lowered his voice. "Look. I'm not superstitious or anything, but this town has some pretty gnarly ghost stories, and I'm not sure they're all *just* stories."

"I thought you weren't afraid of no ghosts," she said with a wink, and took his hand.

He squeezed hers and said, "I don't want to end up like your old man—sitting here alone with a cinnamon roll."

"But then you'd have the whole cinnamon roll to yourself."

"I'd rather have you."

She smiled and kissed his hand. "It'll be fine. If there was some creep kidnapping people back then, they would've moved on by now. It's been closed for *ten* years." Elly waited for his reply, knowing full well she'd go alone if need be, but she hoped to have him by her side. "I've thought about this a lot, Josh. I really want to try."

After a long moment, he let go of her hand, sat back, and tapped a finger on the side of his empty to-go cup. "If I'm gonna face ghosts tonight, I'm gonna need a pop for the road."

Elly smiled wide and craned her neck to hail the server. "Can we get this man a refill?"

The evergreen horizon swallowed the last of the sun, making room for the dark of night. Josh and Elly climbed into the Silverado and started for Josh's house to pick up flashlights. Once at home, Josh grabbed his backpack to smuggle the flashlights out. When asked where they were off to, Josh told his parents he was taking Elly to the movies.

"Oh," Mr. Janowski said, peeking out from behind the June issue of *Car and Driver*. "Any chance you're seeing the new Rambo?"

Mr. Janowski had regaled Elly with more than a few of his rants on modern movies, claiming actors like Michael J. Fox and Tom Hanks were push overs, comparing them unfavorably to the likes of John Wayne and Steve McQueen. "Now, those were *real* men," he'd say.

Josh, a notoriously terrible liar, attempted a reply, "We're, er, going to see—"

"*Big*," Elly said. "It stars Tom Hanks. He's a boy trapped in a man's body, pretending to be a grown man."

"Should be an easy role," Mr. Janowski said with a grunt and retreated behind his magazine.

Josh and Elly beelined for the front door, but before they could make their exit, Mrs. Janowski chimed in from the kitchen. "I don't want you two out late. When is that movie over? Don't you think it's a little late for the kids to be seeing a movie?"

"Okay, thanks!" Josh said, ignoring his mother and rushing out the door with Elly.

"Remember your curfew!" Mr. Janowski shouted as the front door slammed shut behind Josh.

Josh and Elly scrambled for the truck, climbed in and shared a hard kiss.

"Good save," Josh said, turning the key in the ignition.

"Thanks for doing this," Elly said, momentarily aglow in that euphoria that only comes with young love.

"Please. We could be tightrope walking over a volcano and it'd be fine, as long as I'm with you. Well," he said pausing, "as long as I'm with you *and* home by midnight."

Elly kissed him again, fished a bootleg cassette from her backpack, and held it up to Josh.

He took it and read the handwritten title. "Is this?"

"Yup."

"How?"

"My much cooler cousin who lives in a much cooler town."

Josh shot her an *I don't deserve you* look and loaded the cassette deck. The scratchy, low-fi recording rumbled with crowd noise until the Pixies kicked off "Where Is My Mind?" Elly and Josh shouted with the crowd, bobbing along with the drums as a buzzing electric guitar began to play.

"Let's go find some history," Elly said, turning up the stereo.

With the windows down and the summer air whipping through the cabin, the two sang at the top of their lungs till their voices cracked, and they collapsed into laughter.

It was a short drive, or at least it felt short to Elly, as Josh pulled off the road and parked the truck. The music died with the engine, and the two sat in silence for a moment. The headlights shone on a sun-bleached, red and white steel archway that marked the entrance to the fairgrounds. From the arch hung a sign, faded by the years and coated in a patina of red dust. Graffiti marked the sign with names, hearts with initials and, of course, a penis. Despite the graffiti and overgrowth, the original lettering was still legible. *Grimlock Family Fairgrounds*. Below that was an equally defaced plywood sign bearing a command in red spray paint. *DO NOT ENTER*. Beyond the gate spread a forest, thick with old trees dressed in moss. The red dirt road that wound back to the fairgrounds lie obscured beneath a blanket of ferns and fallen branches. Josh killed the headlights.

"You know," he began. "This would be pretty cool if the fairgrounds weren't haunted."

Elly looked out and saw fireflies. She took Josh's hand and squeezed it. "Are you kidding? It's kind of romantic."

"*This* is romantic?"

"And you're here, supporting me," she continued. "That's *very* romantic."

Josh forced his best smile, clearly struggling to mask his anxiety.

"It'll be fine," Elly said. "If we don't find anything, we call it a night. You might even get me home by curfew."

"Oh, dude. Curfew!" Josh said, flying out of the truck and slamming the door shut in one swift motion.

Elly had meant it as a joke, having forgotten Josh would lose his truck privileges if he missed curfew, but seeing him nearly rip the door off in a rush out of the vehicle had granted Elly an insight into the priorities of a young man. *Losing the truck is scarier than ghosts. Got it,* she thought and climbed out of the truck to join him.

"You ready?" she said, clicking on her flashlight.

Josh switched on his flashlight. "Ready."

Side by side, the two passed under the archway and proceeded down the overgrown path through the forest. It was a short walk made longer by their cautious pace, their attention often arrested by rustling leaves, the creak of tree limbs, and what Elly thought sounded like whispers that seemed to be leading them toward the fairgrounds. The pair sighed in shared relief after stepping into a clearing, where the long abandoned Grimlock Family Fairgrounds waited in decay.

Empty flagpoles encircled the fairgrounds. Strings of dead lights connected the poles like a spider's web. Red and white canopy tents stood between empty lots that were once home to food carts. While the forest had grown thick and wild around the place, and vines had wound their way up lamp posts along the perimeter, no grass or weeds or any kind of overgrowth had encroached upon the fairgrounds. Though the place stood in neglect and decay, the forest had refused to enter.

"I kid you not," Josh said, standing with Elly at the entrance. "I hope there's still some cotton candy."

Elly gave him a look.

"What?" he said. "I don't think it goes bad."

"Let's not eat anything, okay?"

Josh shrugged and the pair entered the fairgrounds.

"It's not so scary once you're here," Josh said, glancing around.

"Maybe some ghost stories *are* just stories," she said, swinging her light left and right, illuminating empty tents and vacant lots.

"See anything your dad might like?" Josh asked.

Elly shook her head. "Let's go up the main drag. That's where they had all the games."

The two stepped onto the wide footpath that ran the length of the fairgrounds. Abandoned carnival booths and sun-bleached, candy-striped tents lined the track. They passed empty booths once occupied by ring toss and pellet gun games. The prizes had all been taken save for a few stuffed animals now covered in mold. Despite a decade of neglect, the place showed signs of recent life. As they reached the heart of the fairgrounds, they found crumpled beer cans and crushed cigarette butts scattered around—the remains of keggers past.

"What the hell?" Elly said.

Josh kicked a beer can aside. "I'm kinda feeling left out."

"We need cooler friends."

Josh laughed. "In Grimlock?"

Elly turned her flashlight up the path to the far end of the fairgrounds.

There, at the end of the main drag, a conspicuously clean tent waited. Unlike the other dusty, candy-striped tents, this one was a deep, emerald green with gold piping glinting along the edges. The tent appeared spotless—even better than new. A swarm of fireflies danced around the front of the tent, lighting a sign above the entrance Elly couldn't quite make out.

"Unreal," Elly said. "Do you see that?"

Josh moved to her side and looked in the direction of her light. "I see," he paused, squinting, "another old tent?"

"Seriously?" Elly said, switching off her light. "There. Do you see it now?"

"I— uh," Josh said, continuing to squint down the row of tents and booths. "What should I be seeing?"

Elly looked at him, incredulous, and looked back at the far tent. How could he not see the conspicuous tent or the fireflies? "You might need glasses, babe," she said, clicking her light on and starting toward the peculiar tent. As they drew near, Elly could make out the sign above the tent's closed entrance. The sign read, *Madame Myrna's Things Remembered*. Elly lowered her light. While the rest of the fairgrounds appeared cold in the silvery moonlight, Madame Myrna's tent was warm, even welcoming, patiently waiting in the glow of the fireflies. "This doesn't seem at all unusual to you?"

Josh aimed his light at the tent, inspected for a moment, and turned to Elly. It was clear he neither cared about the fireflies or appreciated the uniqueness of Madame Myrna's immaculate tent. "We passed by a lot of stuff back there," he said, avoiding the question. "We might've missed a tent with prizes or something. So, if you want to check out *this* tent, I'll go search the others."

"Fine," she said, annoyed but not at all interested in helping a boy see the obvious.

"I'll shout if I find anything," he said as he doubled back.

After Josh had vanished into a nearby tent, Elly turned to face Madame Myrna's. Something tugged at the back of her mind, like a buried memory struggling to resurface. Though she could swear she'd never been inside the tent before, the closer she moved to the entrance, a feeling of nostalgia swelled. Elly clicked off her flashlight and stepped up to the tent. The swarm of fireflies parted, making way for her. She wondered at the little sparks of light twinkling all around her, flecks of gold glinting in her eyes. She reached a hand out for the tent flaps. The tent's fabric was velvet instead of the usual canvas. As Elly's fingers graced the fine, gold threads, the sense of nostalgia overwhelmed her. In that moment, she was a child again. All of the magic, mystery, and wonder of a life barely lived returned. The sensation was positively enchanting. She was back in that night ten years ago—it was her last night at the fair. The warm summer air around her cooled. The passing aroma of funnel cake almost spun her on her heels as the sound of a bustling crowd rose all around her. Elly let go of the flap and twisted in place, turning her flashlight on the fairgrounds behind her. There was no crowd, no funnel cake, and no cool breeze.

"Josh?" Elly felt a touch foolish calling for him, but she needed to hear his voice—to ground herself in where or *when* she was.

A crashing sound came from the nearest tent followed by cursing. "What?" Josh shouted back.

Elly sighed with relief, the sense of disconnection fading. "Nothing!"

"Okay," he said, grumbling something about *stupid fairgrounds*.

Elly turned back to face the entrance to Madame Myrna's, the signage still beckoning her. "Things remembered," she said to herself, thinking back to the last time she'd been at the fair —the last time she'd seen her mother. There'd been a cacophony of carnival games, the rumble of the crowd, and the dissonant clash of music sounding from the many rides and attractions. She remembered the smell of frying bread, the delight of licking powdered sugar from her fingers, and her mother's annoying insistence that she use a napkin. Elly recalled her mother, napkin in hand, tending to her daughter's sticky face. "Remember the good times, Elly," her mother had said. "They're good medicine for the blues."

Children know very well when their parents are happy, and children know very well when their parents are sad. After losing Mom, Dad had found his own blues. For years, Elly had wanted her father to be happy again—like he was that night— but her mother had taken a piece of his happiness with her the night she'd left, leaving only memories.

"Memories," Elly said, thinking aloud. "Mom wanted to remember that night forever. That's why we crammed into that photo booth. Then she left for a tent to find a frame for the photo." Thinking *Madame Myrna's Things Remembered* sounded an awful lot like a keepsake shop, she reasoned this would've been a sensible place for her mother to go looking for a frame. If her mother hadn't simply run off, only claiming to have gone looking for a frame, her mother might have visited this very tent. Elly looked up at the sign, where the fireflies still gathered. "What do you remember, Madame Myrna?" Elly said and took hold of the tent flap. Ignoring the swell of nostalgia, she pushed it open, and stepped in, stopping just inside the threshold. The interior of the tent was bathed in the warm glow of kerosene lanterns and a number of burning candles atop tall, spindly candlesticks lighting walls of bookshelves.

"What in the—" she said, her words failing, as she took in the sight. The bookshelves lined the perimeter inside the tent, packed with journals, ornate card stock, quill pens, and inkwells. A glass cabinet stood at the far end, possessing an inventory of shimmering red and gold liquids that stirred within their corked, glass vials. A small, round table flanked by a pair of wooden chairs waited in the center of the tent. An emerald, velvet tablecloth covered the table, bearing an *M* embroidered in gold thread. Breathless, Elly stepped farther into the tent, letting the flap close behind her. Looking up, the canopy overhead seemed to vanish, transitioning from green velvet to an open, infinite sky, where the moon shone among countless stars. The muffled sounds of a jovial crowd, carnival games, and the chorus of rides and attractions rose from outside the tent.

There's no way this is real, Elly thought, moving to inspect the items along the shelves. *Everything looks so old but totally new.*

"Elly?" Josh called from outside, his voice coming over the rumble of crowded fairgrounds.

But Josh's call scarcely registered, as Elly was far too taken with the bewitching little tent. She crossed over to the small, round table. Above the table hung a sign. *Limit One Per Customer.* Beneath the sign, on the table lied a smokey black, radiant cut gemstone. The thing was semitransparent, and most curiously, a scarlet cloud stirred like a tiny storm within the stone. Before the stone was a golden card bearing gleaming, emerald calligraphy. Elly took the card and read.

Wish upon me

*And ye shall see
That which ye seek
Ye shall receive*

Elly picked up the gemstone. The stone was just large enough to fill her palm, and unnaturally warm to the touch. Looking around the preternatural interior of what should've been an abandoned tent, the proposal of a wish coming true seem almost possible—or at the very least worth a try. Elly closed her eyes, held the stone up to her heart, and pictured her father and mother reunited—the Eaton family, whole again.

"I wish," she began, pausing as the stone grew uncomfortably hot in her hand. She opened one eye to see the scarlet cloud like a tiny lightning storm flashing within the stone. Elly's hand trembled. With both eyes closed tight, she summoned her courage and made her wish. "I wish to find my mother."

At once the air changed. The atmosphere grew heavy, pressing in from all sides. The ground pulsed, sending a shock wave up through her feet, vibrating through her bones, chased by a shiver. Elly tightened her grip on the radiating stone. With every muscle tensed, she stood firm as the pressure grew and the ground quaked again. Then all fell still. The pressure eased, and the gemstone ceased to burn, becoming weightless. Elly's heart raced, pulsing in her ears. Every breath came quick and shallow. The once distant rumble of bustling fairgrounds became a distinct, present sound coming from just outside the tent.

Elly opened her eyes to find two women seated opposite each other at the little table. The one on the left was older with silver hair, wearing a flowing, white linen dress with capped sleeves and ruffles around the hem. She had her hands at the center of the table, her fingertips resting on the gemstone.

Only then did Elly realize the stone was missing from her hand. The woman seated on the right wore denim shorts and a yellow, orange, and blue striped sleeveless top.

"Thank you, Madame Myrna," the woman on the right said, withdrawing her hands from the stone and getting up from the table.

"I hope you get all you wished for, dear," the Madame said, pulling the stone to herself.

Elly stood, mouth slack. The woman turned toward the exit, facing Elly. She had Elly's eyes and Elly's hair, or did she have Elly's mother's eyes, her mother's hair? Head to toe, this woman bore the exact likeness of Elly's—

"Mom?" Elly blurted out.

The women looked at Elly, confused, while Elly stood frozen in an impossible moment.

"Do I know you?" the woman said.

"Mom, er, Mary Eaton?" Elly said, catching herself.

"Yes," the woman replied with hesitance.

Elly stood dumbfounded, wondering where to begin.

Josh's small voice came from behind Elly, as though the voice were coming from behind a solid wall. "Elly? Where'd you go?"

Elly glanced behind her. "In here!" she replied, but when she glanced back, where she expected see the empty, moonlit fairgrounds beyond the tent's now open flaps, she instead saw the Grimlock Family Fair teeming with life. Throngs of people passed the tent. Parents carrying stuffed animals and balloons, while their children gobbled cotton candy and savored melting ice cream cones. With all of it came the return of that unmistakable aroma of funnel cake.

"Excuse me?" Mary said.

Elly turned back to face her mother.

"Are you okay?" her mother said, resting a hand on Elly's shoulder.

Her mother's touch cracked something within Elly. Like a time capsule, calcified by years of lying to herself—swearing she was fine—something broke in her, spilling tears Elly had saved for years.

"You poor thing," her mother said, pulling Elly in for a hug, running a comforting hand over Elly's back.

Elly stood in her mother's arms as resentment clashed with the love she had craved since she was a child. For years Elly had wished she could tell her mother off—to tell her mother that she, Elly, was doing just fine without her. Elly had oscillated between resentment and guilt—feeling as though if she'd been a better daughter, her mother would've stayed. All the things she'd wished she could talk to her mother about—the things her father just couldn't relate to. Her father had done his best to be there for her, but try as he did, he could never replace Mom. When the sobbing subsided and the tears slowed, Elly pulled away to dry her eyes, though a part of her hated letting go.

"I didn't know how much I missed you—how much I've needed you," Elly said and looked up at her mother, chin quivering and eyes glistening. "I thought you hated me."

Her mother's countenance changed from compassion to curiosity. Her gaze narrowed, taking Elly in with a more discerning eye—with a mother's eye. Mary cleared Elly's hair, pulling it back behind her ears to get a better look.

Elly smiled, sniffling. "Hi, Mom."

"Elly?" Mary's eyes shot wide open. "But you're— you're so grown. It can't be."

Elly shook her head, another wave of tears threatening to come. "You've been gone so long."

"No. I just left you outside with your father."

"It's been ten years," Elly said.

"Ten seconds, maybe," her mother said.

"Elly?" Josh continued to call out, his voice slipping farther into the distance.

"Josh!" Elly called back. "Come into the tent!"

Her mother frowned. "Who's Josh?"

"My boyfriend," Elly said.

"No. No. No," her mother said, waving her hands. "None of this makes sense."

"I know," Elly said, taking a step toward her mother, "but if you'll just come with me—"

"I'm sorry," Mary said, waving Elly off, moving past her. "I need some air."

"Wait!" Elly said, reaching out for her mother, who stopped at the entrance. Elly turned back toward the table, hoping to grab the stone from Madame Myrna and make another wish, but there was no stone, and there was no Madame Myrna.

Desperate, Elly turned back to her mother who, despite being distressed, waited for Elly. Perhaps she hoped Elly would announce this was a practical joke, or maybe her mother was so upset *because* she knew Elly was her daughter. Elly crossed over and took her mother's hand. Through tears, she explained as best she could something completely and entirely unbelievable.

"You made a wish," Elly said.

"Yes," her mother replied. "Just now."

"What did you wish for?"

Her mother's eyes searched Elly for a moment before answering. "I wished this night would never end."

Elly's heart sank, her legs nearly failing her. "Dad thought you'd been taken. I thought you'd—" Elly stopped herself. "I thought I'd never see you again, but here you are. You've been *here*—living this night—for ten years."

"I only just made the wish," her mother said. "And it's just a silly wish. It's for fun."

Elly shook her head, not understanding how any of this worked. "Maybe we should leave."

"But I don't want to leave," her mother said.

Elly looked at her mother, the sting of abandonment returning. "But you have to, or you'll *lose* us."

"Look— I don't know what this is," Mary said, taking a step back from Elly, "but you're scaring me." With that, Mary backed out of the tent.

Elly wanted to charge forward—to grab her mother—but she stood rooted to the spot, watching her mother vanish. Josh called out again, his voice barely audible. As Elly stood alone in her shock, the crowd noise changed in her ears, sounding more like to a haunting drone than a cheerful rumble. Elly took a step back, stomach sick, and braced herself on a nearby shelf. The truth that her mother hadn't abandoned her sank in slowly, bringing some relief. But instead of reuniting with her mother, she'd stood here, watching her mother disappear. Elly felt stupid. She'd wasted a truly once in a lifetime opportunity. How could she have expected her mother to understand? All of the things she wished she'd said to her mother flooded her mind.

"Thank you, Madame Myrna," Mary said from behind Elly.

Elly turned to see her mother withdrawing her hands from the stone and standing up from the small table. She was wearing the same denim shorts and the same yellow, orange, and blue striped top.

"I hope you get all you wished for, dear," Madame Myrna said, pulling the stone to herself.

"Wait!" Elly said, rushing forward. Her mother jerked back, frightened, but Madame Myrna simply cocked an eyebrow, appearing curious more than anything. Elly slapped a hand down on Madame Myrna's. "Don't you go *anywhere*," Elly said.

"Do you know this girl?" Mary said, reaching to pull Elly away, but Madame Myrna waved Mary off and left the stone on the table.

"Go on, child," Madame Myrna said, watching Elly, as though interested to see what might happen next.

Elly nodded, took a deep breath, and turned to her mother. "Okay. None of this is going to make any sense, but you wished this night wouldn't end, and that wish has trapped you here in this moment for ten years."

"That's ridiculous," Mary said. "I—"

"Only just walked in here."

Her mother paused. "Well, yes. I—"

"You haven't been happy. You hate living in Grimlock Cove, but at this fair—" Elly broke off.

"I'm happy," Mary said in a small, bewildered voice.

"But you can't *stay* here."

"I know," Mary said, scoffing and playing off the absurd notion that her wish could come true. "Look. My husband and daughter are waiting for me—"

"You don't have your daughter," Elly said.

Mary looked alarmed. "Excuse me?"

Elly struggled with how to explain. "I mean, she's not here. She's growing up," Elly's voice cracked. "She's growing up without you."

"I don't know who you are or what this is," her mother said, drawing herself up, "but my family is waiting for me, and I will not let you spoil our night."

"Please, don't go," Elly said as her mother turned to leave. "Please don't trade our future for the past."

Mary hurried out of the tent, vanishing once again.

Elly clenched her fists, cursing, and charged after her mother. As she stepped through the threshold and out of the tent, the lights dimmed and the crowd grew semi-transparent. Her mother was certainly gone. Elly stumbled to a hard stop, feeling if she took another step, the past moment she'd found herself in would vanish along with her mother.

"Thank you, Madame Myrna," Mary said again from inside the tent.

Elly drew in a deep breath and released it slowly. She should've known her mother wouldn't respond well to the rantings of a self-proclaimed time traveler. Who would? With the loop of her mother appearing and then leaving being so small, how could Elly, in such a short time, explain something so fantastically unbelievable?

"I hope you get all you wished for, dear," Madame Myrna said, and the scene played out with her mother exiting the tent, excusing herself past Elly and fading from view.

"Screw it. I won't explain anything. I'll grab the stone and wish for us to be home in 1988," Elly said to herself and marched into the tent, lunging for the table. Mary stumbled back, shocked. Madame Myrna, however, waved a hand over the stone, leaving the table empty.

The Madame, still seated, looked up at Elly and said, "You may not make another wish."

"Says who?" Elly fired back.

Madame Myrna calmly pointed to the sign that read, *Limit One Per Customer*.

"I'm going to get help," Mary said, moving toward the exit.

"No, wait!" Elly said, causing her mother to pause.

"Girl," Madame Myrna said. "Do you think a power that could grant the impossible is too weak to deny *your* will?"

Elly looked to the Madame. "I just want her to come home with me. It's wrong for you to keep her here."

"What are you talking about?" Mary said.

"You're trapped in some kind of time loop here, Mom," Elly said, keeping her eyes locked on Madame Myrna.

"Are you on drugs, young lady?" her mother said.

"Not at the moment," Elly said.

"I've done nothing but grant wishes," Madame Myrna said. "Not once have I imposed my own will, but I will uphold the rules agreed upon."

Mary Eaton, seeming to have heard enough, exited the tent, leaving Elly to pace the floor, wracking her brain to find a way to undo her mother's wish.

"Thank you, Madame Myrna," Mary said once again.

Elly moved up to the table as her mother made to stand up. Elly put a hand on her mother's shoulder and pushed her back down into the seat. "Make one more wish."

"Take your hand off of me," her mother said.

"Make one more wish," Elly insisted, her tone dangerous.

"Okay," Mary said in a soothing tone. "I will. Just please take your hand off of me."

Elly withdrew her hand, and took a step back. "Okay. Now, wish to be back home with your family."

"But my family is—"

"Just make the damned wish, *please*," Elly said, her desperation overflowing.

Mary nodded and reached for the stone, but there was no stone. Both Elly and Mary looked to the Madame, who once again pointed up to the sign. *Limit One Per Customer.*

"There are," the Madame said, pausing to look Elly in the eye, "rules."

Elly's urge to strangle the Madame sent her hands flying for the Madame's throat, but as Mary ran out of the tent, frightened and calling for help, the scene reset, and Madame Myrna vanished. When Elly attempted to steal the stone and wish her mother away, the stone did nothing, and the Madame reminded Elly that there is only one wish allowed. Every subsequent attempt ended with her mother leaving frightened or confused, and the Madame vanishing, having been no help at all. Feeling defeated, Elly sat on the ground, hidden amongst the shelves, and wept. At the end of each loop, after her mother had left, Elly would scream, venting her anger before her mother would reappear at the table.

As the loop began once again, and Mary Eaton thanked Madame Myrna, Elly could see no way out for her mother. What she knew was, her mother's loop reset every time she left the tent. Josh's voice hadn't come for a while now, and Elly feared if she stayed in this place much longer, she might be trapped in her mother's endless loop—if she wasn't already. There were no wishes left, her mother couldn't accept the fact that her daughter had aged ten years in a moment, and there was no way to strong-arm Madame Myrna, so Elly accepted defeat. She couldn't bring her mother home, that was true, but at least now she knew her mother hadn't abandoned them. Elly continued to think on it as another loop played out. Elly couldn't have a mother-daughter heart-to-heart, but perhaps she could have a moment she'd dreamed of since losing her mother. How could she say the things she needed to say?

"I hope you get all you wished for, dear," Madame Myrna said.

Elly took a deep breath, got to her feet, and approached her mother, who was just standing up from the table.

"Hi, jerk face," Elly said under her breath to Madame Myrna.

The Madame gave a knowing smirk.

"Mrs. Eaton?" Elly said.

"Yes?" her mother said.

"You're Elly's mom, right?"

Mary cocked her head, smiling. "I am. Do you know Elly?"

Elly nodded and continued, "She goes to school with my little sister, and my sister thinks Elly is the coolest."

"You know what? So do I," Mary said, beaming.

A lump filled Elly's throat. "My sister has a few friends. Is Elly the one with curly black hair?"

Mary scrunched up her face. "Not my Elly. Here," she said, withdrawing a photo strip from her pocket and holding it up. "That's her."

"May I?" Elly asked, reaching for the photo strip. Mary reluctantly agreed. Elly took the photo strip and looked it up and down, holding back tears. "You all look so happy."

"We are," her mother said.

At that, Elly broke and the tears fell. Without hesitation, Mary threw her arms around Elly, who confided in her mother. "My home isn't happy—not like this."

Mary held Elly tighter.

"My mother left us when I was young," Elly continued.

"That's awful," Mary said.

"Would you ever leave your family?"

"Never," her mother said with iron resolve. "Never in a million years."

Elly sobbed and sniffled and clung to her mother. "You know your family loves you, and they always will."

"I know," Mary said, patting Elly's back.

After a long moment, Elly said, "Even though I lost her, I still love my mom."

Mary pulled back, keeping a hand on the other's shoulder. "Would you like to join us for some funnel cake? You can meet Elly."

"I would," Elly said, collecting herself.

Mary waved goodnight to Madame Myrna. Elly looked back at the Madame, who waved a hand over the wishing stone. The stone disappeared, and the Madame looked up from the table, unmoved.

"Give Josh my best," Madame Myrna said. "He's a good boy. Deserves a better fate."

"What?" Elly said, but Mary turned Elly toward the exit.

When Elly looked back over her shoulder, the Madame had vanished.

"Now, I don't know how you feel about funnel cake," Mary said, ushering Elly forward, "but my daughter *loves* any kind of sugar and bread—donuts, cinnamon rolls, cupcakes— but she *especially* loves funnel cake. And I think you could use some right about now. My treat."

Forgetting about Madame Myrna and the surreal nature of all that had transpired, Elly took a deep breath, released it, and said, "I would like that very much."

Elly walked out of *Madame Myrna's Things Remembered* arm-in-arm with her mother. As the pair stepped out of the tent, the ensemble of carnival games and crowds began to fade. The lights died, the music stopped, and the arm holding Elly's arm faded away.

Elly put her right hand on her arm, where her mother's had been.

"Elly!" Josh said, rushing forward. He took her by the shoulders and looked her over. "Are you okay?"

Not ready to speak, she nodded.

"You scared the crap out of me," he said. "I thought— I thought you'd been taken. I ran all over the place looking for you. Where were you?"

"It's hard to explain. I was looking for my mother—" she broke off, her voice cracking.

Josh pulled her in and held her. "You don't have to explain. I'm just glad you're okay."

Elly rested her head on his shoulder, trembling, overwhelmed.

After a moment, Josh said, "All I found was an unopened pack of smokes. Did you find anything?"

After a deep, shuddering breath, Elly said, "Actually, I did." She pulled away and cast a glance back at the now empty lot where Madame Myrna's tent had been. Elly looked down to find she still held the photo strip her mother had handed her. She held it up, each picture vivid in the ghostly moonlight.

Josh leaned in to see. "What'd you find?"

Taking a breath to steady herself, Elly sighed and said, "I found my mom."

THE MANY-EYED MOTEL

Grimlock Cove, 2019

―――

Atop a hill, autumn leaves lie scattered across a two-lane blacktop. Fiery orange, yellow, and red leaves appeared almost gray under a pale moon. Carpenter houses lined the dark street, where children dreamt of wondrous things such as flying like a bird, while their parents dreamt of wondrous things like retirement. All was still, save for a light breeze rustling the leaves, and all was quiet, save for the songs of restless crickets and the distant sound of an eight-cylinder engine approaching. Like a cannonball blasting through a glass house, a blacked-out Mercedes-AMG barreled over the blacktop, shattering the serenity. The leaves blew up into a flurry and swirled around the car as it roared into the sleeping town of Grimlock Cove.

Blake Gall sat in the passenger seat, checking the comments on his latest video. He was a rising influencer whose channel just hit one million subscribers before his twenty-fourth birthday, but for Blake, one million subscribers was a milestone—not a finish line. He brushed a tuft of straw blond hair out of his blue eyes as he skimmed the comments, getting stuck on every negative one he saw. "Why'd this girl call me a vapid dick?" Blake looked up from his phone, confounded. "I don't vape."

"People are stupid, bro," Chaz said from the driver's seat. Chaz Garcia was a member of the *Galler's Ballers* entourage. He'd been earning more screen time after some of the subscribers commented on how much they loved his big, brown, puppy-dog eyes.

"Yeah, but she's hot, so it matters," Blake said, refreshing his view counter. "I need more views, man—all eyes on me."

"You'll get 'em, bro. You're gonna be trending."

"I'm not *just* another star, you know? I'm the Sun, bro—the center of the universe. You feel me?"

Chaz nodded. "All eyes on you, bro."

Blake sighed. "They better be." He set his phone aside and turned his camera on.

Chaz turned into another neighborhood, where patio homes lined the winding road, lit only by porch lights. The AMG's cold, xenon high beams shone into windows, indifferent to the late hour. Chaz, at Blake's insistence, floored the gas pedal, and the 525-horsepower engine roared obediently. Blake hit *record*. Chaz drifted through a turn, tires screeching, slipping until they found purchase, and the car rocketed forward.

"Punch it again!" Blake said, turning the camera on himself, pulling his best shocked face.

Chaz complied, as did the car, but the sudden burst of speed caused the car to fishtail, careening through several mailboxes before Chaz could regain control. Blake cursed, acting surprised, but inwardly he relished the clickable content.

"Bro! I think that's gonna leave a scratch," Chaz said.

"Go! Go! Go!" Blake said, laughing and waving a hand forward. He turned the camera on the rubble left behind as the lights inside a number of houses switched on. Turning the camera off, Blake twisted back around and settled into his seat, laughing. "That's gonna be so sick, bro."

"So sick," Chaz said with a note of relief, letting off the gas. The wreckage left behind disappeared in the rearview, and after a moment, Chaz cleared his throat. "Hey, bro. I want to thank you for bringing me along. It really means a lot since my dad disappeared, and you're like a bro—"

"Yeah, totally. So, where are we?"

Chaz fell silent.

"Hold on," Blake hit *record*, turned his camera on Chaz, and started again, but this time with more energy. "Yo! Where the *hell* are we, bro? Like, where have you taken us?"

"Uh—We are on our way to the . . . eh . . . hold on," Chaz said, faltering. "Can we try that again?"

Blake lowered the camera. "Seriously?"

"You caught me off guard. I blanked on the name."

Blake groaned. "We're on our way to the freakin' convention."

"Sorry," Chaz said, eager to please. "I got it."

Blake snapped into character, hit record, and said to the camera, "Yo! Where the *hell* are we, bro? Where have you taken us?"

"Bro! We are on our way to MeCon, where the world's top influencers are celebrated."

"Right. Right. But I mean, where are we right *now*?" Blake whipped the camera to himself and pulled a face before turning the camera back on Chaz.

"We're in Grimlock Cove, bro."

"What the hell is Grimlock Cove?" Blake asked, laughing into the camera.

Chaz played along. "Bro. They say this place is actually haunted."

"No way! We're not staying here, right?"

Chaz, perfectly on cue, turned to look at the camera. "Yeah, bro. *This* is where we're staying tonight."

"But like a nice hotel, right?"

"Nah, man. A haunted motel!"

"Motel? Bro. Motels are for hookers!"

This back and forth continued until Blake, feeling he had sufficient material, switched off the camera, his voice returning to his usual tone. "We'll edit it. It'll be dope. But for real, how far to the hotel?"

Chaz kept his eyes straight ahead, fingers tapping on the wheel. "We . . . uh . . . we don't have a hotel."

"Wait. For real?"

"There're no hotels here, and you said you wanted Halloween-themed content, so—"

"For the *camera*, bro. I'm not actually sleeping in some trash-ass motel."

Chaz sighed. "They don't got nothin' else."

Blake shook his head. "You're unbelievable, bro."

Chaz kept his hands on the wheel, casting tense glances between the road and the GPS. "I heard they got rooms with an ocean view."

Blake showed his continued disappointment by ignoring Chaz, and turning to his phone to check for new comments on his latest upload.

"If it's no good, I'll find somewhere else," Chaz said. "I'll make it right, bro. I swear."

Blake refreshed the comment section again before saying, "So, is this motel actually creepy or just trash?"

"People love your content, man, and they straight-up *love* Halloween crap. This'll be something fresh for your channel."

Blake kept his eyes on his phone. "Why's it haunted? Ghost kids? Axe murderer? Ghost-kid axe murderers?"

"The wiki said people who stay there never leave."

Blake considered this for a moment. "Let's go with ghost kids. Ghost kids creep everyone out."

After cutting through town, the pair reached the cove, where The Red Water Motel waited. Gravel crunched as the AMG rolled into the parking lot and slowed to a stop. A neon vacancy sign buzzed overhead, casting a red glow on a welcome sign bearing an anchor entangled in squid-like tentacles. The outer walls wore a salty patina, and every window stood dark. Blake counted thirteen rooms as his eyes moved along the length of the old motel. The unlit front office appeared empty behind hazy windows.

Blake sat slack-jawed, taking in the place as Chaz killed the engine. The two sat in silence for a moment until Blake said, "Is this place even—"

But before the word *open* fell from Blake's lips, a neon sign lit up in the office window that read, *OPEN*.

"I think this place might *actually* be haunted," Chaz said.

"It *might* be haunted, but it's *definitely* trash, bro. Oh, hey!" Blake said, smacking Chaz's arm. "Didn't your dad run off to a trash motel like this?"

"I should get the bags," Chaz said.

"Maybe he's still in there with your new mom," Blake said with a smirk as he hit record. "Yo! We're here, and what is this? Look at this place!" Blake turned the camera on the motel sign, zooming in and out. "Chaz. Are you serious?"

As the two played their parts for the camera, a light came on in the front office, bringing their exchange to a halt. Blake spun the camera around and panned between himself and the office. "Looks like it's time to check in."

The two filed out of the Mercedes, pulled on their matching *Galler's Ballers* hoodies, and checked their hair in their selfie cams. After preening for a solid minute, Blake hit *record* and panned across the front of the motel.

"I'll get the bags, bro," Chaz said, "and no stress. This is gonna be good."

"Shut up, Chaz. You're talking over the B-roll," Blake said, watching shadows, creeping overgrowth, and filthy windows in the camera's LCD display.

"Sorry, bro."

"Dude," Blake said, lowering the camera and glaring. "Shut. Up."

Chaz winced, mouthed, "Sorry," grabbed the bags, and shut the trunk.

Turning the camera on himself, Blake did his best to act anxious as he pulled the front office door open. While the exterior of the motel was a showcase of neglect, the inside was something else entirely. Navy blue, velvet curtains covered numerous windows—more than Blake remembered seeing from the outside. The richly dark, hardwood floor bore no dust or dirt. A circular rug lay in the middle of the room. The rug was intricately woven, featuring a squid-like creature, its tentacles reaching all around. The outer edge of the rug was framed by a ring of open eyes. Beyond the rug stood the front desk that matched the floor, more resembling an executive desk than a typical motel desk. The wood face was adorned with intricate, nautical carvings framed in brass. Atop the desk sat a brass inkwell and fountain pen. Beside the pen waited a call bell, begging to be rung. Behind the desk stood a wooden door with a circular, hatch window.

Blake stared into the camera, "Okay, Gallers and Ballers.

Y'all saw the outside, right? How does this room exist inside a meth-head motel?"

Chaz stepped in, mouth agape as he turned to take in the room.

"Crazy, right?" Blake said, crossing the room to an oil painting that hung on the far wall. The painting was of a middle-aged man. A plaque mounted on the bottom of the frame had no name, only dates: *1920–1972*. The man in the painting wore a navy pea coat, a white button-down with a navy blue tie. His hair was cropped high under a tweed flat cap. The man's Bandholz beard reached down past his collar.

DING! DING! DING!

Chaz drummed the call bell to Blake's amusement.

DING! DING! DING!

"Hello?" Blake called. "This service sucks. I don't think I'm leaving a good review."

"Hello?" Chaz said, parroting Blake.

"Well, I guess we're sleeping in the lobby tonight," Blake said, dropping to the floor and pretending to cuddle the creature depicted on the rug.

Chaz dropped to the floor beside Blake, and the latter turned the camera around and pulled it back to include Chaz in the shot. "Alright, guys. We're calling it a night here in this *insane* motel in Grimlock Cove. I'm not gonna lie—it's weird as hell, but we're here. Don't forget to smash that subscribe button, leave a comment, and don't forget to hit up the dopest merch in the game. Get over to gallsquad dot com and get yourself this hoodie—"

"Welcome," a voice said, cutting Blake off.

Blake and Chaz screamed in unison, hamming it up for the camera. Together, the two leapt up and rushed to the front desk.

An older man stood waiting behind the front desk. He wore a navy pea coat over a tattered, white turtleneck. His hair was cropped and dark with gray around the temples that matched the gray in his wooly beard. His eyes hid behind circular, gold-framed glasses with mirror reflective lenses. The man continued, his voice weathered, and his tone indifferent. "Welcome to The Red Water Motel. I'll be your concierge."

"Yes, Jeeves," Blake said, fished cash from a pocket, and slapped a hundred dollar bill on the desk. "We'd like a room for two, please, and your finest hookers!"

The concierge stood unmoved. "Our guests make payment when the terms of their stay have been agreed upon."

Blake rolled his eyes for the camera, planted a finger on his hundred dollar bill, and dragged it back to himself. "Very well, Jeeves."

"We do have a place for you both," the concierge said, pulling open a desk drawer, withdrawing a sheet of parchment, and spreading it on the desk. Ornate calligraphy covered the page. "Do the gentlemen agree to the terms of the Motel?" the concierge asked, taking the fountain pen from the desk, drawing black ink from the brassy well, and offering the pen to Blake.

Blake took the pen and glanced over the sheet, unable to comprehend any of what was inscribed. Upon closer inspection, he saw the lettering more resembled symbols or little sketches than anything found in the English alphabet. Shrugging it off, he found a signature line at the bottom. "So, what's this for? Incidentals? Because, bro," he laughed, pausing to look up at the camera, "you're gonna need something for incidentals."

The man remained stoic and even in tone. "The gentleman seeks a place to stay, but more than that, the gentleman wishes to look out on an adoring world. Sign here, and you will behold the adoration of many."

Blake hadn't heard a word the concierge had said. His mind had been on what he'd say or do next that'd be good for content, but once the concierge had stopped talking, Blake signed with dramatic flourish and dropped the pen like a mic. "Okay, Jeeves. Let's go!"

The concierge picked up the pen and handed it to Chaz.

Chaz looked between the parchment and Blake, who waved an impatient hand.

"Does the gentleman have a question?" the concierge asked.

Shedding his on-camera persona, Chaz asked in earnest, "Do you know if Damián Garcia was a guest here? Kind of looks like me? My mom says I have his eyes."

Blake shot Chaz a look, frustrated that he broke character, but Chaz ignored him.

The concierge's expression, however, didn't change. "If the gentleman wishes to discover the secrets of The Red Water Motel, the gentleman must agree to the terms."

"Bro," Blake said, lowering the camera and his voice. "Sign the damned thing and let's go."

Ever obedient, Chaz signed. The concierge collected the pen and returned it to the inkwell. After inspecting the signatures, the concierge rolled up the parchment and returned it to the desk drawer. To Blake's surprise, when the concierge withdrew his hands from under the desk, he held a crystal decanter, with what Blake assumed to be liquor, in one hand and a pair of tulip glasses in the other. Blake turned the camera on the empty glasses. The inky drink poured thick as syrup. Once the concierge had filled both glasses, he served his guests and waited.

Blake turned the camera on himself and said, "Free drinks!" then stopped. "Wait. I can do better."

The three stood there in a pause as Blake searched for the right words. The concierge's face remained blank.

"How about 'this is how we do'?" Chaz suggested.

Blake nodded. "This is how *we* do," he said, and the pair drained their glasses.

The flavor was like spiced rum with a hint of salt, and strangely, a strong note of copper. The drink burned all the way down. Blake put a hand to his chest as his heart beat erratically, followed by a stabbing pain. His eyes lost focus, body tipped back onto his heels, and he slowly fell, weightless, as though sinking underwater.

The motel lobby vanished as Blake found himself standing on the main deck of what looked like a pirate ship. Everything was slick with rain and sea spray. Sheets of rain stung his face and buffeted the sails, as gray, frothy waves crashed over the bow. Blake stumbled around, shoved aside by the panicked crew, struggling to keep control of the ship. Lightning flashed and thunder rolled over the desperate cries of the ship's crew as the bow found jagged, black rocks. The ship hung for a moment, until a choir of deep, droning voices swelled over the din. As the choir grew louder, a number of enormous, black tentacles breached the white-capped waters. The tentacles whipped around, cutting the air and snatching sailors from the main deck. Screams carried over the face of the waters, falling silent as their bodies were torn asunder. The choir sang more excited as bones broke and flesh was rended, leaving a bloody offering of entrails to splash down. The tentacles soon took hold of the ship and pulled it into the open mouth of a yawning cavern. When the song ended, the scene turned black. Blake no longer felt the rain or heard the cries of dying men, and the stabbing pain in his chest had ceased.

"Now, if the gentlemen would kindly follow me," the concierge said, his voice distant.

Blake's eyes fluttered open to find himself lying on the floor before the front desk. No taste of copper remained in his mouth. Blake looked over at Chaz, who lie beside him, and the pair exchanged equally confused looks.

"Gentlemen?" the concierge said, inclining over the desk to see the pair on the floor.

After a moment, Blake found his spark and said, albeit more subdued than usual, "The drinks here are *not* for the faint of heart."

The two rose unsteadily to their feet and met the concierge behind the desk.

"Gentlemen," the concierge said as he pulled the door open and bowed them in, "Welcome to The Red Water Motel."

Blake stepped through the threshold, expecting to find a long hall lined with rooms, but instead he found a small, dimly lit room with an antique elevator. A brassy, metal gate stood shut, and through the gate Blake could see the exposed elevator shaft. Above the elevator was a large, ornate, brass dial indicating thirteen floors. The concierge pressed the call button and stood watching the spindly arm on the dial, that had been at rest on the thirteenth floor, slowly sweep from *13* to *1*.

"Sir?" Chaz said to the concierge. "Are there really thirteen floors?"

The concierge's eyes stayed on the elevator's dial. "This elevator will take us down to the cove."

Chaz turned to Blake. "When we pulled up, I only saw one floor—*one*."

"Tourist trap, bro. It's all for show," Blake said, relishing the content.

"Bro," Chaz said, taking Blake by the arm. "Don't you think this is weird for a motel? We're already on the ground floor. The elevator is coming *up*."

"I know how elevators work," Blake said, pulling his arm

back from Chaz. "Now shut the hell up. You're talking over the B-roll again."

"Blake," Chaz said. "I got a feeling we should leave."

Blake dropped all pretense. "You know what? *You* can leave. You can leave the free room in my house, the free booze, and the free girls."

Chaz shook his head. "Seriously, bro. I don't think—"

"I will cut you off. You will be back at Gino's delivering cold pizzas for shitty tips."

Chaz fell silent as the elevator dinged. The concierge slid the gate open.

"You with me?" Blake said.

Chaz ran his fingers through his black hair. "Yeah, bro. I got you."

The concierge gestured to the open elevator. "If the gentlemen please."

"Thank you, Jeeves," Blake said, marching in. Chaz followed, and with the two young men aboard, the concierge stepped in, slid the elevator gate closed with a clang, and pressed the black and gold button marked *13*. The elevator shuddered and groaned as it began its descent.

The dial inside the elevator indicated they had passed several floors, but all Blake could see through the gate was slick, black stone—no hallways or doors—just stone. The temperature dropped and the air dampened as they sank. When the spindly brass arm finally reached the number *13* on the dial, the elevator jerked to an abrupt stop. The concierge pulled open the gate, exited, and waved an arm to welcome the other two.

The pair stepped out to the thirteenth floor. Instead of the musty halls, dank carpets, and slimy ice machines Blake had expected, he found himself standing on a salt-worn dock that ended at the elevator and stretched out ahead, disappearing in a wall of fog. A row of black lanterns hung above the dock, suspended from posts, and spaced six feet apart. Each lantern held a small, green flame behind leaded glass. Gentle waves lapped against the dock, and splintered boards creaked underfoot as Blake turned to take it all in. The thirteenth "floor" was a cavern, cold and wet. The cave's mouth opened at the far end, where the moonlight glinted over jagged, black rocks.

"Gentlemen?" the concierge said, suggesting the other two follow him, but the two stood dumbfounded.

"Blake," Chaz said, finding his voice. "I think we should look for somewhere else to stay."

"Are you kidding me? Look at this place," Blake said. "This is a viral goldmine."

"But I think—"

Blake ignored Chaz, cutting him off. "Lead on, Jeeves!"

The concierge gave a nod, turned on his heels, and led them forward. Chaz reluctantly followed. As the three made their way up the long dock, disembodied voices rose, growing louder as they approached the fog. Blake strained, peering blindly into the gray. A few steps later, they emerged from the fog, and something grand appeared. Blake and Chaz cursed in unison—one with excitement, the other with dread.

Three masts towered, vanishing into the high shadows. Each mast held limp, tattered sails. The ship's body was long and slender, with a wicked gash splitting the bow. Even at rest, the vessel looked fast. At the rear of the ship, a large lantern hung outside what would be the captain's quarters. At the other end, a wooden figurehead clung to the hull. She held one hand up, while the other covered her eyes.

"Okay," Blake said. "There's a freaking pirate ship! You better be filming this, Chaz."

"This is the legendary clipper ship, *The Lady Myrna*," the concierge said. "In its day, this vessel could carry a bounty of gold from Grimlock Cove to San Francisco faster than any other."

"Actual gold?" Blake asked.

"Indeed," the concierge said.

"Jeeves," Blake said, moving inches from the other's ear. "We could be rich. I mean, I'm already rich, but *you* could be rich, too."

"Are those other guests?" Chaz said, pointing to the people moving along the deck.

The concierge did not answer.

"Aye!" a surly voice called from the ship. "This them?"

The concierge nodded, continuing toward the ship as the elevator dinged behind them.

"Okay," Blake said. "This is a hell of an attraction and all, but I have to know. What's the deal with this place? Is it a dinner theater thing, or some kind of immersive pirate experience?"

"Blake," Chaz said, with a tremble.

Blake turned to see two burly men, blindfolded and dressed like pirates, approaching. Each carried a limp body slung over his shoulder. Blake's insides twisted. "Chaz? Do those bodies look dead to you?"

Chaz let out a string of jumbled curses under his breath, to which the concierge calmly replied, "These are the terms the gentlemen agreed to."

"We're leaving now!" Chaz said. Blake opened his mouth to speak, but Chaz cut him off. "I don't give a shit about your money or your videos or whatever the hell else. I'm out!"

"I'm afraid you are both one irreversible decision beyond the point of return," the concierge said, directing Blake and Chaz to a ramp that led from the dock up to the ship. "Your place is aboard *The Lady Myrna*."

Blake looked between the ship and the concierge. "Cut the bullshit, man. I'll plug your business on my show. You'll get millions of views and all that, but I am absolutely done."

"Pardon, boys," a gravely voice said as one of the men carrying a body bumped into Blake.

Blake stumbled aside, his foot slipping off the edge of the dock. His arms flailed until a firm hand caught him by the wrist. With one foot on the dock and the rest of him hanging over the water, the concierge pulled him back.

"The gentleman would do well not to swim in *these* waters," the concierge said.

Blake jerked his wrist free. "I've got all this on video—you, your cosplay pirates, and everything. I can make or break your business. Over a million subscribers are going to see what I want them to see, so if you—"

"The gentlemen agreed to leave behind their material possessions," the concierge said, cutting Blake's threat short.

Blake paused, confused. He checked himself, and after not finding his camera, he looked to Chaz, who shrugged and said, "I thought *you* had it."

Blake had been certain he'd had his camera with him only a moment ago, but thinking back, each passing moment left the moment before more hazy. The second man carrying a body chortled as he pushed past. Blake, already a powder keg of anger and confusion, reeled around to lay into the man. But as he opened his mouth to rage, his breath was stolen by what he saw. Sandy blond hair. Vacant, blue eyes. The lifeless body slung over the man's shoulder was his own.

"Wait," he said, feeling sick. "Wait!" Blake shot out a hand for the man carrying his body, but the man continued forward. Blake started after, but the concierge's strong arm shot out and held him back.

"That no longer belongs to the gentleman."

"Bullshit!" Blake said, struggling against the concierge's restraint. "That's *my* body."

"*Was* your body, sir," the concierge said. "You parted with it and your material possessions when you agreed to the terms of the Motel."

"Does this mean we're dead?" Chaz asked, inspecting his own hands as though expecting to see through them.

"If the gentlemen will kindly wait here, the ritual is set to commence," the concierge said and moved to the edge of the dock. There he knelt and bowed his head.

Blake trembled. His stomach churned; his mind grasped for reality.

The ship's busy crew fell still and silent. It was then Blake noticed it. Just like the pair of men who'd passed by on the dock, each person aboard the ship seemed to be missing their eyes. The two men carrying Blake's and Chaz's corpses climbed the ramp onto the ship and crossed over to the port bow. The concierge began to hum, keeping his head bowed low. Every man and woman aboard the ship joined in, creating a loud, dissonant drone that carried throughout the cavern.

Blake's attention snapped to the only person moving on the main deck. A silver-haired woman cut a path through the crew, arriving at the edge of the deck, where the two men waited with the corpses. Unlike the rest, she had her eyes.

The crew's cacophonous drone continued, rising with anticipation. Everyone along the main deck placed a hand over their empty eye sockets. The silver-haired woman held up a hand, placed her other hand over her eyes, and sang in a loud voice, with all of the crew and the concierge joining:

> *"We have eyes, but we do not see,*
> *So humbly we give our eyes to thee.*
> *Great god, veiled in mystery,*
> *Unknowable, our great god unseen,*
> *Witness us, as we blind believe,*
> *Receive our meager offering."*

At this, the still, black waters before the dock began to bubble and churn, causing the dock to creak.

Chaz moved to Blake's side and whispered, "We can make it to the elevator. Nobody's looking. No one will see us."

A deep groan resounded throughout the cavern, but it hadn't come from the crew. The water swelled, sending waves into the creaking dock. Blake looked out over the water as the stirring moved from the center of the cavern to just off the port bow of *The Lady Myrna*, where the two men with the dead bodies waited. A pair of black tentacles shot up out of the water toward the bodies. The first tentacle reached Chaz's lifeless body and received it as an offering. Then a great mound of slick, black flesh broke the surface of the water. It was like watching a submarine rise, only the form was bulbous and covered in a wealth of blinking, human eyes. The other tentacle took hold of Blake's corpse, wrapping around and constricting the body until blood seeped through flesh, spilling over the coiled tentacle. The men who had held the bodies stepped back, dropped to their knees, and bowed their heads.

The water around the creature churned as though infested with a bed of angry snakes as its tentacles whipped and thrashed in the water. The crew sang louder, repeating their hymn. The creature lifted the two bodies high over its head, suspended for a moment until the silver-haired woman spoke again, keeping one hand over her eyes and the other held high. "To the most worthy, many-eyed god, Uk'tormu. We give thanks!"

The song ended and the crew threw up their hands, cheering and praising their god. Uk'tormu's tentacles lashed the waters around it, growing more frenzied as though fueled by the fervent worship. Blake watched his body break. Black tentacles dripped with blood and sea water. Finally, a second pair of tentacles rose into the air, each taking a hold of one of the bodies. Like a host popping champagne, the creature pulled both bodies apart with a grisly sound unlike any Blake had ever heard. The bones broke like crackers in a clenched fist. The blood offering showered over the creature like a perverse baptism. Uk'tormu's tentacles quivered with delight. With its many eyes wide open, the creature bathed in the offering of its faithful. After the cheering died down, Uk'tormu searched the cavern with its many eyes as it slowly sank, returning to the depths.

Blake fell to his knees, his mind breaking under the weight of it all. There was nothing good here. This was a place beyond unholy—beyond evil. But after a moment, his breathing slowed and whatever distress he'd felt seemed to wane. He tried to think back, but his memories were indistinct. Like a dream slipping away soon after waking, whatever moments had led up to this—whatever life he'd lived before—it had all faded away. There was only this ship, these gathered faithful, and his god, Uk'tormu. Despite that, something buried in the back of Blake's mind tugged at him. He struggled to tease out that small something until a hand fell on his shoulder.

"Humble eyes stay low," the concierge said.

Blake somehow understood this and lowered his gaze until a tentacle snaked up out of the water, gently latching its suckers onto his eyes. Blake shrieked, but as the tentacle coiled around his head, there was a comfort in its embrace. After a moment, the tentacle released him and retreated into the water, leaving behind empty, fleshy sockets.

"Stand tall, children of Uk'tormu," the concierge said. "I now call you my brothers."

Blake stood on unsteady legs as the concierge placed a strip of cloth over Blake's empty sockets and tied it off. Blake cocked his head and looked around the cave. Where before he'd seen shadows, he now saw light. The moon hit the rocks like sunlight, and the lamps that lit the dock shone like beacons.

"I can see," a voice said.

Blake turned to see a young man with dark hair. He, too, was blindfolded and taking in the new world around him.

"You could not see the value of one faithful to you," the silver-haired woman said to Blake, arriving at the concierge's side. "And you," she said, addressing the dark-haired one. "You could not see your own worth."

Blake and the other one nodded their agreement and introduced themselves to each other with familial warmth.

The woman turned to one of the crew. "Brother Garcia. Please, assist our new brothers aboard."

Brother Garcia was an older man with thick, black hair. He replied, "With pleasure," and hastened to Blake's side.

When Blake saw Brother Garcia for the first time, something about him seemed familiar. "Excuse me?" Blake said to Brother Garcia. "Have we met before?"

Brother Garcia's face wrinkled up in thought as he considered Blake for a moment, but the moment was cut short when Brother Garcia winced in pain, bringing both hands to his head.

"Life begins with Uk'tormu," the concierge said, putting a hand on Blake's shoulder. "The future is not found in the past. The future is found in Uk'tormu."

Blake's curiosity faded as the concierge's words brought a strange comfort.

"Your eyes are his eyes," the concierge continued. "What he sees, you see. When next we bring another into the family, you will bear witness to all the adoration given to Uk'tormu. As we adore him, so are we adored. As we worship him, so we are worshipped. We need only bring new followers."

Blake thrilled at this and said softly to himself, "All eyes on me."

The Touch of
Broken Glass

Grimlock Cove, 1987

———

It's a funny thing how houses of healing make room for the dead. Churches have their graveyards; hospitals have their morgues. These were the musings of Josh and Ethan—two high school sophomores enjoying an after-school smoke.

The two sat alone on a rickety fishing dock, looking out across the foggy bay at Grimlock Memorial. A single bridge connected the mainland to the small island where the old hospital had been passed over by progress. Ethan had once visited his Aunt Marie at Grimlock Memorial after she'd missed the last step on a flight of stairs. Ethan remembered the yellowed halls where either end seemed to reach into endless shadow, and the lone, fluorescent light buzzing over the hospital bed that had left Aunt Marie looking cold and sickly.

"But you made it out alive," Josh said in a choked voice before exhaling a rolling cloud of smoke.

"Because we didn't stay the night," Ethan said, taking the joint from Josh. "Seriously, man. I felt things in there—messed up things. My old man says the hospital loses more lives than it saves. Like, there was this girl in the third grade who went in to have her tonsils taken out."

"I still have mine."

Ethan blew a slow train of smoke that hung in the chilled, salt air. "Her parents found her in a coma the next morning."

"Oh, shit," Josh said, rubbing his throat. "Glad I still have mine."

Ethan passed the joint to Josh, making a point to meet his eyes, and said, "She died three days ago."

At Grimlock Memorial, even the common cold could end in death. While most avoided the neglected hospital, for the unfortunate few, it proved a necessary evil.

Dex Maddox, a reporter for the Grimlock Gazette, began each day at with a musical alarm. His clock radio would sound off with whatever was playing on the local alternative station and let the music play as he rolled out of bed. An attractive coworker had recently described him as gangly, so he'd added push-ups to his morning routine, hoping to be seen as more of an Indiana Jones than a curly-haired nerd with a *Blade Runner* tattoo.

After freshening up, Dex would grab a pair of headphones and settle in at his Casio keyboard. With eyes closed, he would sink into entrancing synthesized melodies. Flashes of white, pink, and blue filled his mind's eye, lighting up with the tones and textures. He'd play covers of Bowie, Floyd, and the like. The music quieted his anxious thoughts and eased his stress. This was his medicine—his shelter from the world and, at times, even from himself.

Every morning played in perfect time with Dex setting the tempo—that is, until the morning of October 29th, 1987. Given the chance, Dex Maddox would look back on that day wishing he'd gotten out of bed ten seconds earlier or ten seconds later, because that particular Thursday morning turned from routine to tragic when an oncoming truck drifted into Dex's lane.

He remembered swerving to avoid it—brakes squealing and tires skidding. His brown Oldsmobile Cutlass had fishtailed over the asphalt still slick from the rain. "Don't Dream It's Over" had been playing on the radio when his front end plowed through the guardrail. Dex remembered watching the horizon slowly rise and fall before him as the sedan teetered on the concrete edge high above the bay. He had unbuckled his seatbelt in an attempt to climb into the back seat, hoping to stabilize the car, but as the belt clicked free, the front end dipped, and metal scraped concrete as the car slid forward into a nose dive off the Bay Bridge. The last thing he remembered was the chorus kicking in and gray water rushing up to meet him.

According to Dr. Wagner, Dex had nearly split his skull on his steering wheel when his car hit the water, leaving him with a severe concussion. Fortunately for Dex, a good Samaritan had been fishing under the bridge—a retired fisherman who'd seen Dex's lifeless body slumped in the front seat. The fisherman had dove in after Dex and came away with the best fishing story of his life. When paramedics had finally arrived, Dex's critical condition merited a rush to the nearest hospital.

Dex struggled to focus as he read all of this from a note the doctor had handed him. He glanced up at the doctor, who motioned for him to turn the note over. Dex flipped it around and read on. Both of his legs and his right hip had been fractured in the fall, and the nurse had installed a catheter. The doctor couldn't conclude whether it was the impact, nearly drowning in the icy water, or both, but Dex had suffered profound hearing loss in both ears. He looked up at the doctor who had been speaking with the nurse. Dr. Wagner noticed Dex, smiled, and handed him some pamphlets on hearing loss. A sticky note on the top pamphlet said the doctor would be by later to discuss treatment options with Dex. The note finished with, "Welcome to Grimlock Memorial."

After an afternoon of fitful sleep caused by recurring dreams of falling, Dex stared out the window, watching the sky purple over Grimlock Cove. Street lights blinked on across the bay, and as the world grew darker, the dull glow of his bedside lamp grew brighter.

Empty, yellowed walls rose from brown linoleum floors. The darker the room, the more the walls seemed to close in, entombing Dex. Coupled with the absolute silence, the whole thing made him think of outer space and a sci-fi movie he'd seen recently. Someone in the movie had said nothing could be heard in the vacuum of space—not even a scream. It hadn't meant anything to him then, but now the oppressive silence of space was an easy thing to imagine. Dex raised a hand and snapped his fingers by his ear, hoping to hear the faintest crack of sound. He felt the friction of his middle finger slipping off his thumb and felt the smack of his finger on the fat of his hand, but every attempt left him alone in total silence. His jaw tightened, and he squeezed his ears until they burned, then clapped his hands on the sides of his head like someone punching a steering wheel, hoping the car would start.

The door to his room swung open, and an older nurse appeared. Dex noticed her and stopped beating himself at once. Her hair shimmered a silvery gray, and though he couldn't imagine why, her green eyes brought to mind snakes.

She crossed over to his bedside with a tray of food that could only be served to someone like himself—someone without options. A mold of green gelatin quivered atop a white plastic plate. A dry slice of bread complemented a warm bowl of chicken broth where a few, drowned noodles waited to be fished out. The nurse situated the tray on the overbed table to his left and said something. He watched her pink lips move, but he couldn't make out a single word. Thin crow's feet spread from her eyes as she smiled before turning to leave. He did not return her smile. Did she not know he'd lost his hearing, or did she simply not care?

Dex ignored the tray of food and laid back as his mood darkened. He longed to fall asleep and awake to find this was all a bad dream. But as he watched the shadows grow in the corners, a poison welled up inside him. A grim inner voice— not his own—yearned to drift off to sleep. But this voice did not wish to escape into dreams. This new, small voice wished for endless sleep.

―――

The next morning, a melody played—a melancholy yet hopeful composition. The smell of brewing coffee filled the small apartment as Dex drummed his fingers along white and black keys. Rich, harmonic chords gave him wings; his soul weightless and without fear. Hope, rare and beautiful, swelled with a chordal crescendo until his whole apartment quaked. Water came crashing in through the windows, shattering glass. Doors blew off their hinges in the surge. The apartment quickly flooded. Dex attempted to shield himself with the music, forcing a melody, but his hands slipped across the keys, giving rise to a dissonant wall of sound. He was pulled under the water, flailing helplessly until a hand grabbed hold of him.

Dex awoke to find a young nurse standing beside his bed.

Her right hand rested on his shoulder, while her other held a slip of paper. She was petite with kind, honey-brown eyes framed by curly, blonde locks. After awaking from a nightmare, her presence soothed him. The nurse handed him the slip of paper and collected the tray of untouched food from the night before. Before he could read the note, she gestured to the food as if to say, *Are you sure?* He appreciated she had sense enough not to speak, and he answered with a polite nod.

Dex watched the nurse leave with the food tray and turned his attention to the note. A message scrawled in blue ink said his mother and father would be coming to visit today. *They must've caught the first flight out*, he thought as the nurse returned with a new tray of food. Dex quickly set the note aside. The nurse situated the tray over his lap and held up a note asking if there was anything else he needed. Dex couldn't help but smile. She seemed genuine, and her gentle manner was good medicine. He held up a hand to gesture he was fine and watched her check his morphine drip, change the drainage bag for his catheter, and scribble something on a clipboard before leaving again.

Left to himself, Dex reluctantly tried a spoonful of runny, scrambled eggs. Though the eggs were bland, the cold toast still crunched, and the small cup of fruit—the kind from a tin can—had those little sliced cherries he remembered enjoying as a kid. He washed down the toast with some room-temperature orange juice and picked the cherries out of the fruit cup.

The door swung open, startling Dex, and his mother appeared in the doorway. She rushed in, carefully took Dex's head in her hands and kissed his forehead. Dex's father entered in his usual, reserved fashion as though he'd walked in on a formal occasion. Mom smiled brightly, but Dex knew better. He knew she'd explored every dreadful what-if scenario on the flight in, but she wouldn't let her son see all that fear and uncertainty. No, she'd had years to master putting on a brave face, but Dex was her flesh and blood. He could see through her because he was just like her. Dad greeted Dex with a handshake and a pat on the shoulder. Dex forced a smile, but the moment reminded him of how disconnected he felt. He could feel his father's hand. He could smell his mother's floral perfume. He could even taste it in the air, but the world made no sound—no notes of empathy or encouraging words—only silence. He sat exiled by circumstance—denied the comfort of his mother's voice. As her lips moved busily, he imagined her saying, "How are you feeling? Oh, we were worried sick. What do you need?"

After passing notes back and forth to update his parents on his situation, Dex's mother took him by the hand. She pointed to him and gestured that he should try to speak, but he feared embarrassment. The words may come out clumsily, or he might speak too loudly, so he refused. After a moment's pause, his mother responded with a bittersweet smile. He could see there was so much she wanted to say but knew her words, no matter how full of love, would be lost in the silence clogging his ears.

When evening came, his mother handed him a note saying they were heading out to grab dinner and asked if he'd like anything. He opened his mouth to answer but snapped it shut before any words could tumble out. He motioned to his mother and mimed writing in the air. His mother handed him her pen, and he scribbled, "burger, fries, milkshake."

The smell of greasy fast food lingered in the room long after his mother and father had bid him goodnight. Dex's mother had left him with an 8 x 10 family portrait. It was a picture of Mom, Dex, and his father in front of the family Christmas tree, framed in lightly stained oak. The three of them had on holiday sweaters and held up mugs of cocoa in toast. Dex wore half a smile while his mother beamed. She was happy any time she got "her two favorite men" in the same room. Unlike Dex and his mother, his father stood rigid and scowling. Dex remembered the moment well. His father had doubted the self-timer on the new Nikon Santa had brought him, so when the camera had finally snapped the picture, he'd been clenched and on the verge of swearing. After a moment, Dex set the picture on the end table atop the stack of pamphlets and switched off his lamp.

As the sun set, shadows swelled from the corners until darkness swallowed the room. Dex's eyes grew heavy, and he'd almost drifted off to sleep when the door opened, letting a cold, fluorescent light in from the hall. The older, silver-haired nurse stood in the doorway. Dex felt his lip twitch as she entered empty-handed. Her face hid in darkness as the hall light cast her shadow over him. She moved to Dex's left, seeming to check a chart or the IV drip, but she hadn't switched on a light, leaving Dex to wonder what she could be checking in the dark. He squinted hard, straining to see her. The nurse held up a syringe; her lips moving rapidly, but why? Who could she be talking to? She couldn't be speaking to him, yet there was no one else in the room. Could she be that incompetent? Had she gotten her patients mixed up and mistaken him for another?

The nurse uncapped the syringe and stuck it deftly into his IV. His body tensed as she depressed the plunger. He knew she was just doing her job and would be fine with her not acknowledging him, but seeing her mouth constantly moving and not knowing what she was saying agitated him. The nurse withdrew the syringe and left without so much as a glance at Dex. Though he was glad to see her go, his mood continued to sour. His thoughts turned dark, and a gloom crept into the room. He pictured his keyboard at home, and how it would feel to sit and play, to let chordal waves and melodies wash over him, but he was lost in space, where the moon carried no melodies, and the stars had never heard of Bowie.

Dex laid back, pulled coarse bedsheets up to his neck and breathed curses. The room hid in perfect dark save for thin lines of light seeping in around the edges of the closed door. He gazed aimlessly into the dark—empty and infinite. He imagined himself becoming weightless, lifting off, and drifting out into the void. As Dex teetered on the verge of sleep, a small shudder moved through his bed.

Dex's eyes shot open and searched the room, expecting a nurse, but the door was closed. The vibrations continued as though something heavy were being dragged across the floor. Dex sat up, wincing in pain, but saw nothing. *Maybe it was the pipes rumbling*, he thought. The tremors grew stronger as the source drew closer. He imagined a sleek, black alien creeping through the shadows. Dex took a breath to shout threats, but what threats could he make? He was laid up in a hospital bed with fractured bones and a catheter. He thought to call for help, but if this thing was real and dangerous, his cries for help might only speed his demise. Was it possible the thing didn't know he was on the bed? What if he stayed perfectly still and quiet? Would the thing leave? Dex gripped either side of the bed frame, feeling the vibrations in his hands until the unseen thing passed beneath his feet, moved under the bed, and stopped.

All was still save for Dex's thundering heart. A few ragged breaths later, and the vibrations started again. First they drifted to his right. Dex carefully sank back into his bed, hoping not to make a sound. His jaw locked, stifling a yelp as pain burned in his hip. The vibrations lingered for a moment before moving from his right to his left. Dex craned his neck to see the light coming in under the door. Beads of sweat stung his eyes. He rubbed them clear and watched the light beneath the door.

Dex hoped to be imagining this—to chalk it up to a side effect of the medicine, or mental wear and tear from the stress. But the cold light flickered when a form moved between Dex and the door. There was something in the room. He wanted to leap out of the bed, bolt through the door, and run like hell, but his fractured legs couldn't carry him. Dex shot a hand up and found the lamp. Dreading what he might see, he switched on the light. Between his bed and the door he saw nothing. He looked beyond the foot of his bed, but the lamp light failed to reach the darkest corners of the room. Moments passed with Dex keeping his eyes trained on the shadows. Had he dreamt it? He wondered what that damned nurse had mixed with his morphine, hoping to blame her. Regardless, the room appeared empty, and he felt relieved he hadn't embarrassed himself, crying out like a child afraid of the dark. With a long sigh, he settled back into bed and reached for the picture his mother had left for him. It was like reaching for an anchor—something real.

Dex took hold of the frame and held the family photo out in front of him. Slivers of glass fell from the frame onto his lap. A tingle moved over his scalp and down the back of his neck. His parents' faces were as expected, but his own face had been slashed. Without a second thought, he shouted for the nurse. It was strange, but he pushed and strained to yell as loud as his throat could manage while searching the room for any sign of an intruder. The door swung open, and the silhouette of a nurse stood at the entrance. Dex fell silent, pointing erratically around the room. It was like a game of high stakes charades as he tried to communicate. He couldn't make out her expression, but she seemed unconcerned. Exasperated, he blurted out, "Intruder!"

The nurse jerked as she was clearly startled, but he wasn't

sure if it was because she believed him, or because he'd suddenly shouted. Either way, as she approached, Dex groaned, realizing it was the silver-haired nurse. She took the picture, looked it over, and offered a peculiar smile as she left with the defaced photo.

Dex cursed and hammered the bed with his fists, wincing when something sharp bit his hand. He felt around gingerly and found a long shard of broken glass from the picture. The shard was about six inches long and an inch wide coming to a fine point. He grabbed napkins off of his dinner tray and wrapped them around the thick end of the shard, fashioning a shiv. The door swung open again, and Dex slipped the shiv under his pillow. The silver-haired nurse swept in followed by a tall, solidly built orderly. The orderly put thick hands on Dex and held him down as the nurse found a vein. Dex struggled and shouted again, "There was someone in here! Stop! STOP!" Though his throat stung, his screams felt faint. The orderly kept a firm grip on Dex until the drugs set in. Dex's muscles soon relaxed, his eyes rolled back, and his body melted into nothing.

Dex awoke to gray morning light and a wave of relief. *What a nightmare*, he thought. *Monsters creeping through the dark.* He smirked, almost laughing to himself, realizing he'd actually dreamt that there was a monster under his bed. After a moment, he made to rub his eyes, but something caught his wrists. Leather restraints bound his hands and feet to the bed frame, and scant memories of the night before came swimming back.

The door opened, and Dr. Wagner stepped in looking concerned. He stopped at the foot of the bed, withdrew a pen from his shirt pocket, and wrote on his clipboard. After a moment, the doctor flipped his clipboard around to show Dex the message.

Do you know why you were restrained?

Dex shook his head. Dr. Wagner frowned, flipped the clipboard around, and resumed writing. Dex noticed the younger nurse waiting in the doorway as Dr. Wagner turned his clipboard around again.

Did you do this?

The doctor nodded toward the door. The nurse stepped in and held up the picture of Dex and his parents, where lacerations marred his face. The doctor tapped the picture with his pen to reaffirm his inquiry.

Dex fought looking away and shook his head.

The doctor looked disappointed, returned to writing, and turned his board around again.

Do you have something sharp in your possession?

Dex remembered the shard of glass beneath his pillow and shook his head. He tried to raise his hands as if to say he was unarmed, but they caught against the straps. Dr. Wagner seemed to consider Dex for a moment before addressing the young nurse. Reluctantly, she moved around the foot of the bed to Dex's right, unbuckled his wrist, detached the strap from the bed, and stepped back. Dex let his hand lie limp beside him and remained still. The doctor directed her to the other strap. The nurse nodded and stepped around Dex's bed as if he were feral. She freed his left hand, detached the strap, and held both straps close as she backed up to the door. Dex remained still and watched the doctor turn to the nurse, and a low rumble percolated in his ears. His heart leapt. Dex focused hard, trying to make out any word or phrase, but the rumble stayed low and indistinct. He jammed an index finger into either ear and twisted as if to unclog them, but the rumble died as Dr. Wagner and the nurse exited the room.

Dex wanted to call out to them, to tell them to keep talking, but the straps the nurse had just removed gave him pause. He didn't want to appear unhinged or easily excited. So in the privacy of his room, he raised a hand to either ear. What if the low rumble had been a side effect of being sedated? Then again, what if his hearing was coming back? His fingers twitched reflexively as though dancing atop keys. He imagined soaring through the chorus of "Life On Mars."

I need the music back, he thought, and with each hand at the ready, he drew in a breath, closed his eyes and snapped his fingers. His eyes shot open as a muffled sound thumped. The snap sounded as though it had come from the next room. He snapped again, and again, and his snapping turned into clapping, and the clapping turned to laughter. Though it all sounded as if it were miles away, it all had a *sound*, and he'd heard it.

Dex's parents arrived shortly after the hospital had removed his restraints. His mother had brought in a small plastic jack-o'-lantern bucket filled with Halloween candy. Judging by his mother's festive demeanor, it was clear the hospital hadn't mentioned his episode to his parents, though he did notice the nurse checking in more frequently throughout the day. When his mother asked him about the missing family portrait, Dex scribbled a note to say he'd knocked it over and broken the frame. He assured her the staff had disposed of the frame but were holding on to the picture for him. This seemed to satisfy her, and she popped a carton of candy cigarettes and offered Dex a stick. He accepted, and the two proceeded to puff on their candy cigarettes as they passed notes back and forth about his hearing recovery. His mother would occasionally speak to Dex, hoping he might have gained more of his hearing back, but he heard only distant rumblings.

As the evening settled in, the young nurse checked in one last time before her shift ended. The room smelled of Pizza Hut, and Dex offered her a leftover slice. The nurse politely declined, and like the warm sun leaving to make way for a cold night, she concluded her last visit for the day. Dex's parents left soon after. His father gave a nod and stepped into the hall without waiting for his son's reply. Dex redirected his goodnight wave to his mother. She handed him a note promising to bring breakfast in the morning, and kissed his forehead to bid him goodnight.

After the nurse, his parents, and any sign of light had left the room, the silver-haired nurse returned, but this time Dex switched on his lamp. As she spoke, he watched her mouth closely. There was a cadence to her speech. Her words rattled off like a recitation—like a memorized prayer or a speech. But as she continued to speak, Dex grew irrationally agitated, finding it hard to focus on her. Once again, she injected something into his morphine drip. He watched her turn and leave without acknowledging him. Glad to see her go, he switched off the lamp, raised his hands to either side of his head, and snapped his fingers.

Snap.

Every time he snapped his fingers, the distant, muffled crack stoked a fire inside him.

Snap.

He wondered if it were possible. Could he make a full recovery? If he could get out of Grimlock Memorial, and get to a real hospital, would he have a chance?

Snap.

The prospect of turning up his stereo and playing along with his favorite songs thrilled him. Dex relaxed and tucked in, hoping to find more of his hearing had returned by morning. Despite all the strange, nightmarish things that had happened during his stay at Grimlock Memorial, the possibility of hearing music again made the bed feel a bit more comfortable and the room less gloomy.

Snap.

Dex's eyes went wide. He sat up, wincing in pain, and looked around the room.

Snap.

He could hear it, but it wasn't him. The vibrations returned, and with them, the sound of a snap. Vibrations shivered through his bed as the sound moved closer.

Snap.

The vibrations became tremors. The frame shook, and Dex braced himself. The mattress sank on either side of his hips as a creature crawled onto the bed, straddling him.

Snap.

Something like great spider legs—two or three of them—moved in an elegant, controlled motion on his left. He could see the black silhouettes pass between him and the thin lines of light around the doorway. Dex drew in quick, ragged breaths, heart thumping wildly. Wet, putrid breath blew into his right ear and low rumblings like a voice arose. The cadence of the speech seemed strange to him—inhuman. Though muffled, the voice's pitch was erratic and unlike anything he'd heard before.

The light from the door eclipsed as the creature moved over him—pressing down on him. Sour breath rolled over his face, leaving a trail of hot, stinging droplets on his skin. The smell of rotten meat filled his nostrils causing Dex to wretch. He waited for the thing to bite and tear flesh, but the creature did not attack. It merely continued speaking its strange, erratic language, and Dex wondered if the thing was trying to communicate. Had the creature been testing his ears? Perhaps the effect it had hoped for had been hindered. Then Dex's heart sank, realizing the creature's voice had been growing more distinct as it continued to speak.

Dex urgently dug beneath his pillow for the glass shiv. The bed trembled as the creature shifted in place. Dex felt the weight of the creature pressing against him—pinning him down. The creature's body felt solid and prickly like a bristly shell. Dex found the shiv he'd fashioned. The glass edge cut into his hand as he took hold and withdrew it from beneath his pillow, but before he could drive it into the creature, something pricked his right ear. A knife-edged appendage angled through the dark, drifting into his right ear. Dex grappled the appendage. Flashes of pain warned him to let go as it cut into his hand, but he only gripped tighter. Whatever cuts he suffered would be nothing compared to this creature impaling his head.

The creature's breath rolled over Dex again as something sharp pressed into his eardrum. Dex cried in anguish, his face twisting, and slowly, relentlessly, the monster pushed deeper into Dex's ear. A current of warm blood rushed out of his ear and pooled behind his head. The blinding pain sent shocks through his body. He convulsed, struggling against the creature's advance, but the sharp point only sank deeper. Dex's fractured legs cracked as he kicked, and his eyes rolled back as the creature pressed deeper. After a moment, his body relaxed, his hand fell by his side, and the pain ceased.

The creature was gone. Dex blinked, watching the ceiling slowly shrink away, as he sank through his mattress. He continued down, passing through the linoleum floor and into an empty hospital room. A pale halo of fluorescent light hummed as he passed through the first floor and into the morgue. Dex reached out to grab hold of something—anything—but his hands passed through the world just like the rest of him. He flailed about like a man drowning, attempting to swim to the surface, but still he sank. His body passed through a pale cadaver lying atop a gurney, through the gurney, and through the ground floor.

Dex opened his mouth to scream, but his screams gave no sound. He was lost, drifting through infinite nothing. An impassable expanse spread between him and the world he knew and the people he loved. All around him faded to black. He thought of a dead satellite drifting aimlessly through space, but this wasn't space. There were no stars or moons, only empty, lifeless black, but then he heard a sound—a string of musical notes. Dex Maddox closed his eyes as he had all those times hunched over his keyboard. He saw flashes of white, pink, and blue as the music came swimming back, and the memory of a melody held him like a dear friend as he drifted in the void.

―――

Gray clouds blanketed Grimlock Cove. Gulls called overhead, and waves lapped gently against creaking, splintered docks. It was there Josh and Ethan sat, legs dangling over the water, sharing a smoke. The two looked on from the mainland at Grimlock Memorial.

"What'd you do for Halloween?" Ethan asked.

"Seriously? The house party?" Josh said as his lighter flickered. "Remember?"

"No. Was it good?"

Josh drew in, held it for a moment, and exhaled saying, "Dude. You were *there*."

Ethan wrinkled his nose. "Really?"

"Yeah. I met a girl," Josh said and handed him the joint.

"Nice," Ethan said, taking a drag.

Somewhere over distant waters, thunder rumbled behind Grimlock Memorial.

"So, did you hear the news?" Josh asked.

Ethan shook his head and exhaled.

"It was on the radio this morning." Josh took back the joint. "You know that dude who drove off the bridge?"

Ethan looked across the water at the bridge where police tape and traffic cones still marked the broken railing. "Yeah?"

"They found him dead in his bed this morning at Grimlock Memorial."

"Well, yeah. The dude drove off a bridge."

"No way, man. *That's* not what killed him." Josh fixed his gaze on the gloomy hospital across the bay. "They say he dug into his own head with a piece of broken glass."

The Investigation at St. Julian's

Grimlock Cove, 1977

———

"How much farther?" Jack asked as the black '64 Riviera cut a blind path down the highway. The Buick's high-beams lit up the midnight fog and little else. "One Of These Nights" played on the AM while Jack watched the fog in the rearview, swirling red in the taillights, and he wondered if this would be a dead end for both of them.

"Looks like we're heading into a horror movie, Jack," Rhett said, keeping his bloodshot eyes on the road and his hands fixed at ten and two.

"We might be," Jack said.

Jack Durant was a tall, black man of thirty-five years, once known for his easy smile. They'd said that wouldn't last long after his promotion to Detective, but he'd lost it long before then. His partner, Rhett Kesler, looked as though he'd fallen out of a twenty-five cent pulp detective novel. He had aching, blue eyes with a hard-lined jaw and a pale face with more lines than any man ought to have in his forties. But each of those lines told a story—stories of lies, betrayals, and buried bodies. His newest wrinkle told of a girl gone missing nearly six years ago.

The young woman's case had been assigned to a tired department veteran who, as Rhett had described him, "spent his last year on the job with his thumb up his ass, waiting for retirement." Once the local papers had lost interest the missing girl, the public had, too, and not long after the people had forgotten her, the file had been buried in the basement with all the other cold cases. But one man couldn't forget.

The missing girl had had Jack's eyes, his easy smile, and had taken with her a piece of his heart. He'd lost his little girl. Jacqueline Durant would have been twenty-one this year. The department hadn't let Jack work the case. They'd said he was too close to it, but Jack bided his time—time that had allowed him to do his own digging while the loss ate at him like an untreated wound. After Jack had made Detective, he'd appealed to Rhett's disdain for unsolved cases and his sympathies for a grieving father. Rhett had agreed to help, and the cold case had become their top, albeit unofficial, priority.

Jack was not even a week into his promotion when a letter had arrived at his home. It'd come in response to his request to speak with the staff of a small Catholic church a few towns over. The envelope had arrived with no return address, but the postmark had confirmed it'd arrived from Grimlock Cove. The sender had claimed to know the whereabouts of the missing girl and provided a time and a place to meet.

Meet me in St. Julian's
at the witching hour,
October 31st,
and you will find her.

As Rhett often said, it's better to be lucky than good. With no other leads, the pair planned on calling in sick, and instead of spending Halloween weekend with family and friends—or in Rhett's case, alone with a bottle of Kentucky's cheapest—the two detectives left town and hung their hopes on this mysterious note.

"Did you know Grimlock Cove has had at least one person go missing every six years for as long as they've been keeping track?" Rhett said.

Jack nodded, resenting the anxious churning in his gut. "And even though it happens every six years, nobody in the town seems to give a damn because it's often out-of-towners who go missing."

Rhett glanced over. "*We're* out-of-towners, Jack."

"So was my daughter," Jack said, keeping his eyes fixed on the passing gloom.

Rhett fell silent.

Jack noticed a lone crow perched on an approaching billboard for The Red Water Motel. The bird's eyes glinted bright green. Jack blinked, doubting what he'd seen. Looking again at the passing sign, he saw no crow.

"Is there a reason your mysterious pen pal can't do this in the morning?" Rhett said as another sign approached, welcoming them to Grimlock Cove.

"They're skittish because they know something," Jack said.

"How can you be sure?"

"They clearly don't want to be seen talking to cops."

"That's strangely reassuring," Rhett said. "This might be the break you've been waiting for."

"Maybe," Jack said, though he hadn't been entirely truthful. There had been more than an invitation in the envelope. There'd been a letter. The letter had explained that Jacqueline had been abducted by a cult. The sender said they were protecting Jacqueline from the people who took her. The letter also claimed Jacqueline could not be released without something to appease the cult—like an exchange—or the sender would be sorely punished for "losing" the girl. The sender had wished to meet in secret and had instructed Jack to bring one person with him as an exchange. The letter closed with a clear warning: Any deviation from the terms would cost his daughter dearly, but if Jack showed up under the terms as dictated, he would be reunited with his daughter. For credibility, the envelope had contained something that had belonged to Jacqueline—a purple, woven bracelet.

In better days, Jack wouldn't have believed a word in that letter. He would've planned to arrive with back up, treating this anonymous person as a suspect, but his jurisdiction didn't reach Grimlock Cove, and Jack's better days were well behind him. The piece of him that made sane decisions had vanished along with his baby girl. Moreover, his loss hadn't left a scar. It'd left a festering wound. He'd hear Jacqueline's voice from time to time—be it in a dream or on the wind. He'd see her in the window of a passing school bus or hear her speaking to him from another room in the house. For six long years, she'd haunted him. Let the dead lie, they say, but her body had never been found. Then again, it'd been years since her disappearance. If it'd been anyone else's daughter, he'd tell them to accept the hard truth: She's dead. But this wasn't someone else's child. Jack now fully understood the truth: You'll do anything for your child.

"What'd you tell your old lady you were up to?" Rhett said. "She's not going to worry with you being gone overnight?"

"A stakeout. Said I'd be home later this weekend," Jack said, omitting that his wife had moved in with her sister. Jack hadn't found his way back to her since losing Jacqueline, but he knew if he could get his daughter back, he could get his family back.

"So, nobody knows we're out here," Rhett said.

"I didn't want to get her hopes up. Ya know?"

Rhett glanced over at his partner. "We're going to find out what happened, Jack."

"No," Jack said. "I'm going to find *her*."

Rhett nodded, but Jack knew better. Rhett was here to solve a cold case, hoping to provide the Durant family some closure. Rhett was practical—a pragmatist at best, but Jack had something Rhett didn't. He had faith. As the two sat quietly, the radio played, and the passing rural outskirts turned into a small town of dark windows, creeping shadows, and lifeless streets.

"I thought small towns were supposed to be charming," Rhett said. "This place is creep-city."

"Speaking of creepy," Jack said, nodding to the church up ahead.

Rhett pulled into the parking lot of St. Julian's Catholic Church, slowed to a stop, and killed the engine. Gravel crunched underfoot as the pair stepped out. Jack tucked his white button-down into his brown slacks, and pulled on his corduroy sport coat.

Rhett pulled on his wrinkled gray suit coat, straightened his black tie, and stretched till his back popped. He then took a cigarette and flicked open his brass lighter. The warm light glinted in his yellowed eyes. After a long drag, he blew gray smoke that mingled with the fog and said, "We should go in through the back."

"Why not the front?" Jack asked as Rhett popped the trunk.

Rhett grunted with disapproval as he sifted through his leather duffel. He withdrew two flashlights, handing one to Jack.

"I read the file," Rhett said. "She was last seen at this church. If it'd been my case, this would've been the first place I looked." Rhett withdrew his .38 special, checked the cylinder to make sure it was loaded, and returned it to his holster. "For all we know, some sicko priest could be our perp, or your contact could be. We don't know, so you have to ask yourself: Do you trust this mystery person?"

Jack looked around at the church and the cemetery—the headstones peeking out from a blanket of fog. His palms were sweaty, and his stomach churned, but he gave no reply.

Rhett dropped his half-smoked cigarette to the gravel and snuffed it out under his shoe. "The place looks empty, which means either they're lying low inside, aren't here, or we're being set up."

Jack checked his revolver, holstered it, and stood shoulder-to-shoulder with Rhett, eyeing the moonlit church.

"St. Julian's Catholic Church," Rhett said, his lip curling. "You should feel right at home."

"I'm Lutheran, Rhett."

"Toe-may-toe. Toe-mah-toe," Rhett said, starting froward.

Jack shook his head and reassured himself. *You can do this. You can do this for her.*

―――

The old church steeple held its iron cross up to the October moon. Beneath the steeple was a circular window, and beneath that stood the red, double doors that led inside. The two detectives stepped quietly around the right side between the church and the cemetery. They passed bails of hay and pumpkins stacked beneath tall, stained glass windows. The overgrown cemetery lie beyond a brown and orange banner that read, *FALL FESTIVAL '77*. A low fog snaked between the tombstones. Two beads of green light blinked from behind a

Celtic cross headstone, reminding Jack of the crow he'd seen on the drive in. He paused, turning his flashlight toward the green flicker, but it vanished as the flashlight's beam passed. Jack swept it across the graveyard once more, revealing the hunched form of a pale old man with matted, silvery hair that hung down past his shoulders. The old man held a shovel, and appeared to be digging.

Jack stumbled to a stop, calling in a hushed voice for Rhett, but Rhett kept moving forward, seeming not to have heard Jack. Directing his light at Rhett, Jack discreetly called again, but there was still no reply.

Jack reached for his gun, turning his light back toward the man in the graveyard, but the graveyard appeared empty. He twitched the light left and right in disbelief. *That old man couldn't have moved that fast*, he thought.

Feeling a bit foolish, Jack took his right hand from his gun and placed it over the woven bracelets he wore on his left wrist. His daughter, Jacqueline, had made them. She'd woven three of them—one for herself, one for him, and one for the green-eyed monster hiding in her closet. Jack had thought her too old for imaginary monsters, but Jacqueline had been sure of the monster and its intentions. Jack had reluctantly climbed out of bed and answered her call despite the late hour. When he'd arrived in her room, she'd promptly requested he shoot the monster.

"Sweetheart, we should try our words first," he'd told her.

"Dad," she'd said as though he were being obtuse. "Words don't work! It's a monster. Monsters don't listen because they don't care."

He'd laughed, prompting a scowl from the deadly serious Jacqueline.

"Okay. I hear you, but let me try to talk sense to the monster," he'd said. "I bet we can make a deal." After a moment of negotiating with an empty closet, Jack declared they had reached an agreement. He'd said if she made each of them a friendship bracelet, the monster would leave her alone. The next night, he'd placed a little purple bracelet in the closet, slipped one onto his wrist, and slid the last bracelet onto Jacqueline's wrist.

"The monster said it's leaving," he'd said. Seeing relief wash over her was all the confirmation he'd needed. Jack had brokered peace between an empty closet and his little girl.

The following morning, Jacqueline had seemed well-rested, confirming the monster had left. "It took the bracelet, Daddy."

Jack had smiled, playing along.

A chilling wind swept around the church, rustling leaves and calling Jack back to the present. His hand still rested on the purple, woven bracelets on his left wrist—the one Jacqueline had given him, and the one from the mysterious letter. Thinking of Jacqueline centered him, reminding him why he'd come to this place, why he'd agreed to the offer in the letter, and why he'd brought his partner. He'd come for the one thing he wanted more than anything else in this life: to have his baby girl back.

Rhett rounded the corner to the back of the church. Jack caught up just as Rhett slipped a lock pick set from inside his coat pocket and went to work on the back door. The sound of the lock pick sent Jack's pulse racing, thinking he could be moments away from finding Jacqueline.

"Almost got it," Rhett said just as the lock's tumblers fell into place, and the door unlocked with a *click*. Rhett put away his lock pick, withdrew his flashlight, and opened the door with a slow, steady push. "Head on a swivel," he said as he stepped into St. Julian's.

Jack followed, stepping into a kitchen area, complete with a stock of wine bottles, a bread basket lined with linen napkins, and a coil-top stove. The church was still, silent. It felt empty. Jack's eye twitched, his nerves on edge. If this proved to be some sick prank, it would do more than crush him.

Rhett moved around the kitchen, checking drawers and cabinets.

"You think my contact is hiding in a drawer?" Jack said.

Rhett shot him a look. "You're a detective now. Why don't you try detecting something?"

Jack looked around, frustrated, knowing if his contact was here, they certainly weren't waiting in the pantry.

"You know," Rhett said, reaching for a bottle of communion wine, "this is the first time I've stepped foot in a church since I was a boy." He held the bottle up. "This is your kinda thing?"

"Our church uses grape juice," Jack said.

"Not the wine. I mean religion," Rhett said. "This stuff makes sense to you?"

"Sure. What's your point?"

"I always thought it was strange to pretend to drink blood," Rhett said, setting down the wine.

"Wait," Jack said, waving his hand over the burners atop the stove. His put his hand closer and gingerly tapped the coil. "It's warm."

Rhett cracked half a smile. "Good job, Detective." He motioned the door that led deeper into the church. "Let's find your contact."

Jack nodded, followed Rhett out of the kitchen into the nave, and looked around the place. The altar was situated to their right. The front entrance lie ahead beyond some twenty-odd rows of pews. A winding, wooden staircase stood to the left just shy of the entrance.

"Looks empty," Jack said.

Rhett moved to the center of the room and slowly turned, taking it in. "Blood sacrifices for forgiveness, blood on the doorpost to keep the Angel of Death away. You ever notice how God always demands blood, and it's always the innocent ones doing the bleeding?"

"Damn, Rhett. You break into one church, and suddenly you're a theologian," Jack said.

"I'm just saying," Rhett shrugged as he flicked his light around the room. He stopped at the center of the nave and turned toward the high altar. His flashlight shone upward, illuminating a large, crucified Christ hanging behind the altar. "It's never a statue of Jesus feeding the hungry or healing the sick. It's always him suffering, paying for our screw-ups."

Jack moved his light around the church, his nerves already strained to their breaking point. "You got a point to all this, Rhett?"

"Nah," Rhett replied. "Just rambling."

Jack ignored Rhett's barbs as best he could and moved his light along the length of the walls, looking for a side room.

"And another thing," Rhett continued, clearly unable to help himself. "This free pass for forgiveness doesn't make sense. I mean, if I'm drinking on someone else's tab, I'll *always* order another. Right?"

Jack bit his tongue and turned his light upon the anguished Christ above the altar. The figure was the product of crude woodworking completed over a century ago. The piece wasn't precise enough to be realistic, nor could it pass as abstract. But Jack thought the eyes captured genuine pain. It wasn't the look of one being tortured, or the look of one being publicly ridiculed. It was the aching of one suffering alone—a son who, for the first time, was cut off from his father. "There's no greater love than to die for another," Jack said and turned to Rhett. "When you love someone, you'd do anything for them. So, while you look around and see suffering, I see sacrifice."

Rhett offered a patronizing smile, turned, and called out, "All right. Cut the crap. If you're here, identify yourself."

The pair waited in a long pause. After a moment, Rhett turned to Jack. "It's looking like a dead end."

Jack leaned to one side to peer around Rhett, when a faint warm light spilled down the spiral staircase at the front of the church.

Seeing Jack's gaze, Rhett turned. "Well, I'll be damned."

"We might both be," Jack said and started forward.

"Hold up, partner," Rhett said, throwing a hand out to stop Jack. Rhett drew his gun and motioned for Jack to draw his. "We don't know who's up there. Don't let hope make a fool of you."

Jack drew his gun and let Rhett take the lead. As Rhett stepped forward, Jack kept his revolver trained on his partner, not knowing how or when the exchange for Jacqueline was to take place.

Rhett called out, "Come downstairs."

After a moment, tired floorboards groaned overhead. Footsteps grew louder as someone drew closer to the top of the stairs.

"Move slowly and keep your hands where I can see them," Rhett said.

The stairs creaked as the stranger descended.

"I am alone," a man said from the stairs.

Pale, bare feet appeared first, followed by a tall, thick frame in dirt-stained, denim overalls. The man reached the bottom of the stairs with his elbows at his sides, one hand raised, the other holding a lit candlestick. The man's sallow skin appeared cold even in the warm candlelight. Vibrant, blue eyes sat sunken in dark circles, framed by loose, silvery hair that fell just past his shoulders. His sharp nose seemed too small for his square head, and he had oddly full, pink lips.

"I am unarmed," the old man said.

"I saw you outside earlier, digging in the graveyard," Jack said. "Why didn't you identify yourself?"

"You startled me," the man said. "Why didn't *you* identify yourself?"

"You saw this guy?" Rhett said quietly to Jack.

Jack nodded. "I wasn't sure then, but now—"

"How'd you get in here without us seeing you?" Rhett said to the man.

"Another entrance," the man said. "Please, unless you fear an old, unarmed man, could you lower your weapons?"

The two detectives exchanged a look and holstered their revolvers.

"Excellent," the man said. "My name is Chester Allen. I apologize for the strange nature of our meeting. It is for fear of repercussions that this must be done in secret."

"Awfully eloquent for a groundskeeper," Rhett said under his breath.

"I came as agreed," Jack said, with a subtle nod toward Rhett.

Chester smiled and motioned up the stairs. "I've made tea. Allow me the privilege of hosting you. Goodness knows the trouble you've gone through to be here tonight."

As Chester turned and slowly climbed the stairs, Jack resisted the urge to charge forward and beat every secret out of the old man. At this point, Jack was fine with being the loose cannon detective who drove several towns over to beat up an old man in a church—if it got him his baby back. But aggression could cause Chester to clam up tight—too tight to be of any use.

The two detectives followed Chester to the space upstairs. Moonlight fell in through the circular window Jack had seen from the outside. Chester placed his candlestick on a nightstand beside a ceramic tea kettle and an old, claw hammer and took a seat on his twin-sized bed. A pair of empty folding chairs waited. He waved a hand, inviting the others to sit. Jack sat, but Rhett ignored the invitation.

"What's with the hammer?" Rhett asked.

"The stairs have a few loose boards," Chester said. "Absent-minded me. I'd grabbed the hammer but forgot the nails."

"You live here, Mr. Allen?" Jack said, motioning to the bed and nightstand.

"I do," Chester answered. "Would you like some tea?"

"And the church knows about it?" Rhett said.

Chester laughed, revealing a mess of yellow teeth. "They do."

"Not doing a great job with that cemetery," Jack said.

"Never had much of a green thumb, I'm afraid," Chester said. "But so long as I keep the church clean, they keep a roof over my head." He paused, with a nod to the kettle, and offered again, "Tea?"

"No, thank you. Now, there's no one else here, Mr. Allen. How about we turn on the lights and have a chat?" Rhett said, in a more professional tone.

"I'm sorry, Detective. The church never ran electrical to the attic. So," Chester paused, motioning to the candle. "But please, have a seat."

Rhett acquiesced and took a seat in the chair beside Jack. Chester folded his hands in his lap, looking pleased. Rhett continued, "In your letter to Detective Durant, you asked to meet here after midnight. Why the cloak and dagger act?"

"There's a cult hiding within these holy walls," Chester said. "Their eyes are everywhere. I've garnered their favor, but that doesn't afford me freedom."

"Right," Rhett said, sounding unconvinced. "What do you know about the disappearance of Jacqueline Durant?"

"Young Jacqueline was here visiting a friend," Chester said.

"That's right," Jack cut in, looking between the other two. "A school friend. Her family had moved from our town to Grimlock Cove. The girls missed each other, so we'd planned on meeting their parents halfway. It was a—"

"An All Hallows Eve sleepover," Chester said.

"In this century, we just call it Halloween," Rhett said.

"He's right," Jack said. "About the sleepover. It was on a Saturday. We were supposed to meet again to pick her up on Sunday, which was—"

"Halloween," Chester said, casting a patronizing glance at Rhett.

Jack cursed under his breath. To shield his family from thirsty journalists, the sleepover had never been mentioned. The only way Chester could've known was if he'd talked to the family, or more likely, to Jacqueline. Between the sleepover and the bracelet sent in the mail, Jack was convinced.

"We'll need the names of the people working the festival that night," Rhett said.

"That won't be necessary, Detective," Chester said, pausing for another sip of his tea. "One of us in this room knows exactly who did what to little Jacqueline Durant that night, *and* where she is now."

The two detectives looked at each other and back at Chester.

"Well?" Rhett said, his voice growing gruff. "Tell us everything you know, Chester."

"Every six years," Chester began, his voice calm. "It happens every six years."

Though he knew, Jack asked, "What happens every six years?"

"Some unfortunate soul goes missing." Chester sounded like he was explaining something mundane.

"And you're saying this cult is behind these disappearances?" Rhett said.

Chester nodded.

"Does this cult have a name?" Rhett said.

"There is a reason there must be a sacrifice every six years, Detective," Chester said, looking to Jack. "To get what we want, we must all make sacrifices."

Rhett looked to Jack, confused. "You following this?"

"Where is she?" Jack said.

"I spoke to her just before you two arrived," Chester said. "She is well, but I don't know for how long."

"Where *is* she?" Jack said and shot up from his seat, drew his gun, and leveled it at Chester.

"Whoa," Rhett said, rising to his feet, hands up. "Easy, Jack. Let's lower that gun and—"

Jack thumbed the hammer back and the cylinder clicked, ready to fire.

"Jack?" Rhett said, his voice rising.

"We're not talking in circles. We're not playing cat and mouse," Jack said to Chester. "You're going to take me to her, and we're going to make our exchange."

Rhett took a slow step closer to Jack. "Listen. I want to find her, too, but—"

Jack swung his gun from the unbothered face of Chester to Rhett. The candlelight danced in Rhett's wide eyes.

"Not another step," Jack said. "I'm getting my baby girl back." Jack kept his eyes and the gun on Rhett, and said, "Chester? Where the *hell* is my daughter?"

"I swear to your god, Detective," Chester said, his voice calm, almost soothing. "I *will* reunite you tonight, but you may not have what you want most without a sacrifice."

"Why does it sound like he's reminding you of something, Jack?" Rhett asked, his voice a mix of fear and anger.

Jack swallowed hard, a tremble moving through his hand, causing the gun to waver. "I thought it was an exchange."

Chester shook his head. "Every six years, Detective. It's been six years, and it's time for a sacrifice."

Jack eyed Rhett, watching a range of emotions flooding through.

"She asks about you, Jack," Chester said. "She asks how you are doing, and if we think you're proud of her."

Rhett's eyes locked onto the stainless steel barrel pointed at him.

"I saw how special Jacqueline was when I first laid eyes on her. That's why I protected her these last six years," Chester said. The bed creaked as the groundskeeper stood up and crossed over to Jack's side, where he continued softly, "She learned to play the piano, Jack. She plays beautifully. And she's no longer afraid of the monsters in her closet."

Jack's heart hammered, his veins throbbing, sweat beading all over.

"You're not thinking straight, Jack," Rhett said.

"I can't protect her any longer," Chester said. "They all know how special she is, but they're zealots. If they find out I've talked to the police, they will kill her and they will kill me."

"He knows where she is," Jack said, feeling certain he was right—as sure as he'd ever been of anything. This would be the night he found his daughter.

"Then point the gun at *this* asshole instead of me, and make *him* tell you where she is," Rhett said.

Jack's hand wavered.

"Rhett doesn't understand," Chester said. "He's not a believer, is he, Jack? He doesn't *believe* you can get your daughter back. He can't see a miracle right before his eyes. What was lost *can* be found."

Jack imagined holding her again, hearing her laugh.

Chester continued, "How could a faithless, childless man ever understand your god's ways?"

"Are you insane? Are you—" Rhett began, but Chester cut him off.

"Time is running out. There *will* be a sacrifice tonight, and it's time for you to choose. Will it be this man or your daughter? Will this alcoholic go home to drink himself to death, or will you bring your beautiful Jacqueline home?"

Rhett grunted, signaling he'd reached his limit. Maybe it was decades of muscle memory, but the veteran detective drew his revolver faster than Jack would've ever imagined. The old man's gun was drawn and cocked in a half second, but in that small fraction of time, Jack saw the end of everything. Rhett's bullet, no matter who it hit, could cost Jack his daughter, his wife, his family.

The dark room lit up white with the muzzle flash. Jack's ears rang. The Detectives' eyes stayed locked on each other's. For a long moment, neither breathed, neither moved, neither blinked. As the pair stood, gun smoke between them, memories came flooding back. Jack saw Rhett recommending him for promotion. He saw the look in Rhett's eyes when he, Jack, had asked him to help find Jacqueline. Jack had missed it at the time, but now, in a moment of clarity, what had seemed to be pity had actually been compassion. Jack's stomach sank. He felt sick, as he watched Rhett collapse. Rhett's gun tumbled aside as his head thumped against the wood floor. After a brief moment, a pool of blood spread from beneath his body. Jack's grip loosened. He let go of his gun, leaving it to hit the floor with a *clunk*, and planted his hand over the bracelet on his left wrist.

It was like waking from one nightmare to another. Jack dropped to his knees, his will broken, his delusions shattered. "I killed him," Jack said to himself. "*I* . . . killed him."

"You did what had to be done," Chester said, taking a step behind Jack, who kept his gaze on Rhett's body.

Jack felt alone, despite the other in the room. He'd lost his daughter, he was losing his wife, and his losses had consumed him. But now he saw it. He had shut out everyone around him, leaving grief to be his only companion. That grief had festered, becoming an emotional necrosis that had eaten away at Jack's compassion, his empathy, his humanity. He had become numb, but now he felt it all. A knot formed in his throat. Choking back tears, he rubbed the bracelet on his wrist.

Chester put a hand on Jack's shoulder. "Jack." The old groundskeeper's sickly sweet voice changed, becoming inexplicably feminine. This was not a voice coming from Chester, but a voice coming from inside him. The voice said, "I am a witch of my word. It's time for you to be reunited with your daughter."

Thinking he must've heard wrong—that this voice couldn't have come from the old man, Jack turned his head to better incline his ear toward Chester. Though his vision blurred with welling tears, he noticed the hammer was missing from the nightstand. Twisting in place, he saw the hammer aloft, and the groundskeeper's once blue eyes flashed bright green. He threw his hands up to shield himself. A loud *crack* sounded as his right forearm broke. Chester hammered again and again, cracking bones. Jack tried to grab Chester by the wrist but was met with another crushing blow. Finally, Jack glanced to see his revolver just in reach. He fell toward the gun, snatched it up, and rolled onto his back, struggling to take aim with his broken arm. He managed to get two shots off, both missing, before Chester landed a hammer blow to Jack's nose. Jack crumpled. The gun tumbled aside, and the room fell black.

Jack's head throbbed, and his arm ached. He opened his eyes but saw only black. It's a strange sensation to stare into perfect darkness. There's no sense of height or depth—just an endless void in every direction. Trying to sort out what time of day it was, or even *what* day it was, he struggled to recall anything leading up to the moment he came to. He remembered riding into town with Rhett. It'd been foggy. The Eagles had played on the radio, and he and Rhett had stopped at an old church. Then the attic, the gunshot, and the old groundskeeper all came back. Jack dry heaved, sickened, remembering what he'd done.

"Rhett," he said, barely getting the name out.

Jack heard the crack of bone and the bloody hammer.

"One of us in this room knows exactly who did what to little Jacqueline Durant that night," Chester had said.

Jack tried to sit up, only to find solid wood above him. He felt around in every direction and found solid wood on all sides. His pulse quickened. *A coffin?* There was a weight on his chest. He felt around to find a collection of small bones scattered on top of him.

Chester's sickly sweet voice echoed in Jack's ear. *"I am a witch of my word. It's time for you to be reunited with your daughter."*

Jack seized up, stricken by the realization. Refusing to accept it, he moved a trembling hand to his wrist for comfort —to feel the bracelet Jacqueline had woven for him. But where he'd expected to find two bracelets, he found three. One for him, one for Jacqueline, and one for the green-eyed monster.

THE HALLOWEEN MIRACLE

Grimlock Cove, 1978

These were the last few minutes of calm. All along Witchwood Drive, jack-o'-lanterns waited with candles flickering in their wide smiles. Cotton ghosts hung from the trees, gently swaying in the autumn breeze. Soon, the sun would vanish, and the day would succumb to nightfall. Then the children would arrive, let loose in the streets, haunting each home with a bewitching proposition: trick or treat?

Among the old craftsman homes that lined the street sat one with a drab, olive green face and a red door. Inside the musty bungalow, cranberry walls stood cluttered with commemorative plates and faded photographs in antique frames. While the home sat still and quiet most nights, this was not just another night. The widow, Barbara Bane, bustled about, preparing for what she considered to be the most magical night of the year. Barbara was a stout woman in her golden years with light blue eyes, thin, ruby lips, and a round nose. Though she'd accepted the fact that her bouffant hair had gone gray, she insisted on burying her wrinkles beneath a heavy layer of foundation and pink rouge, which left her face a shade lighter than her neck.

"Tonight is for the children."

That's what Barbara Bane's mother had always told her, and that's what repeated in Barbara's mind as she took her daily aspirin. Barbara rubbed her head, as her mother's voice seemed louder, clearer, and closer than it ever had since the day she'd died. After washing the pill down with a glass of water from the tap, she gathered bags of candy and emptied nearly two pounds of colorful suckers, peanut butter cups, and taffy into a large, ceramic serving bowl, filling it to the brim. "Tonight is for the children," she said as she carried the bowl from the kitchen to her front door. She set the bowl on a credenza. Beside the bowl sat a cupcake atop a china saucer. Barbara straightened her eyeglasses and took a step back to admire her preparations—especially the cupcake.

The homemade fudge cupcake was topped with chocolate buttercream frosting and covered in orange candy sprinkles. Barbara had, in her opinion, vastly improved the old family recipe, though she knew her mother would've never approved. As the widow of a pharmacist, Barbara understood the importance of precise measurements and what a drastic difference an errant dash of sugar, a pinch of too much spice, or too little a dose of medication could make. Unlike her mother, Barbara carved out the heart of the cupcake and carefully filled it with a dollop of perfectly prepared milk chocolate fudge (the secret was to not stir the fudge while it was cooking, but to wait and beat the fudge after it had cooled). When served with a tall glass of cold milk, she'd concluded it was the culinary equivalent of a pitch-perfect siren song, and she had the track record to prove it. After updating the recipe with her own personal touches, the cupcake became the cornerstone of her forty-four-year Halloween tradition. Though many children came to her door each Halloween, only one child, if any, would be welcomed into her home to enjoy her All Hallow's Eve double fudge cupcake. Most years, the cupcake would sit uneaten after the last trick-or-treater had come and gone. Not many children proved deserving, but this night felt different. There was a kind of spark in the air—a kind of magic like she had never felt before.

The laughter of excited children echoed up Witchwood Drive, tugging at Barbara's ear. She moved to a window at the front of the house and pulled aside the drapes just enough to peek through. The sun had set, the street lamps had lit up, and the children were free to haunt each house for candy. Barbara paused a moment to take in this year's costumes: a clown stood chatting with an angel; a little ghost walked hand in hand with a half-pint princess; and an astronaut hurried to catch up to a raggedy, red-haired doll. Barbara's heart quickened, anxious as she looked up and down the street from her window, but she found no cause for concern. There wasn't a parent in sight. Relieved, she shuffled away from the window, collected her candy bowl, and crossed to the front door to await the night's first group of trick-or-treaters.

A knock soon sounded at the door, thumping with urgency—the kind of urgency that should be expected when the promise of candy is involved. Barbara answered the door to find a knot of children squeezed onto her front porch. With the precise execution of a well-rehearsed stage troupe, the children held their candy bags aloft and said together, "Trick or treat!"

Barbara smiled, craning her neck to inspect each of their earnest faces before digging a handful of candy from the bowl. One by one, she dispersed suckers and taffy among the eager trick-or-treaters. Some thanked her, but others said nothing as they as they turned to leave for the next house. She'd thought them all lovely children, yet behind the costumes and masks, she saw the entitled eyes of healthy, well-to-do children. They were nothing like little Billy Badowski. Billy would have been thankful for anything she'd given him—even a handful of rocks.

It'd been decades, yet she remembered the night well. When Barbara had first clapped eyes on Billy, he'd approached her door all by himself. He stood in a plaid, flannel button-down, with blue jeans cuffed at the bottom, and a coonskin cap that sat lopsided atop a mess of curly brown hair. The blue-eyed, freckle-faced boy announced himself as Davy Crockett—after which he'd whispered his real name just in case Barbara had mistaken him for the *real* Davy Crockett. A Daisy pellet gun had rested on his shoulder, which he'd been sure to inform Barbara was not loaded.

Though that had been the first time Barbara had met the boy, word travels fast in a small town, and she'd known all about his affliction. Billy had been diagnosed with epilepsy, and in those days, treatments included bloodletting and skull trephination, which would've involved some barbaric surgeon drilling a hole in the boy's head. Barbara couldn't stand to see such a sweet child suffer and knew she had to do something. She'd also known that children—all children—go to Heaven. As she saw it, she had delivered the poor boy from needless suffering, ushering him into eternal rest. If his grieving parents had known or understood the kindness she'd done for them—for Billy—they would've been thanking her.

Another flurry of knocks came from the front door, and Barbara answered, swinging the door wide open. Two children, possibly a brother and sister, held up paper bags from a nearby grocery. The little boy wore a sheet over his head with holes cut out, revealing big, blue eyes. The little girl, who stood an inch or two taller than the boy, had blue eyes much like the other. Her costume consisted of a plain white dress with a wire coat hanger that had been twisted up to resemble a crown. Her Highness's crown sat atop wavy blonde hair that framed her round face.

"Trick or treat," the kids said at once.

"A ghost and a princess?" Barbara said with candy in hand.

The pair nodded.

"Did you make your costumes?" Barbara asked.

The two nodded again.

Barbara's neighborhood was situated on the edge of Grimlock Cove. A few hundred yards away, on the other side of a dense forest, a trailer park sat at the end of a dirt road. Given the kids' tattered shoes and homemade costumes, she concluded the pair must have come all the way through the woods from the trailers. As Barbara considered the two, neither of the children said a word, but as they waited patiently, the princess fished an inhaler from her candy bag and took a puff.

"Asthma?" Barbara asked.

The little princess, still holding her breath, nodded.

That must be such a burden for a family without means, Barbara thought. *It'll be a challenging life for them—unfairly so, but I've never taken in two before. One cupcake won't be enough.* After a brief moment of internal deliberation, Barbara found a solution and asked, "Do you two like chocolate cupcakes?"

The little ghost was quick to nod, but the princess hesitated.

Barbara bent down to the princess. "Do you not like chocolate?"

The little princess seemed to think for a moment before saying, "I do, but we're not supposed to take food from strangers."

Barbara smiled. "On any other night, you would be

correct, but tonight is *Halloween*. Didn't your parents give you permission to collect candy from strangers?"

The little princess considered this with her face scrunched up in thought.

"And candy is food, yes?" Barbara said.

The little ghost certainly agreed with an enthusiastic, "Yes."

The princess shrugged. "I guess so."

Barbara dropped her candy back into the bowl and held up a finger, asking the two to wait, and retrieved the cupcake from the credenza. When she returned, she held it out before the children like a prize. The ghost's eyes lit up, and the princess licked her lips.

"Now, you can't put a cupcake in a paper sack," Barbara said, pulling the cupcake back a bit like an experienced angler twitching their bait. "You'll have to sit at the table to enjoy."

Without hesitation, the little ghost started forward, but the princess shot a hand out to block him. "We can't," she said to him. Looking to Barbara, she repeated herself in a more respectful tone. "We can't. We're not allowed to go into a stranger's house."

Barbara scoffed playfully and held out a hand to the princess. "My name is Barbara Bane, and you are?"

The princess eyed the old woman's hand before extending her own. "Jenny Williams, and this is my brother, Jimmy."

After shaking hands with the children, Barbara said, "Now that we're no longer strangers, would you like to come in and eat a gooey, melt-in-your-mouth cupcake?"

Jimmy nodded and started forward again. Barbara smiled, waving a welcoming hand toward the dining room.

"Take a seat at the table. I'll fetch you each a tall, cool glass of milk. You can't have a chocolate cupcake without milk," Barbara said, handing Jimmy the saucer with the cupcake. "Now, not a bite until I can join you."

Jimmy nodded obediently and rushed around Barbara, cutting a path into the dining room. Jenny followed after, albeit less enthusiastically. The pattering of little feet paired with the children's hushed, excited whispers gave Barbara such a thrill.

A voice came from behind Barbara saying, "Tonight is for the children." Barbara turned to find the room empty, though the voice had sounded so real and present. She rubbed her temples, and with a deep breath, Barbara steadied herself, locked the front door, and shuffled into the kitchen for milk. In passing, she heard Jimmy asking if he could take just one bite of the cupcake, but Jenny urged her brother to remember his manners and to wait for Ms. Bane.

"Just a bite!" Jimmy shouted, his voice carrying from the dining room.

"It's rude to shout at a princess," Jenny said sternly.

"You're not a *real* princess," Jimmy said.

"But I'm older, and Ms. Bane asked us to wait," Jenny said. "So, we have to wait."

Delighted, Barbara hummed a tune as she stood before her open refrigerator. Two cartons of milk waited side by side. One marked with a big, black *X* and one without. She took the one with the black *X*, gave it a shake, and grabbed a pair of glasses from beside the sink. Her eyes twinkled as a concoction of milk, diazepam, and hydrocodone filled the two glasses.

"Who wants milk?" Barbara called, taking the drinks and starting for the dining room.

"I do, Ms. Bane!" Jimmy said.

Barbara's heart raced with anticipation. This had always been the most exciting part of the night. It had been so long since a child had accepted her hospitality, but to have two? This would be a magical night to be sure. After delivering the glasses of milk, she held up a finger and urged the children to wait one moment longer. "I need to cut the cupcake, so that you each have an equal share."

The two looked up at her and nodded, though the waiting was clearly testing the last of Jimmy's restraint.

Barbara returned to the kitchen and retrieved her prized Garven chef's knife. The handle was a rich rosewood, softened by years of use. The blade was eight inches of glinting steel that Barbara kept as sharp as a razor's edge. The knife had been a Christmas gift from her late husband. At the time, the Garven name had been known for its durable blade, impeccable German craftsmanship, and hefty price tag. *Whether you're carving the holiday turkey or cutting the crusts off a sandwich, sharp minds choose Garven knives*, the ads had claimed. *They're good to the last cut.*

Barbara's wide eyes stared back madly from the reflective blade. "Tonight is for the children," she said in a low voice and started for the dining room. But as she rounded the corner from the kitchen to the dining room, a knock came from the front door, stopping her dead in her tracks.

Barbara, you old fool, she thought, realizing she had forgotten to leave the bowl of candy outside the door. "Stay put, kids," she said to the two in the dining room and crossed over to the credenza, exchanging the knife for the bowl of candy. Arriving at the front door, she hastily opened it, ready to throw candy into hungry sacks and dismiss the trick-or-treaters. The door swung open, and Barbara froze as a chill swept up her spine. A boy, stained with mud from head to toe, stood at the threshold of her house wearing jeans cuffed at the bottom, a plaid flannel shirt, and a coonskin cap. A putrid, black slit stained by old blood marked his chest. His eyes were cloudy and gray, his lifeless face a mess of dirt and freckles.

As Barbara breathed his name, "Billy," the candy dish slipped from her hands and shattered at her feet, sending candy shooting across the floor in every direction.

From the dining room, the ghost and the princess yelped at the sound of the shattering dish, but Billy stood unmoved. Barbara kept her eyes fixed on Billy, as she blindly reached a trembling hand for the door. Neither the boy nor the old woman blinked, as she slowly shut the door between them.

"Is everything okay?" Jenny called from the dining room.

Barbara ignored the little princess. A high-pitched ring swelled in Barbara's ears. She placed a hand on her chest and felt her heart thumping against her palm.

"Are you okay, Ms. Bane?" Jenny said.

Barbara turned to find Jenny standing there. The little princess looked deeply concerned. Barbara said nothing. She couldn't process Jenny's concern while struggling to comprehend who or what was waiting at her front door.

Billy Badowski was dead—dead and buried. Barbara was sure of it, so who could *that* have been? Certainly not an angel. Perhaps it was a grim coincidence—a child dressed up like the living dead, and he happened to resemble Billy Badowski.

"Ms. Bane?" Jenny pressed.

"Go wait in the dining room," Barbara said coldly, her thoughts remaining on the first child she'd ever saved.

As Barbara reminded herself why she'd set Billy free all those years ago, another knock resounded like a hammering fist, causing Barbara to jump, cursing. Jenny, frightened, retreated into the dining room.

Barbara turned to face the door, reminding herself that the dead stay dead. *I'm going to see normal children waiting for candy, and that will prove that I did not just see a dead child at my door.* As she opened the door, Barbara felt the full weight of dread fall over her—the feeling of a nightmare coming true. The corpse of Billy Badowski remained, waiting on the front porch, but now, he was not alone. At his side stood the mud-stained corpse of eleven-year-old Grace Lín. She wore a pointed witch's hat, black and violet robe caked with dirt, dried blood, and a stab wound in her chest that matched Billy's. Her eyes were also milky, empty, and the two children kept their vacant gaze on Barbara.

"I laid you to rest—both of you," Barbara said, quavering as she leapt to her own defense. "You were afflicted, Billy. They would've tortured you. And you, Grace. I saw the signs. I knew there was something wrong with that mother of yours. She belonged in a nuthouse. I was certain of it. It was only a matter of time before you lost your mind, too. Is that the life you wanted? To end up like your crazy mother?"

The children said nothing and took a step forward. Barbara stumbled back, grasping for a handhold.

"Not another step," Barbara said and backed into the credenza. The Garven knife slid off the credenza and clattered to the floor. Barbara bent over and snatched it up. Rising unsteadily to her full height, she pointed the knife at the two children and said, "I told you, not another step." Though her tone was stern, Billy and Grace stepped closer and reached out for the old woman. Barbara reeled around as quickly as her body, aged and rigid, could manage and made to escape. Careening through the house, she arrived in the dining room, swinging the knife wildly. Jenny and Jimmy let out a scream and bolted out of the dining room. Their screaming sustained all the way through the kitchen and out into the backyard, and their voices soon faded from earshot. While only moments ago that would've disappointed Barbara, now she wished to do the same, but she didn't have the heart for it. Her erratic palpitations were joined with short, shallow breaths. She needed to slow down—to lie down, but the floorboards creaked behind her.

With great effort, Barbara hobbled into the kitchen, hoping to escape into the backyard. She pushed her way through the screen door and staggered outside, one hand clutching the knife, the other clutching her chest. If she could make it across the yard, she might reach the neighbor's house, but she couldn't manage another step. Barbara stood stunned at the state of her yard.

Over the course of several decades, Barbara Bane had laid to rest five children, but as she surveyed the yard, four of the five graves were open, vacant, surrounded by mounds of upturned soil. A little ways off to her right, where she'd laid to rest the fifth child, the ground began to bulge. A small patch of grass rose and fell, until finally the soil broke, and a little, pale hand shot up out of the earth as though it were reaching for the moon. Barbara shook her head and rubbed her eyes, not wanting to trust a thing she'd seen. The shrubs rustled to Barbara's left, drawing her attention. The familiar face of the third child, little Jessica Thompson, peeked out from around the greenery. Muddy, matted hair framed cloudy eyes that peered off into nowhere.

"You were blind!" Barbara shouted. There was a note of pleading in her voice, as she thought perhaps the dead were more understanding than the living.

Another child stepped into view from behind Jessica. It was Isaiah Green. The fourth child. Clumps of dirt fell off him as he limped up to Jessica's side and took her hand. Barbara glared at the child, indignant.

"You had cancer, Isaiah!" Barbara said, waving a dismissive hand. "You would've been an impossible burden." The bushes behind Barbara rustled. She twisted around to find the fifth child, nine-year-old Buster Barnett, had managed to crawl from his grave and amble across the yard. Barbara jabbed the knife at the boy, shouting, "Get back in your hole, you—you —mongoloid!" Barbara kept the knife pointed out at the children as they pressed toward her. "I saved you—every one of you—from years of suffering!"

Buster continued his approach, as Jessica and Isaiah closed

in on Barbara. Barbara turned, directing the knife between the three children as the screen door creaked open. She looked to find Billy and Grace standing in the doorway. Surrounded, Barbara's wrinkled, red lip curled. She turned, and with everything in her, Barbara Bane plunged the eight-inch Garven blade into the chest of Buster Barnett. She let go of the knife and stumbled back, gasping for air. The blow had sent a sharp pain through her left arm, but she hoped the attack would be enough to scare the little monsters away.

Buster, so precious in life and still so precious in death, looked down at the knife planted in his still, cool chest. The look on his wrinkled-up face suggested he wasn't scared. He looked confused, as though he wondered why Ms. Bane had put a knife in his chest. He then looked around at the other children, seeming to imply he hadn't any idea what he should do with the knife now that it was there.

Frustrated, Barbara sputtered, "Oh, just move, you little fool."

But Buster didn't move. He stood uncertain, looking between the knife and the other children.

Grace moved to Buster's side, laid a hand on his shoulder, and gave him a look as if to say, "It's okay. I'll help you." Gently, Grace wrapped a hand around the handle and pulled the knife free from Buster's chest.

Seeing Grace with the knife, Barbara cursed, her words tumbling out in a heap. A cold sweat beaded from head to toe. Her struggling heart thundered. Grace looked up, knife in hand, and the other four turned their attention to Barbara.

"You mean to kill me," Barbara said, wheezing. She pushed past Jessica and Isaiah and stumbled into the yard. "Get . . . away . . . from me."

She wanted to run, but the world seemed to turn around her, and in a heartbeat, Barbara knew it was too late. Just as she'd feared, a cold, stabbing pain shot through her chest. She might've prayed or screamed or even wept, but all she could do was exhale a wet, rattling breath. Barbara Bane fell to her knees, her right hand a rigid claw hovering over her idle heart.

A chorus of trick-or-treaters resounded from Witchwood Drive, free from fear—their hearts and candy sacks overflowing. Soon, the astronaut and the cowboy, the superhero and the monster, would be sifting through mounds of candy, trading pieces with their friends or defending their treasure from their parents. But beneath the clear, starry sky, under a gleaming, Halloween moon, Barbara Bane found herself kneeling before one of the empty graves she'd dug so many years ago. On the other side of the grave stood a hunched, barefoot old woman in a homemade dress. Her eyes were hazy, skin pallid. "Mother?" Barbara said, and her eyes rolled back, her clenched hand fell to her side, and she tumbled forward into the open earth. After a moment, the five children, Billy, Grace, Jessica, Isaiah, and Buster, approached slowly, each as innocent as the night they'd died. Behind them laid the shiny knife, gleaming in the grass. Before them laid the still body of Barbara Bane. The children looked at the old woman and then at one another. Without a word, they all got on their knees, pushed the loose soil back into the open grave, and buried the dead.

As Barbara Bane's body cooled beneath the soil, awaiting the worms, the last flicker of thought came low and distant in the familiar voice of her mother. "Tonight was for the children."

THE PROVENANCE
(PART ONE)

Grimlock Cove, 1999

In the heart of Grimlock Cove, on the historic main street where gas lamps still flickered over glistening cobblestones, stood The Witch Bottle Cafe. Churning storm clouds rumbled overhead, as sheets of summer rain battered the windows. Inside the cafe, safe from the storm, Sarah McLachlan's "Angel" played. An espresso machine hummed along, pulling shots. Floral art nouveau prints hung on brick walls between violet curtains, and the last of the day's pastries sat unwanted atop pedestals under glass. A pair of baristas worked behind the bar—a stocky young man with a sandy blonde bowl cut restocked shelves, while the other, a tall, blue-eyed, broad-shouldered man, prepared a double cappuccino.

Tori Gellar sat alone on a red velvet couch, thinking, *Art is magic, taking us places we'd never imagined and leaving us forever changed*. This was the opening line of Tori's application to her master's program, and for some reason, it'd been lurking in the back of her mind all day.

The barista poured four shots of chocolaty espresso into steamed milk, topped it with a layer of thick foam, and read the name scrawled on the side before fitting the to-go cup with a paper sleeve.

"Double cappuccino for *Terry*," the barista called, and set the drink on the bar.

Tori waited a beat after instinctively looking around for a "Terry" to approach the counter. Realizing she was the only customer in the cafe, Tori stepped up to the counter, assuming she must've heard the wrong name. "I think that's my drink," she said sheepishly.

"Are you *Terry*?" the barista asked.

"Well, no. I'm Tori."

"Well," the barista said, pausing to look around the empty cafe, "it's probably your drink." He nudged the cup toward her with a wink. Their eyes met for a moment, lingering, and she felt a little spark she hadn't felt in far too long. Tori blushed, pulling a lock of raven black hair behind her ear, leaving the rest to hang helplessly from her struggling updo.

Tori's day had started before sunrise, and though the sun had clocked out hours ago, not Tori. After twelve hours of forensic research, and two hours on the road to Grimlock Cove, she hoped to look better than she felt—maybe her tussled look would come off more "casually chic" than "hot mess."

"You look familiar," the barista said, leaning on the counter.

"Oh, I get that a lot," Tori said. "Monica from *Friends*, right?"

"Never seen it."

Tori laughed.

"Seriously," the barista said. "I've never seen it."

Tori smirked, very much doubting the man. "*Everyone's* seen it. Come on. Look again." Tori waved her hand around her face and gestured to the rest of her, which was wearing the hell out of her favorite black tank top and jeans.

The barista shrugged. "Never seen the show."

"My last name is *Gellar*," she said.

"Like Sarah Michelle Gellar?"

"No—well, yes. Her, too, but—"

"Hey, Joey," the barista called.

"Wait," Tori said. "His name is *Joey*?"

"What's up?" Joey said, popping up from behind the bar.

"She doesn't believe I've never seen—wait—what'd you call it?"

Tori rolled her eyes. "*Friends*."

"On my honor," Joey said. "Ross has never seen—"

"Ross?" Tori said, cutting Joey off. "Okay. You guys have got to be—" but she stopped, and the three turned to look as the cafe door swung open with a peal of thunder.

An older, lanky man stood in the doorway, wearing a gray, plaid trench coat and a bowler hat. He lowered his dripping umbrella, closed it up, and gave it a shake before tucking it under his arm. Taking his hat in hand, he stepped in, leaving the door to close behind him.

"Mr. Kanival," Ross said, his tone suggesting this wasn't just another regular.

"Good evening, Mr. Laront," Mr. Kanival said. "I'm here in need of one pound of finely ground espresso."

"I was worried," Ross, who Mr. Kanival had called *Mr. Laront*, replied. "I haven't seen anyone from the manor in a few weeks."

Mr. Kanival nodded. "To my delight, the lady of the house wished to explore the world of tea, but her experiment proved to be more of a detour than a journey, and she's *very* much in need of coffee."

As Joey hurried about preparing the order, Tori took in Mr. Kanival. His features were angular, severe. His bespoke suit, impeccable posture, and cordial smile did little to distract from the distinct sense of unease that had arrived with him.

Mr. Kanival's gray eyes fell on Tori, seeming to notice her appraising look. "I don't believe we've met."

Slightly embarrassed, she introduced herself.

Mr. Kanival replied with a cold smile. "And what has you out and about in this horrendous storm?"

"I'm a provenance researcher—freelance," she said. "That is, until I can find a gallery job."

Mr. Kanival's smile was replaced with a look of curiosity.

"What's a provenance researcher?" Ross said.

"I work with art," she said, avoiding the usual, drawn-out explanation.

However, Mr. Kanival seemed most interested, and offered clarification, "A modest reply. A provenance researcher analyzes cultural assets and art to confirm their provenance—that is to say, their true origin and history."

"That's right," Tori said, a little surprised, as few had even heard of provenance research.

"Gentlemen," Mr. Kanival continued, "we stand in the presence of a highly skilled detective, whose research not only roots out forgeries but may well determine if the art was stolen by, say, Nazis. She can ascertain more from wood and nails in a painting's frame than many can from the painting itself."

"That's *amazing*," Ross said, with Joey blurting out, "She fights Nazis?"

"You should meet Mr. Vice," Ross continued. "He's a regular who sells tons of art. He might hook you up with a gallery job."

"Well, actually—" Tori began but was cut off.

"I suspect she's on her way to see Mr. Vice right now, aren't you?" Mr. Kanival said.

Tori said nothing, taken aback. How could he have known?

Perhaps prompted by the look on her face, Mr. Kanival continued, "Mr. Vice is a prolific art dealer. You are a specialist in a fledgling field of art research, and Grimlock Cove is certainly not a town known for its art scene, so it stands to reason."

"You're right. I'm inspecting a new acquisition," she said.

Joey handed Mr. Kanival a pound of espresso beans. The latter put on his bowler hat and received the ground beans with a nod to thank Joey. Looking again to Tori, Mr. Kanival said, "You're a rare bird, little canary. Do be careful in that coal mine."

Tori had no idea what he meant, but still she thanked Mr. Kanival as he turned, and exited the shop, popping his umbrella and disappearing into the storm.

After a moment, Tori said quietly, "He didn't pay."

"He doesn't have to," Ross said. "The Grimlock family owns this place."

Tori's gaze lingered on the door, still processing the peculiar interaction, when Joey piped up. "Wait, you were married to Mr. Vice, right? I heard you were dead. Someone said Mr. Vice *killed* you."

Joey's slanderous gossip pulled Tori's attention. "That's ridiculous. Gerry would never," Tori said, scowling at the notion. Sure, Gerry was selfish, bull-headed, and completely out of touch with other people's feelings, but he was working on all of that. After all, that's why he and Tori had taken time apart. He'd wanted Tori to decide if she really wanted him or his money, which was preposterous. As Tori saw it, he held that concern because all he seemed to care about was money—always chasing the next deal. Which was *another* thing he'd promised to work on. "He's many things," Tori continued, "but he would never intentionally hurt me."

"So, you're still married?" Ross asked.

"We were never officially *married*," she said with air quotes. Tori paused, preparing to explain the complexities of her very modern relationship. "Gerry and I have a sort of unofficial domestic partnership, but right now, we are on a break."

The two baristas exchanged a look.

Tori continued, "In a mature relationship, two adults can step back to reevaluate themselves and their place in the relationship. It's an opportunity to grow individually before coming back together stronger than before. We've just been taking a break, but that doesn't mean we've broken up."

With an obviously pitying tone, Joey said, "I think Mr. Vice traded you in for a new model."

"First," Tori began, "referring to a woman like she's a car is offensive."

Joey shook his head. "I mean, she's literally a new model for Ralph Lauren or something."

It was like an invisible fist had sucker punched her, leaving the pit of her stomach hollow. "He wouldn't," she said. "We were just on a break."

Joey offered a pitying smile and stepped away.

"It's on me," Ross said, nodding to Tori's cappuccino. "Seems like you had—well—*are* having a long day. You deserve a break." His tone was sincere, almost making up for Joey's out-of-line accusations.

"Thank you," Tori said.

"And remember," Ross continued, "I'll be there for you . . . you know . . . when the rain starts to—"

"Okay," Tori snapped. "What are your *real* names?"

Ross laughed. "I'm Shawn Laront, but that really is Joey," he said thumbing to the other barista.

"It's true," Joey said. "I've been Joey my whole life."

"And of course we've seen *Friends*," Shawn said.

"So you *are* fans," Tori said.

They shook their heads.

"Not really," Shawn said.

"Overrated," Joey said, and Shawn agreed.

"I hate you both," Tori said, resenting the smile she couldn't hide.

As Tori turned to leave, lightning flashed with a boom of thunder. Tori flinched as the cafe shook.

"Seriously, though. Be careful out there," Shawn said. "Tonight's gonna get a lot worse before it gets better."

"What do I get if I survive the night?" Tori said, surprising herself with her flirtatious tone.

Shawn's eyes met Tori's, and he said to Joey's surprise, "A lot more than a free coffee."

―――

Growing up, Tori had enjoyed watching thunderstorms from the safety of her bedroom. Outside, mournful winds would howl, and rain would pepper the windowpane, but it was all just bluster. She'd felt safe inside her home. Sometimes, she would wrap herself up in a blanket, curl up by the fireplace and watch gray clouds rumble as they rolled by. She'd grown to find storms soothing—the rain becoming a kind of meditative white noise. Storms had been cozy and welcome . . . until she had to drive through one.

The drive from The Witch Bottle to Gerry's house was typically ten to fifteen minutes on a good day, but this was not a good day. Tori sat tense, guiding her Civic around flooded curves and up slick inclines, as her trip approached the forty minute mark. The barrage of rain breaking over the windshield reminded Tori of driving through a car wash. Each lightning flash left an imprint on Tori's eyes, compounding the stress. But her head-to-toe tension relieved a bit when the Civic's headlights fell on the turn in for Gerry's house. Tori pulled off the main road. Towering evergreens provided some relief from the rain, but the familiar, snaking drive toward the coast was barely recognizable through the downpour, so she proceeded with caution.

The unrelenting storm seemed intent on testing Tori's limits, as she winced at another peal of thunder. Exhausted, she shot up a middle finger and cursed the clouds, Mother Nature, and any other parties responsible for the nerve-wracking drive. But her flurry of incoherent swearing was cut short, when hope sprang anew by the light of Gerry's $1.8-million-dollar cliffside mansion.

Tori pulled up to the double-wide iron gate marked with a large, brass letter *V*. She rolled down her window and punched the code into the keypad, the rain falling into the car. The brass *V* split, and she hurried to crank the window up, watching the gates open. As she pulled up to the house, she had to admit, even in the heavy rain, it was a sight to behold. The unmistakable influence of Frank Lloyd Wright set it apart from the rest of the traditional craftsman-style homes of Grimlock Cove. The contrast was stark between this house and the dark, Victorian stylings of Grimlock Manor. Unlike Grimlock Manor, Gerry's house was hidden by the coast—not set on a hill, visible from the town. Still, rumors persisted that the Grimlocks resented Gerry's house. Some had said the Grimlocks coveted the land, and when Gerry had outplayed them and closed on the property, they'd been furious.

Tori parked in front of Gerry's closed four-car garage and glanced at the rearview to see her overnight suitcase in the backseat. Her satchel, which held her forensic tools, and her purse sat in the passenger seat. Sadly, the cappuccino waited in the cupholder, untouched. All of it needed to be lugged through the downpour, and the walk up to the front door was flooded. A light was on inside, so needing a helping hand, Tori grabbed her mobile and called Gerry. After a few rings, he answered.

"Tori?" Gerry said.

"Hey," Tori said, relieved, and began collecting her things. "I'm outside. Can you—"

"Outside the house?"

"Yeah. Can you help me in or open up the garage?"

There was a muffled, rustling sound, followed by static.

"Hello? Did I lose you?" she said, pulling the phone back to check her signal. Seeing three bars, she tried again. "Gerry? Did I lose—"

"Shhh."

"What was that?" Tori asked.

"What was what?"

"Why did you shush me?"

"What? I didn't shush you," he said, laughing. "Probably just static on the line. Look, sweetie. I hate the timing, but I had to leave town."

"What?" Tori said, a bit harsher than she'd intended.

"I know. I know. But I have a huge opportunity in New York. There's this woman representing a seller from Ecuador or Mexico or something—I don't know—but I know she's looking to move a goldmine. I'm talking about *unreleased* masterpieces that have never entered the marketplace."

"That sounds too good to be true," Tori said. As a provenance researcher, every red flag waved furiously.

"Look. The Knoedler—that's a super famous art gallery in NYC—"

"Yeah, I know The Knoedler."

"Okay. So, the Knoedler already bought some Rothkos and a Pollock off this lady."

At that moment, Tori forgot about the storm and how cold, damp, and utterly exhausted she was. "Did you say *Rothkos* . . . as in more than one?"

"That's right. Never before seen."

"And a *Pollock*?"

"That's what I said."

"And the Knoedler confirmed they're all real?"

"The Knoedler is waltzing straight to the bank with this lady, so I'm in New York to see if I can have the next dance. Know what I mean?"

Tori sighed. "I do." It meant she was, yet again, alone while Gerry chased another deal.

"You don't sound too excited for me."

"Oh, no. I totally am. I'm sorry. It's just that I worked all day out of town. Then I drove four hours to get home, and you would *not* believe this storm. It took me almost an hour to—"

"Uh-huh. So you're all set, then?"

"Oh, sorry," she said, wondering why she'd apologized.

"We're good to go, right, sweetie?"

Tori killed the engine and eyed the house key dangling from her keychain. "Yeah, babe. I'm good to go."

A pouty, feminine voice came over the line, but Tori couldn't quite make out what'd been said. Keeping her voice light, she asked, "What was that?"

"What was what?" Gerry said.

"Are you watching TV?" A small part of her—a part she chose to ignore—knew it wasn't a TV.

"Uh, yeah. Listen. The piece I need you to look at is in my vision room. You can't miss it. If you could get started tonight—"

"Tonight?" Tori said, her voice rising. "Babe. I'm pretty tired. It's been a long, long day."

"Same here, Tori, but do you know what I'm going to do when I get off this call?"

Tori let her head fall back against the headrest, knowing what he would say next.

"Hello?" Gerry snapped.

For the sake of peace, Tori chose to indulge him. "No," she said in a soft voice. "I don't know what you're going to do after this."

"I'm gonna work. I'm gonna nail my sales pitch because that's what I do. I work. Then I win. Then I do it again."

"I know, and I admire your work ethic, but you remember we talked about this, right? This is exactly the kind of thing you were going to work on during our separation."

There was a knocking sound on the other end.

"Ah, that's my suit," Gerry said. "Had the hotel press it."

"Oh, what hotel are you staying—"

"Look. I gotta go. Can't wait to hear what you figure out about that piece. It's a wild one, and you'll never believe who the buyer is."

"Who?"

Tori heard a muffled voice in the background call, "Room service."

"The Grimlocks," Gerry said. "Can you believe it?"

Tori perked up, her voice high. "Seriously?"

Gerry laughed. "Yeah. The pricks are buying from *me* now."

Tori had never figured out how Gerry had managed to snatch this cliffside property out from under the Grimlocks, but that was Gerry. He had always said with a wink, "They say you can't make an honest living in this country, but look at me."

"So, what do you need from me?" Gerry asked.

Tori pulled the phone away, sighed, and slipped into her professional tone, though without her usual enthusiasm. "Is there anything you can tell me about the painting?"

"My storage guy called me about an abandoned unit going up for auction. He said the Grimlocks had been asking about it—a painting they believed the owner had stored there. I came to check it out and found this wooden shipping crate. The damned thing was nailed shut, with a bunch of 'Do Not Open' stickers plastered on every side. Naturally, I opened the crate and there it was. This was the only painting in the unit, so I snatched it up, nailed the empty crate shut, and listed the painting. The Grimlocks found out and made an offer contingent on the provenance."

"Whose storage unit?"

"Belonged to a guy named Crowley. His son had inherited it. I asked around about the son, but it was all dead ends. Checked online, and looks like Crowley was heavy into some occult nonsense. My bet is the guy's dead, but he still has a whole following of weirdo fans—like Trekkies but for occult crap."

"Anything else?"

"That's all I got."

"Room service," the voice called again.

"Oh, hey. I really gotta go, but—" Gerry paused.

"Yeah?" Tori said eagerly, as in that moment, for the first time all night, Gerry sounded like he was thinking of her instead of the deal.

"Good luck," he said as the knocking continued. "You're gonna need it."

"Thanks, babe," she said but only to herself, as Gerry had ended the call.

———

Tori's footsteps sloshed as she stepped into the biting cold of Gerry's aggressively air-conditioned home. After a quick glance around, nothing seemed to have changed since she and Gerry had taken a break. The white walls held no pictures of family or friends . . . only art. The art that hung had nothing to do with Gerry's appreciation for a piece—such as the

Warhol in the entrance. He'd positioned it to greet guests as a statement piece, and that statement, however unnecessary, was, "I'm rich." Tori understood this, but she'd always looked past it. She believed a good heart hid somewhere in Gerry, and with a little patience and time, that heart would grow—even if that'd meant time apart.

Tori stripped off her rain-soaked layers, tossing them into the laundry room, and scurried to the shower, leaving a path of damp footprints on the wooden floor. But as she hurried down the hall, a *slam* resounded from inside what Gerry called his vision room. Tori slid to an unsteady stop and peered into the room for the source of the noise. The vision room featured a panoramic wall of windows that overlooked the ocean, where white-capped waves crashed over great, black boulders —only visible with the occasional crack of lightning. The forty-foot long wall reached from one end of the room to the other. Remote-controlled blackout curtains hung above every window. A white sectional couch ran parallel, facing the windows, and behind the couch, waited the painting in question. It sat atop an easel, beneath a white sheet. Seeing the room undisturbed, she concluded the sound she'd heard must've been thunder. Though Tori wanted to see the painting, she was shivering in nothing but her skin and rushed out of the room for the shower.

A long soak in a hot shower drove the chill from her bones. Afterward, Tori wrapped herself in a fluffy Ritz Carlton towel (Gerry liked to "collect" hotel towels) and moved to the kitchen to reheat her cappuccino. Realizing she had a long night ahead of her, she also prepped a pot of coffee. The microwave dinged, and with her freshly reheated cappuccino in hand, Tori went to the bedroom for clothes, as she'd left clothes behind when they'd decided to put the relationship on hold. Tori fished through a dresser drawer and blindly grabbed a pair of underwear. She slipped her feet through and made to pull them up, but the pair stopped short—not even halfway up her thighs. Tori stood mortified.

How infinitely rude, she thought.

Sure, the break from Gerry had been stressful, and yes, her work had her pulling long hours, often relying on fast food for meals, but she still fit just fine into her favorite pair of jeans. Tori slipped the underwear off and held them up to inspect.

Silky, lacy, and extra small.

Tori's stomach sank. She hadn't been an extra small since high school. She rifled through the drawer, looking for another strange pair and instead found Polaroids of a young, tan woman who looked as though she'd fallen out of a Victoria's Secret catalog and into Gerry's bed.

Tori, hands shaking, fumbled her cell phone as she tried to call Gerry. Her stomach churned, sick and hollow. Arms, legs, the whole of her trembled.

"Tori?" Gerry answered, sounding pleasantly surprised. "You're done already?"

Despite the fire in her belly, she stood silent.

"Hello?" Gerry said.

I hate you. How could you? Why would you do this to me— to us? Is she worth it? Was I not worth it? All the things she wished to say proved too heavy to get out.

Gerry said again, "Tori? Are you—"

Tori hung up. She clutched the phone in her shaking hands, eyes welling with tears. A whirlwind of questions churned. Was he really in New York? Was that the TV she'd heard—of course not. He'd taken *her* on his trip after having told Tori he preferred traveling alone. Could she, Tori, have been so gullible? Panic swelled, mingling with anger, as every unanswered question grew louder. Guilt swept in, feeling as though this was her fault. Overwhelmed, Tori did what she'd always done in a situation like this. She made excuses for

Gerry, attempting to reason away what she knew to be true. *We've been apart for too long. I should have come back sooner.*

Tori's phone lit up. She listened to it ring a second and a third time. If she answered, maybe Gerry could explain everything and dispel a potential misunderstanding. Or maybe, if confronted, he would break down, having seen the error of his ways. Maybe this could be the catalyst for change that he needed. Maybe this would be his rock bottom.

Tori felt a touch lighter at the prospect, but then again . . . what if he didn't care to explain? What if he no longer cared for her? He might've used her and decided he was done with her. He might be using her now. *Might be?* she thought. *Of course he is.* Tori's grip on her phone tightened. *Of course he's using me now.* In that moment, she turned her anger on herself, spiting herself for every tear and every *I love you* she'd wasted on this man.

The phone stopped ringing.

When Tori was a child, long before she'd outgrown her father's advice, he had said something that'd stuck with her. After Tori'd had a nasty falling out with a friend, her father had sat beside her on her bed and dried her tears. When he'd dried the last tear, he'd said, *It's good to open up to people—to take that chance, but remember that your heart belongs to you. If you've given it to someone who's not careful with it, you can take it right back.*

But Tori couldn't self-soothe any more than an active volcano could simmer down. Still, she took a deep breath, let it out slow and steady, and focused on her breathing. In and out . . . slow and steady. Her phone rang again, announcing Gerry's second attempt to call back, but she ignored it, choosing instead to just breathe. When he tried a third time, Tori opened her eyes and took the call.

"Hello?" Gerry said, sounding annoyed.

Tori said nothing and took another long breath.

"Tori?" Gerry said again. "If you're saying something, I can't hear you."

Tori exhaled and said, "Who is she?"

There was a moment's pause, and Gerry answered, "Who is who?"

"The woman you've been sleeping with," Tori said. "Who is she?"

"Where's *this* coming from?"

"Gerry," she snapped, catching herself before her voice cracked.

"What?"

"I found— I found the pictures. I am asking you plainly—and please don't lie to me—who is she?"

"Well, shit," Gerry said, exhaling hard into the phone. "I was going to tell you after—"

"After what? After another anniversary apart? Or after another—" Tori stopped, feeling as though she knew why he'd waited.

"I was waiting until this job was done," he said, "because I know how much you need the money."

Tori flushed. "So, you strung me along for *my* benefit?"

"Come on, sweetie." His tone was unsurprisingly condescending. "That art degree ain't paying for itself."

"What's her name?"

Gerry groaned.

"Tell me her name," Tori said.

"Bianca," he said, and continued with the phone clearly pulled away. "No, sweetie. I'm not talking to you. Go back to sleep."

Tori fought back tears. "She's very petite."

"She's a model. Doesn't sit around eating junk food all day."

Tori's jaw tightened.

"Look," Gerry continued, his tone having turned formal.

"I'll level with you. I *really* need the provenance for that painting done, so I'll pay you twenty grand if you get it done by the time I get home tomorrow. Deal?"

"How are you *still* talking business?" she said, abandoning restraint and letting her voice rise. "I just caught you in an affair!"

"An affair?" Gerry laughed. "We've been over for a while. Maybe if you weren't so wrapped up in your career, you might've seen that."

The whole of Tori shook. "Wrapped up in *my* career?"

"Look. I close with the Grimlocks tomorrow. They're sending a rep over to pick up the piece. Have the provenance done, take the twenty grand, and be grateful. Or, do nothing—but I swear I will ruin your name coast to coast with every museum, every gallery, and every dealer I know. It's up to you." And with that, Gerry ended the call.

Tori cursed at the top of her lungs. Fists clenched, she screamed into nothing and resented every tear.

After a couple of hours with her thoughts, letting the initial shock settle, her relationship with Gerry gained the unflattering benefit of hindsight. Was she the only one who hadn't clearly seen their dysfunction? Had every listening ear pitied her when she'd explained the relationship as something "progressive" and "mature"? Had everyone but her known it had only been business with benefits?

Tori's blood simmered. She looked around the bedroom in disgust and imagined setting fire to the house—emptying lighter fluid on the bed, around the bathroom, and on anything else Bianca might have touched. She could sip French wine and watch the whole damned thing burn. Maybe the fire would take some of the memories with it. She savored the thought—the wicked delight of watching Gerry on his knees before his multi-million-dollar pile of ash.

After a long moment of entertaining diabolical, yet deeply

satisfying, ideations of crimes she knew she'd never *actually* commit, Tori pulled on her jeans and a top, packed her things, and lugged her belongings to the front door. The rain hadn't let up a bit, though the thunder had become less frequent. But as she stood in the open entryway, the rain blew in, needling her arms and face. With her arms at her sides, she closed her eyes and turned her palms outward to feel the rain. Lightning flashed, but she didn't flinch. The thunder boomed, but she didn't back away. She simply breathed and allowed herself a moment to feel something other than anger, betrayal, and humiliation.

The hard rain and cold winds brought clarity, reminding Tori that her world was so much bigger than Gerry. The thunder crashed again—this time shaking the walls—and Tori opened her eyes. Floodwater rushed steadily past the front steps, spilling around the edges of the house. Her car hid in the heavy rain. She remembered what Shawn, the barista, had said: "Be careful out there. I think tonight's gonna get a lot worse before it gets better."

Though she hated Gerry and loathed spending another minute in his house, leaving wasn't worth potentially dying. Tori closed the door and cut a path to the kitchen. She stopped at the wine rack and looked until she found Gerry's prized bottle—a rare French vintage. She remembered taking him to a wine tasting class as a couples activity, where he'd confessed he preferred body shots over tasting notes. Thankfully, his clients preferred a good red over house tequila, so Gerry had paid a sommelier to source a particularly exquisite Bordeaux.

"It's the very least you could do, asshole," she said and uncorked the bottle.

Leaving no time for the bottle to breathe, Tori snatched a glass, filled it nearly to the rim, and retired to the vision room. On the back wall hung various paintings and sculptures. It was

Gerry's own private gallery. Tori took a seat on the couch to watch the storm through the windows, intending to give the wine time to do its thing before deciding what she wanted more: twenty thousand dollars or the satisfaction of screwing Gerry out of not just any sale but a sale to the Grimlocks.

With the lights on, the room reflected in the windows. Tori raised her glass, toasting her reflection, and there, alone with herself, she drank to the end of another failed relationship. The times she'd shared with Gerry came back to her uninvited, but the old memories looked different, recast in a new light. Without the rose-colored glasses, she could see the red flags that she'd dismissed. In hindsight, it all seemed so obvious—so much so, she wondered how she hadn't seen it sooner.

Moment after moment replayed between sips of bloodred wine, but her exploration of the past ended sharply when the painting behind her shuddered. Tori jerked in her seat at the sudden sound, sending red wine splashing down her front. She cursed and rushed into the kitchen to blot up the wine as best she could. When she returned to the main room, she saw, for the first time, the painting Gerry had hired her to research. The sheet that had covered the painting lie in a heap at the foot of the easel.

After a long pause to rationalize the sudden noise, Tori decided it must've been the sound of the sheet hitting the floor. With her sitting in dead silence with her thoughts, the sound must've seemed much louder. Approaching the painting, she said to herself, "Twenty thousand dollars." She thought about that number for a moment, tallying up the many ways that money could change her life. She counted the months of rent that would cover versus how many student loans she could pay off. Perhaps it was Gerry's influence finally taking hold, or perhaps her latest heartache had delivered a final blow to her naiveté—either way, a realization sank in.

Twenty thousand dollars was a lot of money for Tori, but it wasn't a lot of money for Gerry. With no formal contract between them, and Gerry's payday on the line, she could agree to research the provenance as requested, but not for twenty thousand dollars.

The hour was late, but Tori knew Gerry was open for business twenty-four-seven. She paced the length of the windows, strategizing, casting the occasional glance at the painting. He had been using her and was likely using Bianca now. Tori finally stopped and faced her reflection in the dark windows. She determined this would be the last time she worked for Gerry Vice, and that she was going to get everything she could out of him.

Tori made the call, and Gerry picked up.

There was a rustling followed by Gerry's disoriented, "Hello?"

"Half," she said.

"What?"

"Half."

"Tori?"

"You heard me," she said. "Half."

There was a pause before he answered. "Oh, you want half of the *sale*."

It didn't surprise her that he was quick to recognize her opportunism, but the "proud papa" tone in his voice made her skin crawl.

Tori kept her sentences short to hide the nervous tremble moving through her. "Half or I walk."

Another long pause ensued. Tori waited, saying nothing. She'd learned from watching Gerry: Never ask for what you want. Tell them what you want, and never tell them more than three times. If the other party thinks you're asking, you've already lost. Your "ask" is a demand—it's simply the price for whatever it is you have that they want. And when there's silence, you embrace it. Only the party negotiating from a point of weakness would feel the need to fill the silence.

"Can't do half," Gerry said. "Forty thousand. That's the best I can do."

"My bags are packed. Good luck with your sale," Tori said and ended the call.

Her heart thumped in her chest, her hands trembling. *What if he doesn't go for it? No. He has to. I just have to wait*, she thought. After pouring another glass of the French red, she swallowed a mouthful and watched her cell phone. If she knew Gerry, he needed a moment to get past the shock, but he wouldn't sacrifice his payday for anything—not for ego, not for pride, and not for spite. She knew that when Gerry said, "It's just business," he truly meant it.

Her phone rang. Taking intentionally slow, calming breaths, she let it ring three times before answering.

Tori was quick to speak first, keeping her tone flat and the conversation in her hands. "We're both short on time, so I need your decision now."

After a moment, Gerry replied, "I gotta admit, this new you is turning me on."

Tori's stomach twisted, her knuckles going white. "Your lawyer can draft the contract and send it via courier in the morning. Half of gross proceeds from the sale for my time." Tori hoped he wouldn't catch that her "time" didn't necessarily guarantee a successful provenance.

"You know . . . I bet Bianca would be open to the three of us—"

"Goodbye, Ger—"

"Half," he said before she could end the call. "Have your findings recorded, signed, and provided in a sealed envelope. I'll have the contract there by noon."

"Once you've signed, I'll hand over the provenance. Agreed?"

"Agreed," he said. "Anything else?"

With her heart racing, she fought to keep her voice even. "What price did the Grimlocks agree to?"

Gerry was slow to answer, as it clearly stung to give up half. "Two million."

Tori swayed on the spot, planting a hand on the cold window pane to catch herself. The words fell out of her again, nearly breathless, needing to exit the conversation fast, "Half of gross proceeds from the sale in exchange for my time."

"I got it," he said, lacking his usual superior tone.

There was a pause. She knew she didn't have the time or resources on hand to complete the job tonight, but she hoped what Gerry had told her earlier about the painting might be enough to provide a provenance that could satisfy the Grimlocks. Even then, their satisfaction wasn't *her* problem. She wasn't getting paid for completing the provenance—just for her time. She only had to be present in the morning to receive her check.

"Well?" Gerry said. "Anything else?"

"I'll be looking for the contract in the morning."

Gerry laughed and said, "Well, you're officially doing business with the Grimlocks, kid. Good luck," and ended the call.

Gerry's uncharacteristic laugh in the face of paying out one million dollars hardly registered. Tori, stunned, repeated under her breath, "A million dollars." She remained braced against the window, struggling to process how her life might have just changed. All the Grimlocks wanted to know was that the painting Gerry had taken was *the* painting they'd expected to find in Crowley's storage unit. Assuming this was the painting the Grimlocks wanted, the family's willingness to pay millions suggested they certainly knew something about the painting that Gerry didn't. More than their bid, their willingness to pay *Gerry* millions showed how deadly serious they were in acquiring the painting. But why *this* painting?

Tori's high-flying moment was swiftly grounded by a realization: She needed more information in order to sell the Grimlocks on her provenance research. If they backed out of the sale, she got nothing. Tori needed as much forensic information as she could tweeze out in one night.

So with one million dollars on the line, she corked the wine, retrieved the tools from her backpack, and went to work.

The Provenance
(Part Two)

Tori began her research in Gerry's office with the information he'd given her over the phone. A tangerine iMac sat ready with what was likely one of the few dial-up connections in Grimlock Cove. A search of "Crowley Grimlock Cove" returned a small message board dedicated to occult paraphernalia. From what Tori could gather, Mr. Crowley had been a collector of occult wares and had written a book on the matter decades ago. *Witches Among Us: A Guide* had garnered a meager following of tinfoil hat enthusiasts with a taste for the supernatural. "Like Trekkies but for occult crap," Gerry had said. Crowley's sudden disappearance shortly after publishing had only fueled his fans' suspicions.

Disappointed by the lack of new information, she returned to the vision room to inspect the painting in question. The face of the painting was a mess of drab green and brown oils with seemingly no intent or purpose in the composition. The frame was nondescript wood. Nothing ornate or particularly remarkable. After carefully removing the backing board, she found no stamp on the canvas identifying the canvas-maker, nor was there a gallery or auction label. *I'll have to work with what I've got*, she thought, reassuring herself, and moving to inspect the components of the painting.

She started with the wooden dowels used to stretch the canvas. The imperfect cuts at the joints had left small gaps where the wood met. Machines would create near seamless lines, which an artist wouldn't have access to until the 20th century. The back of the canvas hadn't been preserved under backing paper, leaving it to oxidize—to darken with the decades. All of that, along with the apparent old age of the wood and the use of hand-wrought nails, led Tori to believe the piece likely dated back to the 18th century.

Inspecting the back of the canvas more closely revealed something peculiar—four markings, each resembling a rune—possibly Celtic. The four runes were arranged in a diamond formation. At the center was a circle, and in that circle was what Tori assumed to be a name. Tori's first thought was that it might be the artist's signature, but even for an artist, this would've been unusually elaborate. Perhaps she was feeling the aftereffects of having spent too much time on the occult message board, but something about the presentation of the runes and the encircled name invoked mental images of occult rituals.

Tori sat close to the painting and read the name on the canvas, "Myrna."

Returning to Gerry's office, Tori searched "Myrna." The search delivered a site listing old Hollywood stars, which was easy to rule out, given the centuries-old age of the canvas and stretcher. After a short time, "Myrna" proved more of a dead end than "Crowley."

Tori returned to the vision room and flipped the painting around. The front of the canvas was a mess of angry brush strokes and globs of oil paint. The oil exhibited the expected deep cracks that ran along the grain of the canvas. She knew these cracks, called the "craquelure," could be faked, but given the depth and how random the cracks appeared, Tori felt increasingly confident in her assessment that this piece was well over a hundred years old.

Looking closer, Tori noticed something irregular—an intentional, raised pattern in the oil. Retrieving a magnifying glass from her toolkit, she inspected the canvas to find a diamond shape resembling the one on the back that framed the name. The shape appeared to be made of thin braids of hair that would've had to have been pressed into the paint while the oils were still wet. The few sections of hair that weren't submerged in the paint appeared silvery. Tori had known artists to infuse animal and even human remains into their work, so this was nothing unusual to her, but it raised questions.

"Is this the artist's hair, or maybe a lover's?" she wondered aloud, pausing to consider all the evidence she'd compiled so far. *I bet the Grimlocks know exactly who the artist is—why else would they pay millions? What else could make this worth so much to them?* She reached for her UV light. "Let's see if you have any secrets."

Under ultraviolet light, a painting may exhibit various colored hazes, which might indicate repairs had been made, restoration work performed, or whether or not the painting had been painted over another work. A truly valuable work could have been painted over for any number of reasons—a scorned lover, a bitter rival, or even an impoverished painter in need of a canvas. It wouldn't be the first time a hungry artist had painted over what would have later been regarded as a masterpiece. Perhaps the real work—what the Grimlocks sought—hid beneath what Tori could see. That could explain the value. Though older paints would not fluoresce under a UV light, more modern paints would, which, if nothing else, could strongly suggest this was a newer painting concealing an older work.

Tori killed the overhead lights and switched on her UV flashlight. She passed the light over the face of the painting in slow, even movements, interrupted by intermittent flashes of lightning. Under the UV light, the canvas remained dark, failing to fluoresce. This confirmed the oils used were older. She leaned in to inspect more closely with another pass. Again, much of the painting remained dark, but then a mark—reminiscent of the runes on the back—appeared in the top right corner. The mark lit up a fluorescent green. Moving the light around revealed three more rune-like markings—one in each corner of the painting. Tori checked the markings on the front against the ones she'd seen on the back of the canvas and found they matched. She wondered if the runes had been part of the original work, and this aggressive slop of oil over top of them had been to conceal them, but that didn't add up. Leaning in, she inspected one rune to find it hadn't been painted over. One by one, she confirmed each of the four runes had been painted on the face of the painting. Given the manner in which the runes lit up under the UV, she wondered if they had been painted with blood.

Continuing her inspection, Tori noted the fine cracks in the oil, which suggested that if the work had been painted over, it couldn't be Mr. Crowley's handy work. The random nature of the craquelure couldn't happen in Mr. Crowley's lifetime. The painting would have to be much older than Crowley himself.

Tori passed the light over the canvas again and froze. Something was staring back at her. She held the light as still as as she could over a photorealistic likeness of an old man hidden in the painting. *It looks so real*, she thought, moving in for a closer look. The excruciating detail in the wrinkles and fine hairs was outstanding, and the eyes—Tori felt as though this terrified man gazing back at her were alive. He appeared weathered, worn down. His face seemed entirely three dimensional, as though she could reach into the painting and touch him. She recorded her findings in her notebook—the runes, the strands of silver hair, the age of each component, and the remarkably detailed face.

Tori wondered what could have been used to paint such a detailed face and still show up so clearly under the UV. It made no sense. If newer oils, maybe no more than thirty to forty years old—were used to paint the face, how did this work end up behind a layer of much older paint—oil paint that had cracked over what appeared to be more than a century. She took in, with great admiration and curiosity, the impressive detail in the old man's iris. Somehow, the artist had manipulated the perspective until the face, when viewed up close, retained its three-dimensional quality from every angle. "This is too cool," Tori said, having never seen such an effect achieved on canvas. She moved closer until she was nose to nose with the mysterious face in the painting. Squinting, she peered into the flawlessly painted eyes shimmering under the UV light. "Who *are* you?"

The eyes blinked, and in a moment of panic, Tori thrust a hand out to shove the painting away, but a cold, sticky hand shot out of the canvas and caught her by the wrist. She screamed and pulled back against the hand, but the hand refused to let go. The old man's face pressed out of the painting, a head slowly emerging, becoming fleshy and tangible as it passed from the painting into the world. The man clutched Tori's wrist like one would cling to a lifeline, bruising and damn near breaking her arm. She continued to scream, struggling to pry herself free.

The old man shouted, his voice raspy, "Let me out!"

Tori writhed frantically, struggling against his hold. She kicked her feet, almost knocking the legs out from under the easel. The painting rocked in place, and the old man's mad eyes bore into her, as he pulled until his upper half protruded from the canvas. It was then that Tori jerked forward, pulled into the painting as the man flew past her. Heart racing, she flailed, off balance in a short free fall, before landing with a solid thud.

Scrambling to her feet despite the pain, she looked around and found the frame of the painting before her. The frame hung, suspended in air, with no canvas. From where she stood, what had appeared to be a painting from one side was a window of sorts from the other. She was peering through a kind of portal into Gerry's vision room.

Tori tried to make sense of what had just happened. The best she could come up with was that the old man had been trapped inside the painting, and she and the old man had just traded places, though she wasn't sure why. Tori shouted to him, but he ignored her, celebrating his freedom. She tried to reach through the portal, but if this portal was a door, the door was closed.

After his celebratory moment, the old man turned to face the painting and peered in at Tori. He was careful not to get too close.

Tori glanced at the strange new world surrounding her, her anxiety rising. Looking back at the portal, she implored the old man. "Please. I don't understand what's happening, and I'm scared."

"I am truly sorry," he said, his hands up as he backed away from the painting. "I never intended this for anyone but the witch. I would try to pull you out, but the painting requires a soul. It will not go without, and—" The old man looked away. "I cannot go back in."

"Please," Tori said again. "Please, don't leave me."

"I saw you studying the painting. You're highly skilled and well-suited for this. Remember the stories behind what you see." The man took another step back from the painting. "Whatever you see is meant for *you*." And with that, the old man hurried away.

Panic threatened to overtake Tori, who stood helpless, staring through this strange portal into the empty vision room. But she refused to give in, choosing instead to breathe. After a quiet moment, a thought occurred to her. *That old man could've been here for years—decades even. He was probably trapped in here the entire time the painting was locked up in storage.* With that realization, the panic won. Tori threw herself forward, screaming, beating her hands against the closed portal. A bruised elbow and a bloody fingernail later—she relented. Nothing left so much as a mark on the wood frame or the invisible barrier preventing her from reaching through into her world. She tried shouting, though she knew it was pointless. Even if the old man had stuck around, he clearly had no intention of getting near the painting, and if the old man had run off, then Gerry's house was empty. After a moment of staring helplessly into the portal, she turned to face the new world that awaited her.

An old gas street lamp flickered before a shadowy, three-story house. All but two of the shutters were closed, with light coming from the two uncovered windows. Behind the house, the sprawling, pitch-black silhouette of a tree line stood in stark contrast to the bright blue sky overhead. Cumulus clouds hung equally spaced in the sky. She looked down. Her bare feet stood on what appeared to be a damp cobblestone street, yet her feet weren't cold, and the stones felt more like hard clay than solid rock. There was no breeze and no scent of the nearby grass or trees. She pulled her hair up to her nose and sniffed. There was no trace of the shampoo she'd used in the shower. The air was odorless and unmoving. Looking up again at the clouds, she noted how still they hung in the sky. The world was surreal and unlike anywhere she'd been before, and yet, the scene was unmistakable. It was as though she'd stepped into a painting—into Magritte's *Empire of Light*.

Tori squatted and ran her fingers along the cobblestone street. The surface of the stones felt like dry oil paint. She wondered if the world around her shared anything with the real world she knew, or if this was something else entirely— something like a painted world.

There were no signs of life, other than the light in the windows of the nearby house. Tori approached the house, in awe at the sight of Magritte's painted work looming large before her—fully realized and tangible. Stepping up to one of the first-floor windows, she cupped her hands around her eyes and peered in. Despite having moved closer, the light inside the house looked the same as it had from a distance. There were no walls, doors, furniture, or people inside. There wasn't even a source for the light. It was as though she'd zoomed in on a still picture.

Tori stepped back from the window to look for a door, but as she did, she backed into something or someone solid. She reeled around to find a man in a black suit, white button-down, and black tie. A white sheet covered his head and wrapped around his neck. In his hands, he held another white sheet, holding it taught. The sight of him stole the air out of Tori's lungs. She stood frozen. The man raised his hands and pushed the sheet toward her, as though he meant to wrap her head like his own.

Tori ducked under his reach, turned, and ran. She raced up the sidewalk for the open gate, hoping to find more than a painted door. She hoped to find help. Anchoring herself on the iron gate with her right hand, she swung around the corner, her feet slipping over the stone path. Out of the corner of her eye, she could see the man approaching, sheet held out, his steps quick and sure. Inside the gate, she saw steps leading up to a red door. Tori crashed into the door, twisted the brass knob, and fell in as the door swung open. Getting to her hands and knees, she looked back and saw the man striding toward her, unwavering intention in every step. As he reached the steps, Tori rolled onto her back and kicked the door shut. Scooting away, she eyed the doorknob, waiting for it to twist —waiting for the faceless man to enter. But the knob didn't move. It seemed he'd stopped at the door. After a moment, Tori's racing heart slowed a bit, and she got to her feet and took in her surroundings.

The place was dreary, empty, with no windows, no doors, and no clear source for the dull, amber light filling the room. Where the red door had stood was now a smooth, stone wall. From somewhere in the room, she heard what sounded like someone carving meat. Tori turned toward the sound to find a man laid across a bed. Shining sheets of linen wrinkled beneath him as he resisted his attackers. A woman in a red dress stood over him, pinning his left arm to his chest while the man used his right to shove her away. But his struggling was all for naught. A second woman in a gold dress held the man by his hair, forcing his head to one side. Rivulets of blood ran over the sheets, as the woman in gold dragged a short sword along his neck, sawing through flesh and tendons, down to the bone.

Tori's stomach lurched, and she gave a shriek, drawing the attention of the woman in gold. Tori caught herself and froze. The woman in gold grit her teeth, pressed the sword deep into the man's neck, withdrew the blade fiercely, and released him. The man lay sputtering, his hands twitching. Tori swayed, queasy and cornered, feeling helpless as the woman in gold approached, but then she remembered what the old man had said.

Just lean on your understanding—remember the stories behind what you see. Whatever you see is meant for you. Tori closed her eyes and tried to see the scene as a still painting and not a tangible blood bath. She opened her eyes to find the woman in gold nearly upon her, but she recognized the scene. She knew which painting she'd stepped into. "This is *Judith Slaying Holofernes*," Tori said, her excitement overriding her nerves for one brief moment. "*You're* Judith."

The woman in gold shook the dripping blood from her sword as she closed in on Tori.

"Artemisia Gentileschi painted you. Some say it was because of her suffering—the betrayal. Artemisia—" Tori faltered for a moment, noticing the anguish in Judith's eyes. "She was only seventeen. Her chaperone betrayed her to a family friend who forced himself on her."

Tori found herself cornered by Judith as the woman drew her sword back. There was no prayer to offer and no cry for help that could be heard. Tori looked Judith in the eye, the bloody blade braced to fall, and said, "You are the rage of one treated like property. Used and discarded."

Judith stayed her hand, the sword still held aloft.

"You're the silenced voice of suffering and injustice. And this violence," Tori continued, indicating the savage scene behind Judith, "is the cry of the unheard."

Judith lowered her sword and considered Tori for a moment. Tori watched Judith closely, hoping that she, Tori, wouldn't be next on the bed. Judith turned the sword around, and offered it to Tori. Tori received the sword with hesitance. Judith greeted Tori with a kiss on either cheek, put her hand on Tori's shoulder, and directed her toward the man on the bed.

Tori looked at the man, Holofernes. "I— I can't," she said, her voice small.

Judith encouraged her, motioning again toward Holofernes.

But the sword sat heavy in Tori's hand. The weight of it, the blood, the threat of violence was more than Tori could bear. She handed the sword back to Judith. "I'm sorry. I can't."

Judith looked at the sword and then at Tori, her disappointment clear.

"I don't have any monsters to slay," Tori said.

Judith seemed to consider Tori. After a brief moment, Judith slid the bracelet off of her left arm and motioned for Tori to hold out her hand. Tori did so, and Judith slipped the bracelet onto Tori's arm. She thanked Judith, who, without another word, returned to the bed and resumed her task of removing the head of Holofernes.

Tori backed away, the horror of the scene proving more than she could stomach. Glancing around, she saw a door had appeared at the far side of the room. When she reached the door, she stopped and looked back at the women on the bed. Matching the mercy and humanity that had been shown young Artemisia centuries ago, the woman in gold set the edge of her blade against the flesh of Holofernes. Judith, and by extension, her creator, Artemisia, heralded her yearning for justice with a final, ferocious blow.

Tori opened the door and backed into the next room. Just as before, once the door had shut, it vanished behind her. Looking around, Tori found this room to be unlike the previous room. This one featured numerous windows. The floor was made of gold bricks under a patina of ash. A forge stood at the far side of the room with a fire in its belly. Before the fire was a stone workbench. Atop the bench sat an anvil. There was a woman standing at the bench, but nothing of her appearance suggested she was a forge worker. She wore a fine gown of crimson and navy, with a bejeweled gold mesh headdress. Her frame was delicate, and her straw gold hair reached down to her hips. An infant rested in the woman's hands. Tori watched intently, as the woman placed the infant atop the anvil. The baby did not wriggle or kick. It did not cry or coo.

It simply lied still and silent. The woman then kneeled down beside her workbench, drawing Tori's attention to a pile of broken pieces—the arms, legs, and heads of other newborns, piled at the foot of the forge. Hoping to remain unseen, Tori threw her hands over her mouth to catch a scream before it could escape. The woman at the forge then rose to her feet and raised her hammer, as though to strike the infant.

Tori's instincts took over. With a guttural, "No!" she charged forward.

As the hammer came down, Tori caught the woman by the wrist. The woman twisted around. Her hazel and gold eyes bore into Tori. The look was not one of rage but indifference. With one swift motion, she pulled her hand free and delivered a hammer blow to Tori's shoulder. Tori's bones crunched, and she shrieked in pain, stumbling back. The woman turned, her dress billowing, and swung again, striking Tori in the neck. With a cry, Tori collapsed to the ground, her head thumping against the brick floor. Stabbing pains radiated in both arms. Her legs were numb, unresponsive. She watched the woman return to her forge and look down upon the infant atop the anvil. Tori imagined the woman regarded the child with the same indifference she'd shown Tori. The woman's hammer rose once again into the air, and it was then that Tori recognized the scene.

Nature Forging a Baby, she thought, recalling the name of the painting. Tori cursed under her breath, realizing she had picked a fight with Nature itself.

Nature brought the hammer down upon the child. The once silent baby erupted with a throat-rending cry, but not as one wounded. It wasn't a cry of anguish. It was the call of new life. It was the rush of cold air, the flood of blinding light, and the cacophony of new sounds overwhelming the child's senses. It was the cry expelled with a baby's first breath. Tori had watched Nature create life. Nature moved around the bench and placed the baby in the fires of the forge, where it would be refined through life's trials. There, through years that passed in mere heartbeats, the child laughed and wept, rejoiced and mourned, and grew. Nature then gathered new pieces and laid them out on the workbench. With little arms and legs, heart and head in place, Nature created once more.

Tori wheezed. It was difficult to move without pain paralyzing her, but with concentrated effort, she gathered her breath, and said with a raspy exhale, "You're creating."

The hammer continued to clink and thump as Nature worked.

"You . . . creating life," Tori said again, struggling to speak more loudly.

Nature stopped and turned its head, inclining an ear.

"I mistook you for something to fight against—to resist—but you're neither a friend nor an enemy. You are growth and decay, pleasure and pain, life and death."

Nature turned to face Tori, and where there had been indifference, Tori saw intrigue.

"You are heartbreak and healing," Tori continued. "Through pain we're born, and through pain we grow."

Nature approached Tori, who remained paralyzed on the floor, and kneeled down, her gown spreading like a royal train.

"I'm not painted. I don't belong here. My natural place is in *my* world," Tori said, her voice small and shrinking. "Can you help me get home?"

Nature inclined its head to one side, considering Tori, who laid prostrate, surrendered. Without a word spoken, Nature raised her hammer, indifferent, and struck Tori again. She struck Tori's shoulder, her neck, and with a final, swift blow, Nature brought her hammer down upon Tori's skull. With every blow, the throbbing, stabbing pain faded. Bones mended and her wounds healed as though months had passed. Tori moved gingerly, expecting flashes of pain, but to her surprise, she felt better than she had in ages. Nature drew herself up, stepped around Tori, and crossed over to a window at the far side of the room, opposite the forge. Nature drew back and struck the window, shattering the glass. It ran the hammer around the edges, clearing every shard, and then turned to face Tori.

Tori got to her feet and moved to the window. She could see the passage outside—the little portal through which she had entered the painted world. "I don't know how to get back through. It won't let me," she said.

Nature stepped aside.

Tori pressed, "How do I get through?"

Nature said nothing and returned to the forge.

Tori looked again at the little framed portal suspended in mid-air. Through it, she could still see Gerry's vision room. She saw clear skies outside his windows. The storm had passed, and the morning sun had risen over Grimlock Cove. Then she heard a voice, muffled and indistinct, but no less recognizable.

"Gerry?" she said.

A second voice joined Gerry's. The voice was masculine and vaguely familiar, but she couldn't quite place it. Still, hope sparked. Perhaps they could, together, pull her back into the real world. Tori hoisted herself through the broken window and fell out, landing hard on the damp ground. Without pause, she got to her feet and ran to the framed portal. As she approached, the voices coming from the other side grew more distinct.

Gerry stepped into view, eyeing the painting, and for a moment, Tori felt as though he were looking directly at her. She waved like one stranded on an island, but he seemed not to see her.

"As you can see, Mr. Kanival, the provenance is complete," Gerry said.

Mr. Kanival stepped into view, turning a scrutinizing eye on the painting. He was dressed much as he had been the night before. Tori waved again, though less enthusiastically this time, feeling certain they couldn't see her through the painting. She had needed a UV light to accomplish that. These two were viewing the painting in natural sunlight.

"These are the young lady's things?" Mr. Kanival said, pointing at what Tori assumed were her satchel and research tools.

"They are," Gerry said, "and as you can see, there's no sign of her."

Tori wilted, sick to her core. *He knew?*

"Perhaps she left," Mr. Kanival said. "Or she is hiding."

"Good point," Gerry said, looking around, seeming not to have considered that. "Let's check her notebook. She would've recorded her findings there."

"Oh?" Mr. Kanival said. "And is there a note about being captured in the painting?"

Gerry flipped through, scanning the pages. "Here it is!" He held the notebook up for Mr. Kanival to read.

UV light reveals a preexisting work. Beneath the oils is a work of masterful detail. Photo real. A flawless, three-dimensional face.

Gerry slammed the notebook shut, eyes wide with excitement. "She saw someone in there. *This* proves it."

Mr. Kanival appeared unconvinced.

Gerry deflated a bit, but the ever tenacious salesman was far from giving up. "Let's test it out, then, eh?" he said, stepping out of frame for a moment and returning with a small remote. He took aim at the panorama of windows and clicked to lower the blackout shades. As the shades descended and the room darkened, he tossed the small remote on the couch and grabbed Tori's UV light. Looking at Mr. Kanival, he said, "I hope you have that wire transfer ready, because you're about to get all the proof you need. This *is* Crowley's lost work, *The Judgment of Myrna*."

"I can't wait," Mr. Kanival said, checking his watch.

As Gerry leaned in closer, his face nearly filled the portal.

He knew everything, Tori thought. *He knew what this painting was. He knew it was dangerous. He only needed to prove it.* The words of Mr. Kanival came back to her. As he had said during their brief exchange in the cafe, she was like a canary sent into a coal mine.

A fire ran through her veins. She looked down at the bracelet Judith had given her and felt a bond with the warrior she hadn't before—a sisterhood forged in injustice. Tori's hand twitched for want of Judith's sword, but she'd refused it. Thinking over everything she knew about this painting, she remembered what Crowley had said: ". . . the painting requires a soul. It will not go without." Though she had no weapon, she did have two hands and a soul waiting just outside the portal. If old man Crowley could pull himself out of this world, then so could she.

Gerry lingered close to the painting. Seeing her opportunity, Tori charged toward the portal, determined to take hold of Gerry and pull herself out of the painted world and into her own. As she started forward, a flash of white fell over her eyes. The faceless man had wrapped his sheet around her head and jerked her back. One foot shot up, and Tori struggled to keep her other foot planted. The man jerked again, and Tori fell back against him. Pain shot through her spine. The sheet constricted, smothering, threatening to crush her. Though the sheet resembled plain cotton, the thing felt much like the cobblestones had—like hard clay. The sheet compressed against her face, cutting off her air supply. The faceless man pulled again and hoisted her up. Her feet left the ground as she clawed at the fabric tightening around her head. She tried to scratch the man's hands, but it was like scratching wax. His clay-like flesh gathered under her nails, and the sheet remained wrapped around her head—a crushing, asphyxiating vice.

"You're not going to believe this," Gerry said, his voice muffled as Tori struggled. "Take a look, Mr. Kanival."

The faceless man spun Tori around and pulled her close, as though he intended to kiss her. Her head went light, and a sense of helplessness begged for surrender. His assault had thrown her off balance, sending her mind into a panicked flurry, but as she hung from his grasp, she chose to calm her mind. As her thoughts stilled, a work of art came to mind. Magritte's *The Lovers*: a surrealist piece. Unlike the other paintings she'd encountered—Judith and Nature—the man's golem-like, murderous actions weren't true to *The Lovers*. The faceless man treated her with no regard, no respect, like something to be captured and possessed. His was not the touch of a lover.

"I . . . don't see anything," Mr. Kanival said from beyond the portal. His voice was cool, unmoved. "I will not return to Lady Grimlock with a forgery, Mr. Vice."

Tori hung limp, suffocating.

"Are you kidding me?" Gerry said. "She's right there. Look!"

"I see no one," Mr. Kanival said. "You'll have to do better."

Maybe it was the need to breathe or her need to tear Gerry apart. Regardless, something in Tori clicked, like shackles unlocking. She reached up and took the faceless man's right wrist in both hands and dug her nails in hard. She pressed until her fingers had almost met. Then she pulled and pried until she'd severed the man's clay-like hand from his arm. The sheet fell loose, and Tori fell free, gasping and stumbling away from the faceless man.

"Take the damned UV light and look again," Gerry said. "She's in there with some guy."

As the faceless man stumbled about, seemingly without direction, Tori turned to the portal. Mr. Kanival held the light aloft, peering in. Her eyes met his, and the faintest smile threatened to crack on his gaunt face.

"Well done, little canary," Mr. Kanival said under his breath.

"What's that?" Gerry said.

"I do not see her," Mr. Kanival said. "If I do not see her for myself, you will need to swear to what you've seen. If Lady Grimlock sees the same, I will wire payment within the hour."

"So, what then?" Gerry said. "You need me to swear to you on my honor?"

"No, Mr. Vice," Mr. Kanival said. "I need you to swear on your *life*."

Gerry seemed to falter. Clearly, Gerry's impenetrable ego and unwavering confidence could, in fact, be cracked by the Grimlock family.

"One last time," Mr. Kanival said, handing Gerry the UV light. "Look carefully. If she appears again, be quick to hand me the light and let me see for myself. Then I can confirm the provenance for Lady Grimlock. It will be on *my* word, and you may collect your payment."

Tori approached the portal, hands opening and closing with anticipation.

"Payment wired immediately?" Gerry said.

"With great haste," Mr. Kanival said, waving a hand toward the painting and stepping aside.

Tori watched Gerry approach the painting, his face growing larger as though she were watching him through a peephole.

You used me and sent me to die, she thought.

Gerry leaned in one last time.

Tori stepped out of view as Gerry peered into the painted world. She paused for a heartbeat and called his name.

"Wait," Gerry said. "I think I heard something,"

"Get closer," Mr. Kanival said. "Every dollar depends on it."

"I'm practically touching the damned thing," Gerry said.

With that, Tori pivoted into view of Gerry and threw both of her hands through the portal. She could feel the stark difference between worlds. Gerry dropped the UV light and jerked away, but Tori caught him by the neck. Gerry pulled, bracing himself against the painting's frame. Tori dug in her nails and pulled harder, jaw clenched and every muscle tensed. Gerry cursed hysterically. Tori struggled to maintain her grip as the painted world around her quaked. The ground shook, nearly sending her off balance, but in a heartbeat, the painting accepted the exchange. A force beyond the bounds of the natural world took hold of Tori and shunted her out of the painting.

Tori fell into the vision room. The force of the exchange sent her tumbling over the sofa and onto the floor. There she lay still for a moment, disoriented, but the sensation of air moving over her skin, the rush of smells—coffee, cologne, sea air, and the taste in her mouth—all confirmed she was no longer in the painted world. Once she'd gathered her wits, Tori looked up to find Mr. Kanival, hat in hand, offering to help her up. She declined the offer and got to her feet on her own accord.

"Well done," Mr. Kanival said. "Very few find their way out of *The Judgment of Myrna*, or so I've heard."

Tori picked up the UV light and crossed over to the painting, hesitant to lean in, but far too curious not to look. She had to see Gerry—to see the state of him—wondering what kind of painted world Gerry had found himself in. Inching closer, Mr. Kanival offered a verbal warning not to draw too close, but Tori continued. With her UV light aloft, she moved in until she could see him. Through the painting, she once again saw the painted world, but it was nothing like the world she'd found herself in. A knot formed in her throat, and her stomach turned as she tried to recall the name of the painting in which Gerry now found himself. His feet were bound, as he hung upside down from a tree. Several women, children, and men gathered around him. Dogs barked and a satyr stepped into view, holding a bucket. Tori gasped as the satyr placed the bucket under Gerry's head.

"*The Flaying of Marsyas*," Tori said. She pulled back from the painting. "They're going to—" But she couldn't say it. She couldn't say, *They're going to flay him alive.*

"They're going to free his soul from his flesh that he may find enlightenment," Mr. Kanival said. "Titian's most controversial work. I always preferred the *Assumption of the Virgin*, but *The Flaying* feels appropriate here."

"It'll be torture," Tori said, sickened.

Mr. Kanival raised an eyebrow and motioned to the painting. "Do you wish to save the man who would've watched you die?"

"We can't just stand by and watch it happen," she said.

Mr. Kanival nodded. "Right you are." He picked up the sheet that had fallen aside and carefully draped it over the painting. "There we are," he said with a smile.

Tori looked at the covered painting, knowing as she stood there, Gerry's life was spilling red into the satyr's wooden bucket. The dogs would lap up the overflow while the people watched. Tori's imagination sank into the grim scene until Mr. Kanival's mobile phone rang with Tchaikovsky's "Nutcracker."

"Excuse me," he said, stepping away to take the call.

Tori backed away from the painting, made her way around to the front of the couch, and sat, trembling. She noticed the remote to the blackout curtains lying on the cushion beside her. The curtains rose with a click, letting morning light flood the room. Ahead of her, a blue horizon spread as far as she could see, not one cloud in the sky.

"Very good. I'll take care of her. I will see the matter concluded before I leave the residence," Mr. Kanival said and ended his call.

Tori sat still as her adrenaline subsided. Though she could hear his conversation, the words sank in slowly. Mr. Kanival approached, stopping shy of coming between her and the view.

He paused for a moment before saying, "Quite the view."

Tori nodded silently.

"I loathe interrupting your moment," he said, pausing again. "I know you've had a . . . challenging night, yet our business remains unfinished."

"You knew I was in danger," she said, her tone flat and eyes fixed on the horizon.

"I knew it was a possibility."

"How would you feel if you were me?"

Mr. Kanival thought for a moment before answering. "Conflicted."

Tori nodded. "Are you going to kill me now?" Though she sounded hollow, defeated, her hands were balled into fists.

"Do I *look* like a hit man to you?"

She looked from his wing-tipped shoes to his three-piece suit, and up to the bowler hat. "I don't know. I've never met one."

Mr. Kanival smiled, reached into his coat pocket and withdrew a pen. "Lady Grimlock is satisfied—dare I say impressed—with your provenance research. Seeing as you have proven the authenticity of the painting without question, Lady Grimlock considers *you* to be entitled to the full payment of four million dollars."

His words had come so casually, yet they nearly bowled Tori over.

"*Four* . . . million?" Tori said. "Gerry told me he was selling it for two."

"Would you prefer two?"

"No. Four will be fine."

Mr. Kanival smiled and handed Tori the paperwork. "The funds will be delivered directly to the account number you provide."

Tori reminded herself to breathe as she took the paperwork from Mr. Kanival. "Four million dollars?"

"Indeed," Mr. Kanival said, handing Tori his pen. "And per my employer, you are welcome to take with you whatever belongings are in the house."

"Gerry's stuff? Even his Warhol?"

Mr. Kanival nodded. "The house will be foreclosed upon following non-payment from its owner, who had mysteriously disappeared, thus abandoning the property. The bank will then put the property up for auction, at which time the Grimlocks will take possession."

Tori could scarcely keep up as everything moved so quickly. Mr. Kanival waited, appreciating the ocean view, while Tori sat staring at her signature on the completed paperwork. He eventually turned, quietly collected the documents and, seeing everything was in order, placed the call to request the wire. When the order was complete, he shook Tori's hand.

"You've done excellent work," he said. "Good day." And with that, Mr. Kanival tipped his hat, carefully wrapped the white sheet around the painting, and departed with *The Judgment of Myrna*.

The roaring surf and calling seagulls soothed Tori. She sat still and quiet, thinking, trying to process any part of what had transpired. She wondered if the painting had chosen the specific works of art she'd walked through just for her. If so, had the painting chosen Gerry's, as well?

Tori lowered the blackout curtains and laid down on the couch. To her surprise, the bracelet Judith had given her was still on her wrist—a gift from the painted world. Tori contemplated *The Judgment of Myrna* and the many worlds hidden within. She wondered who Myrna was, and how such a painting could've been made, but her questions would have to wait. Her eyes were heavy. Her heart was heavy. So with a deep breath and a long exhale, she curled up and closed her eyes, remembering her thesis: *Art is magic, taking us places we'd never imagined and leaving us forever changed*.

The Wolves and the Sheep (Part One)

Grimlock Cove, 1994

In the neighboring town of Pawkinsville, white cotton clouds graced a blue sky. Robins called to each other through the forest's canopy. By the banks of the lazy Dolonia River, among the slender blades of grass that grew wild on the riverside, flies buzzed excitedly over one hundred and twelve pounds of festering flesh. Milky eyes gazed up toward Heaven. The woman's empty, rigid hand—slightly open as though it had been holding something—rested on her chest. The victim's face had been clawed apart, unrecognizable.

Sheriff Sturgess stood back, holding a handkerchief over his nose and mouth. "Wolf pack?"

The deputy, whose face had been fixed in a grimace since arriving on the scene, shot the sheriff a look and said, "Respectfully, I've never seen a wolf do *that* to a person."

The sheriff grunted his agreement and looked down at the victim. A gold crucifix hung from a thin chain, resting on the victim's blood-stained throat. The sight of it seemed a mockery, juxtaposed with the black iron railroad spikes that had been driven through her hands and feet.

Sheriff Sturgess shook his head and shrugged, admitting to himself that the wolf pack story was absurd at best. But what else could he say? The people of Pawkinsville expected the same two things every small town wanted: peace and quiet, and they expected the sheriff to see to it. The kind of panic this scene could inspire would be anything but peaceful or quiet. A story like this would sully his beloved town with sensational headlines, possibly reducing the town to a macabre tourist trap. Though this wasn't the first time a body had been found like this in Pawkinsville, the times had changed. Local reporters listened in on police radio. They could be on the scene before anything could be done—before any of this could be handled quietly.

The area had been cordoned off so the prying eyes of the media or curious hikers couldn't take in the details of the grisly scene. Still, a lone reporter for the local paper had arrived shortly after the sheriff. She pressed forward, leaning into the police tape and called aloud, "What do you make of it, Sheriff? Care to comment?"

The sheriff and the deputy exchanged looks of concern.

"Well," the sheriff began, turning to face the reporter, "there's no doubt in my mind. What we are dealing with here is a . . . pack of wolves."

The reporter scribbled down the sheriff's every word, stopping at "pack of wolves" and shooting him a look. He held his best poker face, which looked a lot like his usual face. The reporter rolled her eyes and snatched up her camera. Flash bulbs fired in rapid succession, capturing the image of a body obscured by tall grass in 35 mm. The photos would net a decent payday, landing on the front pages of the local and surrounding newspapers, including *The Grimlock Gazette*.

The sheriff turned back to face the scene with his deputy at his side.

"Think one of our own did this—someone from Pawkinsville?" the deputy asked.

"Hope not," the sheriff said. "If so, then they've been living under our noses for thirteen years."

The deputy looked confused. "Sir?"

"We found a body just like this thirteen years ago."

"Here in Pawkinsville?" the deputy said, surprised.

"Yessir. Right here in our little town."

"Was the victim found by the river then, too?"

"Nope. Behind a church."

"Body left naked like this here?"

Sheriff Sturgess nodded.

The deputy put his hands on his hips and looked on in disbelief. "First at a church. Now by the river. Anything else different, Sheriff?"

"Well," the sheriff began, rubbing the back of his neck as he looked over the covered body. "We should probably get K9 out here."

"K9?"

The sheriff stepped around the body and continued down to the river's edge. "Last time there was a body, it was holding a Bible. It was the victim's Bible." Shielding his eyes from the sun, the sheriff looked up and down the river.

The deputy's hurried steps approached from behind, coming to a stop at the sheriff's side. "Maybe this one's different?"

"Maybe."

"Or maybe someone took it?"

The sheriff took another long look both ways, and said, "The body isn't fresh—it's been days or a week, maybe? The deceased's hand is empty, but her hand isn't lying flat. It looks like she was holding something as rigor mortis set in. Now her hand is stuck open. So, Deputy, what was she holding, and who took it?"

"The killer?"

The sheriff grunted.

"Just a thief?" the deputy asked and radioed in, requesting the K9 unit.

"A thief would've taken her necklace, too. I think someone out there came looking for her, found the scene, and took whatever she was holding," the sheriff said.

"You think they knew the victim?"

The sheriff nodded. "Possibly. We'll ID the victim. Then check in on their kin."

"If someone knew her and found her body, why not notify anyone?"

"People get scared, Deputy." The sheriff turned and looked back at the body in the grass, considering the black iron spikes in the faceless victim's hands and feet. The reporter was still waiting behind the police tape with her tape recorder at the ready, awaiting a proper statement from the sheriff.

"What're we telling them?" the deputy asked.

"That it was a plain old murder. No clawed-off face. No mock crucifixion. Just a victim found by the river."

Beams of golden, morning light fell through the canopy of oak trees that hung over Witchwood Drive, where carpenter homes and white picket fences lined the street. Behind the neighborhood, raw forest spread wild and thick with trees and brush and treasures left behind by generations of teens looking for a little independence. Beyond the forest ran Red Road, where mobile homes stood atop concrete blocks along the dead end, dirt road.

Halfway down Red Road, in a brown and yellow trailer, nineteen-year-old Tom Dalton returned the milk carton to the fridge. His cereal crackled and popped as he took a seat across from his mother at the kitchen table. A year ago, he'd been a high school senior, making plans with his friends. Nine months ago, he'd held his mother's hand as his father was lowered into the ground. His mother, Dolores, had struggled to find a decent job. Employers hadn't been too excited to hire a candidate whose experience included to two years behind a cash register and eighteen years managing a home. After expanding her job search to the nearby town of Grimlock Cove, she'd found a teller position at the Grimlock Bank & Trust. The next week, Tom had watched his home town of Pawkinsville disappear in the rearview as he and his mother started over.

Making friends as the new guy in senior year had proven as impossible as he'd expected, but his mother had reassured him that Jesus was a friend to the friendless. Unfortunately for Tom, Jesus wasn't popular at school, either, and the two had regularly sat alone at lunch. After graduating with no plans for what to do or where to go next, he'd found a job stocking shelves at a small, family-owned grocery store. It wasn't the job he'd wanted, but it was a job, and it came with a much needed discount on groceries.

"Did you hear me?" Dolores said, seated in her bathrobe with a hot cup of Folgers. Every Sunday morning, she'd sit and sip her coffee between impatient glances at the kitchen clock, waiting to take out her sponge curlers.

Tom looked up from his cereal, groggy after a late night of stocking shelves.

"They found someone dead in Pawkinsville," she said, tapping a finger on the paper.

"Who found what now?"

"Down by the Dolonia," she said, checking the clock on the wall.

Tom took a spoonful of cereal, and with his mouth full, he asked, "Who died?"

Dolores glared at him.

"Sorry," he said, milk dribbling down his chin. He swallowed and tried again. "Who died?"

Dolores motioned to his chin.

"Oh," he said, and wiped a dribble of milk away with his hand.

"You know I pray for you every night—that God will give you wisdom."

"And I appreciate it," he said, taking another bite and continuing through his mouthful, "which is wise of me, so it must be working."

"I should've been praying for God to teach you manners."

Tom shoveled in another mouthful, and asked again, "So who died?"

His mother shot him a look. "I don't know. It was probably a camper eaten by wolves."

Tom's eyes turned to the newspaper between them, trying to read the caption beneath the picture, despite the paper being upside down. "Does it say they were murdered?"

"This is the second time wolves have gotten someone out there," his mother said, distracted as she checked the clock again.

Tom thought it strange. "Is there some turf war between wolves and campers I don't know about?"

His mother seemed not to hear him, or she ignored him, which she was given to do, as she never showed much appreciation for his sense of humor.

Tom spun the paper around so he could read it right side up. "It does say it was murder."

Dolores said nothing as she took another sip of coffee, watching the clock.

"When a wild animal kills someone, they don't usually call it a murder," Tom said.

"Almost there," she said, her finger drumming faster on the table, her eyes glued to the clock.

"Mom?" he said, trying to get her attention, "it definitely wasn't wolves."

The clock ticked to 8:30 a.m., marking the time each Sunday morning when Dolores could take out her curlers. Without another word, she popped up from her seat and hurried out of the kitchen.

Did she even get past the headline? he wondered, continuing to read the article:

Sheriff Sturgess declined to release the identity of the victim until her family could be notified. Though an autopsy has yet to be completed, foul play is suspected. In a statement to the press, Sheriff Sturgess confirmed, "We have reason to suspect foul play. The investigation is ongoing."

Contrary to the sheriff's statement, an eyewitness, who was present when police secured the site, described the scene as "horrific." The source, who requested not to be identified, said—

"There's a guest evangelist speaking today," Dolores shouted from her bedroom down the hall. "I think you'll like him. Not sure how long he'll be with us. He said he's here for as long as the Lord leads him."

Tom ignored her and read on.

The source, who requested not to be identified, said they believe the deceased was the victim of a Satanic ritual.

"Did you hear me?" she called.

"Yes," Tom snapped back, annoyed.

"Then say something."

"I just did."

"Don't get smart with me."

Tom groaned, took another spoonful of soggy cereal, and continued to read.

According to the eye witness, "It was like something out of a horror movie. Her face was so cut up, it was unrecognizable. She had spikes driven through her hands and feet."

"Whoa," Tom said under his breath and slurped the remaining milk from his bowl.

Authorities are asking anyone with information to call the tip hotline provided below.

As concerned locals process the shocking news, Pawkinsville's own Aksel Eriksson, lead singer of the triple-platinum and five-time Grammy-award-winning band, Hellslayer, announced he will be performing a memorial concert at the Pawkinsville Civic Center Sunday, June 12th. The concert will be open to the public.

"That's next Sunday," Tom said, completely forgetting about the dead body. Now, all he wanted was to get to Pawkinsville next Sunday. Tom had every Hellslayer album, two of the band's t-shirts, and their poster on his wall, but he didn't have a ticket stub. He'd never seen who he considered the greatest rock band alive. They'd never toured this close to home, and in the excitement of the moment, he felt as though this might be his only chance to see Hellslayer. *I'll trade shifts, call in sick, whatever. I can't miss it.*

"It's been years since you've been to church," his mother said, appearing behind him.

Tom jumped, caught off guard by how cat-like she'd crept up. "It's not even been a year."

"You need to go to church," she said, her curlers out and dressed in her Sunday best.

"Well, there's only one church in town, and it's Catholic, so—"

"Actually, a nice, older man came into the bank a few

weeks ago, and he said his church meets in their family's barn. It's small, of course, but he said they have a spirit-filled evangelist visiting."

"Visiting their *barn*?"

"Yes, and—"

"That's kinda weird."

"God can move anywhere," she said, freshening her cup of coffee. "Anyway, the man was nice, so I visited the church."

"The barn church?"

"Yes, and I'll tell you what. I felt the Lord there."

"How did I not know you were attending a barn church?"

"Well, you only emerge from your room for food, so I can't imagine how it slipped by."

Tom looked down at his empty cereal bowl. "Fair enough."

"Anyway. We're going," Dolores said.

"We?"

"We."

"How about *you* go, and I wait to hear all about it?" Tom said.

Dolores raised a brow. "I thought you liked church?"

"I liked the *friends* I had at our *old* church."

"You'll make new friends."

"With the geriatrics or the barn owls?"

Dolores's mouth tightened. "You're going."

Tom groaned and slumped in his chair. "It wasn't wild animals, you know."

"Excuse me?"

"That lady they found by the river," he said. "Someone said she was basically crucified."

"Don't spread gossip," she said, smacking his arm. "I'm sure it was wild animals. It happened when you were a kid, and it's happened again."

"It's happened *twice*?"

"Yes, because people think sleeping in the woods makes sense. Now, go get dressed for church, and I don't want to see you wearing one of those demonic, heavy metal t-shirts."

"Okay," he said, getting to his feet and taking his empty bowl to the sink.

"I wish you'd throw those shirts away."

"I know."

"What about a nice Christian shirt? Oh, who's the band that sings 'Romance Me Jesus'?"

"Faith 4 Ever?" Tom said, hating that he knew the answer.

"They're a cool band."

"They're like a boy band, except they're all old."

"The bands you like have old guys, too."

Tom sighed for want of a rebuttal.

"You've got five minutes to get dressed. Now go, go, go!" she said, clapping. "And no heavy metal shirts!"

———

The Daltons walked up to a whitewashed barn, as birdsong carried on the Sunday morning breeze. Sunlight, broken by the surrounding paper birch trees, fell upon the entrance of the barn. Inside, hay lie scattered across the dusty wood floor. A number of occupied folding chairs faced a stack of empty apple crates that appeared to be a makeshift lectern. Poised at the lectern stood a man in a navy suit and light blue silk tie. He stood out against a backdrop of an axe, old pitchfork, and a rusted crosscut saw. Before him, seated but not quietly, were his few yet fiery faithful. Though the service had yet to begin, some were already praying for each other. As the Daltons took their seats, the man in the suit called the congregation to attention and announced it was time to take up the offering. He paused to thank Mr. DeVille and his wife, Vicky, who sat in the front row ahead of Tom and his mother. Vicky rose from her seat and turned to offer the congregation a prolonged beauty queen wave.

According to Dolores, the DeVilles had opened their barn for services a week ago, and it was right about that time the man in the suit showed up, claiming he was a man of God and had been led to Grimlock Cove by divine providence. The DeVilles had offered their guest room to the man, and the latter agreed to remain in residence, delivering the word.

"That's him," Dolores said in a whisper, her excitement evident. "*That's* Reverend Jesse Cope."

"If you plant an apple seed, you get an apple tree," Reverend Cope began, his chest out, head held high. "If you sow into *this* soil, friends, you *will* reap a harvest. I'm talking about supernatural health. I'm talking about divine prosperity. His promise is to pour out blessings you cannot even contain." The reverend paused, allowing space for a corporate *amen*. "Now, I know I don't need to remind *this* congregation, but . . ." Reverend Cope paused and moved around to the front of his apple crate lectern, dabbed sweat from his forehead, and looked across the congregation. "Do not rob God," he concluded, jabbing a finger to punctuate each word. "That offering you thought you'd spend on a new dress or a fancy steak dinner? Friends, that's *God's* money—not yours. If you rob God, you're robbing yourself of *your* blessing. Amen?"

Hearty amens ensued.

Mr. DeVille retrieved a ceramic serving bowl from beneath his chair. The bowl was white with red roses printed around the rim. Tom noticed the congregation looked to be about as well off as he and his mother, which led him to believe the money being collected was probably better off with the congregants. As the bowl passed from person to person, Tom didn't see seeds being sown. He saw grocery money, rent, and personal savings mingling with the roses in the bowl. Each put in their offering—giving above and beyond their weekly tithe, sure of the blessings that would bloom from the sacrificial seeds they'd sewn. Yes, each was faithful to give . . . except one.

Among the floral print dresses, crisp button-down shirts, and pressed khakis sat Tom, conspicuously out of step without apology. His choice of a Nirvana "In Utero" shirt had managed to solicit more than a few disapproving glances and at least an eye roll or two. When Dolores reminded him in the car that she'd told him not to wear a heavy metal t-shirt, he'd reminded her that Nirvana wasn't heavy metal. They were grunge.

Dolores received the offering bowl from the person seated on her right and passed it left to Tom, urging him to give.

Tom leaned over and whispered to his mother, "As soon as I can afford a suit as nice as the reverend's, I'll consider it."

Dolores rolled her eyes and dropped in a pair of twenty-dollar bills. Tom's stomach sank as she gave away about a day's worth of pay. Thinking fast, he fished around in his pocket for change as he received the bowl. Finding a dollar, he made sure to catch his mother's eye.

"God loves a cheerful giver, right?" he said with a shrug, and lowered his dollar into the offering dish. Dolores beamed, unaware that her son had palmed her offering. He withdrew his hand from the bowl with forty-one dollars in hand and passed it to the next person.

"God will return our offerings ten fold," his mother said, patting his knee.

Tom forced a smile to hide his frustration. As the reverend thanked the congregation for their offerings, Tom wondered, *How can she think this guy needs her money—she needs it. We need it.*

After the bowl had been passed to every congregant and collected by Mr. DeVille, the reverend said, "Let us bless this offering."

Every head bowed and every eye closed except for Tom's. He kept one eye open. He knew people drop their facades when they think no one is looking. Tom looked across the small congregation. Many sat with their lips pursed and brows furrowed, their faces wrinkled up in earnest prayer. Hushed, hopeful petitions ascended in whispers. Hands stretched out to Heaven like hungry infants reaching up from their cribs.

They really believe it, Tom thought.

"Father," Reverend Cope began, "the word says as we give, so it will be given to us. If we sow a bounty, we will reap a bounty. So, right now, we receive—by faith—the *blessing* promised as we give in obedience. And Satan? In the Lord's name, we rebuke you. Keep your filthy hands off of our money. These are *our* seeds and *our* harvest—our harvest of *wealth*—our year of plenty! Be gone, in the mighty name of the Lord!" Shouts and amens ensued, concluding with the Reverend throwing his arms wide and saying, "And all the people said—"

"Amen!" the people called out, but not *all* of the people.

Tom sat with his mouth shut, glaring at Jesse Cope. The reverend met Tom's gaze, and in that moment, Tom felt like a mouse staring down a cat.

"What's your name, son?" Reverend Cope asked.

"Tom Dalton," Dolores said excitedly.

Reverend Cope raised a hand to quiet her. "Let the boy speak for himself, Dotty."

"*Dotty?*" Tom said aloud. Nobody had called his mother Dotty since his father's dying breath. Turning to her, he continued in a hushed voice, "Seriously, Mom? You let *this* guy call you—"

Dolores smacked his leg and shushed him.

"I asked you a question, son," Reverend Cope said, his tone firm.

"You already got your answer," Tom said, crossing his arms.

The reverend smiled, with the look of one tolerating a child. "All right, Tommy. Who led you to The Church of His Word?"

"My mom," Tom said, wanting to correct the reverend. *It's Tom not Tommy.*

"No, son," the reverend said. "That's not who led you." Reverend Cope folded his hands and brought them up to his lips. He closed his eyes tight and shook his head. "Not *my* will but *Thy* will be done." Reverend Cope opened his eyes, having donned a mask of compassion. "It's not by *your* will you are here. It is by *God's* divine will that you find yourself here today."

Tom knew the reverend was at least half correct. It certainly wasn't his own will that had led him to this insufferable moment. *More like Mother's will be done*, he thought.

"Thomas," his mother said, sending an elbow to his ribs, causing Tom to wince.

"Please, Dotty," the reverend said, his hand raised like one training a dog. Dolores shrank into her seat at once, and Reverend Cope directed his attention to the congregation. "Tommy's steps have been divinely ordered. You see, this very morning, while I was in prayer preparing for this morning's service, I received a word from the Lord."

Tom braced himself for what was coming.

"And the Lord said to me," Reverend Cope continued, "'I am sending one whose heart is hard. He will come with a rebellious spirit because his faith is misplaced. His heart is filled with the things of this world instead of the things of Me.'"

The congregation's eyes fell on Tom. He glanced around, shifting uncomfortably in his seat.

Reverend Cope continued, "'But I have called that one mine,' says the Lord."

Dolores teared up as the reverend finished with, "Let's lay hands on our brother Tommy. What this young man needs is prayer."

As the crowd stood and gathered around Tom, he shrank into himself. He wished he could vanish as hand after unwelcome hand fell upon his head, shoulders, arms, and back. The congregation's voices simmered in a cacophony of prayer.

"You foul spirit of rebellion!" Reverend Cope shouted, causing Tom to flinch. "There it is! I see it. Come out of him. Loose him and let him go, in the mighty name of the Lord!"

The simmering crowd rose to a boil. Some called on the Lord, while others shouted at the Devil. Tom kept his eyes closed tight, though not out of reverence. It was a failed attempt to block out the moment, to shelter within himself. Outwardly, he stood blanketed under intrusive hands. He'd been publicly accused of being lost and rebellious and found guilty by strangers who'd learned his name only moments ago. Strange tongues resounded, mingled with threats made to demonic spirits.

Tom's heart beat harder. Pressure mounted from all sides. His breaths grew shorter, coming quicker. Their voices rang in his ears. The air grew thick, and his knees grew weak. Tom fought to keep from screaming, flailing, and barreling his way toward the exit, but as he stood covered in sweaty palms, pressing and groping about his head and shoulders, the tumult slowly died down. Once the congregation's roar fell to a rumble, the reverend declared the work done, and the congregation withdrew. Only a single pair of hands remained.

Tom opened his eyes to find Reverend Cope standing before him, gripping his shoulders tight. "You have been chosen," the reverend said. "There is a plan for you." Reverend Cope paused to flash a smile at Dolores, who stood, hands folded at her mouth, teary-eyed. Returning his attention to Tom, the reverend continued, "I want to see you here next Sunday. It is vitally important to stay connected to the church body."

Tom stood stunned, unable to respond.

Reverend Cope continued, "I want you to promise me you'll be here."

Tom glanced anxiously around at the surrounding press of devout faces, all watching and awaiting his reply. His mother's eyes were lit with a hope he hadn't seen since his father died.

Reverend Cope squeezed Tom's shoulders. "Can I count you?"

Tom looked down, wrestling within himself. Would it feel worse to disappoint his mother or to give Reverend Cope the satisfaction? He glanced at his mother and saw her hope—her joy. As much as he loathed giving in to the reverend, he loved seeing his mother happy again. Defeated, he replied, "I'll be here."

"Hallelujah!" the reverend said with a clap, joined by the congregation. "I'll see you all next Sunday. And remember! Give, and it shall be given unto you! Now, go in the grace and power of the Lord. You are dismissed."

"Can we leave now?" Tom said to his mother, but before she could answer, Tom was pulled into a parade of greetings from the other congregants.

"Bless you, Tommy," one man said, with a full press hug.

Tom tensed. "Thanks."

"Welcome," said a grandmotherly woman, offering a soft, trembling hand to shake.

"Thank you," Tom said.

A gaunt, hunched man hobbled up to Tom, nudging the old woman aside. The man wore a plaid, pearl snap shirt, tucked into dusty Wranglers. The man's thin, gray hair laid flat and slick over his liver-spotted skull. He wore crooked eye glasses that he adjusted before fixing his gaze on Tom. The old man's beady eyes blinked behind smudged, Coke-bottle lenses, and either the wealth of wrinkles on his face were refusing to cooperate or he was not smiling like the rest of the congregation.

Ignoring pleasantries, the old man said, "Matthew 7:15 warns us about wolves in sheep's clothing. Do you understand what that means?"

Wishing for nothing more than to be out of this barn and back home, Tom aimed to appease the man. "Absolutely."

"Do you think *Jesse Cope* is a wolf or a sheep?"

Tom couldn't ignore the old man's disdain when he'd said the name Jesse Cope. And having heard that sweaty, melodramatic reverend affectionately call his mother "Dotty," the words leapt out of Tom. "Definitely a wolf."

A smile cracked across the old man's face that unsettled Tom. He looked Tom up and down, and said, "You're not like them. Not one bit."

Tom didn't know what to say, so he just nodded politely.

The man leaned in closer, his head cocked. "Are you coming to church next Sunday?"

Tom tensed up, holding in a reflexive cough as the stench of old fillings and black coffee rolled into his mouth. "Yes," he said in a choked voice.

The old man continued in a whisper, "Don't come to church."

"*Don't* come to church?" Tom blurted out, taken aback.

The old man planted a hand over Tom's mouth and shoved a Bible into his chest.

"The devil's place is in the lake of fire," the man said, pausing to glance in Reverend Cope's direction. "*That* devil deserves it. I deserve it. *You* don't. Take this and be spared the coming judgment."

Tom took the Bible, absolutely befuddled.

The man continued, keeping his voice low, "Read it *before* next Sunday."

"The whole thing?" Tom said.

The old man jabbed a boney finger into Tom's chest. "Judgment is coming."

Like flipping a switch, the old man let go of Tom and returned to his quiet, unassuming demeanor, and without another word, he turned on his heels, and marched toward the exit, leaving Tom with a Bible and a head full of questions. Tom felt the familiar burden of being assigned homework but not understanding the assignment. He looked down at the Bible and saw tabs marking certain pages and assumed the old man wanted him to read the marked passages.

"Hello, Tom," a deep, firm voice said. Tom turned to find Mr. and Mrs. DeVille—the couple the reverend had thanked earlier during the service. Mr. DeVille was a tall man with salt and pepper hair, broad shoulders, and a firm build that fit well into his gray suit and white button-down. Beside him stood Vicky, who looked to be about half his age. She had golden blonde hair, thick black mascara, and a persistent, bleached smile that was even brighter than her ruffly, fuchsia dress.

"I'm Franklin DeVille," the man said, "and this is my wife, Victoria."

"You can call me Vicky," she said.

Tom greeted the pair, shaking each of their hands in turn.

With a nod toward the old, hunched man as he exited the barn, Mr. DeVille said, "I believe you just met Mort Mackey."

"Wacky Mackey," Mrs. DeVille said, jumping in. "This is actually his first Sunday with us, but friends of ours in Pawkinsville told us all about him. He's one of those 'doom and gloom' types."

"But he did come all the way from Pawkinsville to join us this morning," Mr. DeVille said. "That is a real testimony to what the Lord is doing here."

Tom didn't like the slight on the old man. Though Mort Mackey was unsettling and possibly out of his mind, he seemed to have been the only other person in the room who'd seen through Jesse Cope. If anything, that had put old Mort in Tom's good graces.

The DeVilles continued, so Tom returned to silently nodding along to avoid prolonging the conversation.

"Mort does seem a touch eccentric, but I'd say he's harmless," Mr. DeVille said.

"Franklin is *very* discerning," Mrs. DeVille said, putting an arm around her husband.

"Just don't let him scare you off from the church," Mr. DeVille said, in turn putting his arm around his wife. "We're all just happy to have you with us at The Church of His Word."

"Just pleased as punch," Mrs. DeVille said, her smile never breaking.

"Now, you *will* be joining us next Sunday?" Mr. DeVille said.

Tom, still mindlessly nodding, thought hard for a strong, believable excuse for why there was no way he could possibly make it.

"Wonderful," Mr. DeVille said through a wide, white smile.

Tom's stomach sank, realizing his absent-minded nodding had been taken as a *yes*.

Mr. DeVille put a hand on Tom's shoulder, gave it a squeeze, and began massaging lightly with his thumb. "You should know: We're all family here, Tom."

Mrs. DeVille snatched up Tom's free hand and pulled him closer. "This family has been missing something."

Tom's insides squirmed, as he was no longer sure if Mrs. DeVille was talking about the church family or the DeVille family.

Mr. DeVille's hand slid off Tom's shoulder to the small of his back. "You carry a fire in you that this family needs."

Tom's heart beat in his throat. He glanced toward his mother for help, but she stood out of reach, entangled in conversation with Reverend Cope.

"We'll save you a seat next Sunday," Mrs. DeVille said. With Tom's hand in hers, she brought their hands up to her heart to rest against her chest. Finally, her smile broke, lips parted.

Tom's stomach turned. After a dry swallow, he managed a weak reply. "Cool."

The couple exchanged a delighted look and let go of Tom as Dolores walked up.

"Oh, good," Dolores said, moving to her son's side. "You've met the DeVilles."

"Ready to go?" Tom said quietly to his mother.

"These are the nice folks I met at the bank," Dolores continued.

"We're just pleased as punch to have Tom join the family," Mrs. DeVille said.

"I'm just pleased I could get him out of the house," Dolores said.

"Can we *please* go?" Tom said in a hushed voice to his mother.

Dolores ignored him and patted his back, as if to tell him to behave.

"I feel sick," Tom said, trying to sound normal in a moment where everything felt far from normal. Between Reverend Cope's public shaming, Mort's cryptic warnings, and the DeVilles' advances, Tom wasn't sure what he wanted more: to run and never look back or to burn the world down.

"Teenagers," Dolores said, shrugging.

"I— I'll wait outside," Tom said. At once, he cut a path for the exit before anyone else could get their hands on him. He stepped out of the barn and took a deep, gasping breath, like a drowning soul coming up for air. After taking a moment, he looked back at the barn and thought, *Nothing could ever get me back in there.*

———

Tom's week progressed in its usual, unremarkable manner, with each passing day putting much-needed time between him and his experience at The Church of His Word. Though he wanted to forget it all and never subject himself to another minute in that barn, he couldn't help but notice the change in his mother since he'd agreed to attend next Sunday's service. Though he and his mother's senses of humor had rarely clicked, she'd attempted to make jokes and find common ground with him throughout the week. She'd even had a hot breakfast of bacon, eggs, and toast ready for him on the days he had a morning shift. Though her change was a welcomed one, Tom found it bittersweet. Sweet because he truly wanted his mother to be happy and for the two of them to get along, but bitter because her happiness depended on him being the son he could never be.

———

It was Saturday night, and as Sunday morning loomed large, so did a crossroads before Tom. The Aksel Eriksson benefit concert was Sunday evening. Tom had been scheduled to work that night, but he'd managed to trade his evening shift for the morning slot, but another hurdle stood between him and the show in Pawkinsville. Unlike his short work commute, he couldn't ride his bike forty-something miles to Pawkinsville.

"Oh, by the way, not only am I *not* going to church, but I need to borrow the car to go to a heavy metal concert," he said to himself, falling back onto his bed. He could only imagine his mother's meltdown. What he couldn't imagine was his mother being reasonable.

Lying across his bed, Tom adjusted his headphones, watching the ceiling fan turn. A Walkman rested atop his chest, playing a cassette of Hellslayer's latest album. The song was called "The Devil's Due." It was about a devil coming to claim what it was owed. Over a blistering wall of guitars and thundering drums, Eriksson sang,

> *The devil gave me fortune*
> *The devil gave me fame*
> *I never thought my flesh and blood*
> *Would be the price I'd pay*

Tom drummed his fingers, wondering what, if anything, he could say to persuade his mother to let him take the car. He concocted a number of elaborate lies before considering the uncomfortable truth. If she knew how the DeVilles had behaved toward him, would *she* even want to go back? If he told her how Reverend Cope made him feel, would it mean anything? Would she even hear him, or would she choose the church over her son? After giving it some thought, he abandoned the truth, fearing he already knew who his mother would choose.

So, he turned his thoughts to Mort Mackey. He remembered the Bible Mort had given him, and what the old man had said about deserving judgment. When Mort had given him the Bible, Tom's head had been a mess of stress and anxiety, but now Mort's words rang clear as a bell: *The devil's place is in the lake of fire.* That *devil deserves it.* I *deserve it.* You *don't. Take this and be spared the coming judgment.*

"Why does Mort think he deserves judgment?" Tom wondered aloud as he rolled off his bed to dig through his mess of clothes, comics, and cassettes until he found the Bible Mort had given him. Once he'd recovered the good book from a pile of laundry, he sat on the edge of his bed and inspected the book.

"Read it *before* next Sunday," Mort had told Tom.

Tom saw tabs marking a number of pages, so he opened to the first tab and found a highlighted passage. It was in the book of Matthew, chapter four, verse one: *Then was Jesus led up of the Spirit into the wilderness to be tempted of the devil.*

"King James Version. Yikes," Tom said, finding the King's English cumbersome.

A handwritten note filled the margin beside the first verse: *I was led into the wilderness to be tempted, but the devil won. Marge's blood is on my hands.*

Who is Marge? Tom thought. *And what did Mort do to her?* Tom flipped to the next tab, which was also in the book of Matthew. Chapter seven, verse fifteen was highlighted.

Beware of false prophets, which come to you in sheep's clothing, but inwardly they are ravening wolves.

Tom remembered Mort's questioning regarding the reverend being a wolf. Tom flipped to the next tabbed passage found in the book of Luke and read under his breath, "Then entered Satan into Judas surnamed Iscariot, being of the number of the twelve." A pen line traced from "Satan" to the right margin where *J. C.* had been scribbled.

Tom lingered on the letters *J. C.* Given he was reading a Bible, his first thought was of Jesus Christ, but that made no sense. Mort wouldn't consider Jesus a wolf. Tom reread the note until another name came to mind, and his lip reflexively curled at the realization. "J. C. . . . Jesse Cope."

Tom remembered the reverend's familiar tone, calling his mother "Dotty"—a name only Tom's father had called her. Feeling his temperature rising, he flipped ahead to the next tab in the Book of Revelation. The highlighted passage read, *But the fearful, and unbelieving, and the abominable, and murderers, and whoremongers, and sorcerers, and idolaters, and all liars, shall have their part in the lake which burneth with fire and brimstone* . . .

Ignoring that the passage acknowledged the existence of "sorcerers" and all that implied, Tom's stomach twisted in an anxious knot. The initials *J. C.* appeared again in the margin beside the verse, but this time there was a second set of initials: *M. M.*

"M. M.? Mort Mackey?" Both had been aggressively circled with lines connecting *J. C.* and *M. M.* to "murderers."

"Mort is saying he and Cope are murderers. But why?" Tom asked himself. For a fleeting moment, Tom considered the possibility that Mort might've been properly dubbed "Wacky Mackey."

Tom flipped back to the first marked passage and reread the notes in order.

"What are you getting at, Mort?" Tom said aloud, growing frustrated and increasingly anxious. He fanned the pages under his thumb to look for highlighted passages he may have missed, but page after page flashed by unmarked. Though there was one thing that stood out as he fanned the pages: the back cover felt oddly stiff. Tom opened to the back cover to find a 3 x 5 photo taped inside. In the picture, a woman stood shoulder to shoulder with a man who looked like a much younger Mort Mackey. She appeared to be about the same age as Mort, with bright blue eyes and feathered, black hair. Tom noted the ring on her finger—it was hard to miss, as she stood presenting the ring to the camera. Her other hand was entwined with Mort's, and it was clear this was an engagement photo. Tom flipped to the front of the Bible. There was no photo, but there was an inscription.

To Marjory Mackey.
"This will be your year of plenty!"
Blessings,
Reverend Cope

Beside the handwritten inscription from Reverend Cope was another of Mort's notes: *2 Cor. 11:14 - Satan himself is transformed into an angel of light.* A scribbled arrow once again connected *Satan* to *Cope*.

"Cope is an asshole, but he's not *Satan*," he said, setting the Bible aside to give himself a moment to think.

Tom laid back on his bed just as the song in his headphones faded out. The cassette reached its end and stopped with a *click*. In the silence, he tried to make sense of it all. Cope was a con man preying on the vulnerable. He was slimy, manipulative, and insufferable, but a murderer? *It's not like he's hiding out or on the run*, Tom reasoned, assuming few murderers would hide out in the next town over from wherever they'd committed their crime, but the more he thought about it, the more it seemed most criminals kept up appearances until investigators closed in—at least the murderers in his mother's detective shows always stuck around. He then thought back to the Grimlock Gazette. The newspaper had quoted a source as saying the victim had been a member of a cult, but Tom didn't see Cope as a cult leader—just a grifter, and The Church of His Word was just like Christian television set in a barn. So, he tried to see the little church through the eyes of an outsider. What would that church look like to someone who'd never been to a place like that? *A small group following a charismatic leader who shouts at the devil and promises riches?* With a little reflection, Tom could see how someone might see that church as a cult.

Okay, so Cope is a grifter and the church seems a little culty, but that doesn't make him a murderer, Tom thought. *What would he stand to gain by killing his flock? You can't milk a dead cow.*

Tom considered his source. Mort was grieving his wife, convinced the reverend had killed her while at the same time claiming her blood was on his, Mort's, hands. Last Sunday had been Mort's first time at the church, yet everyone already knew him as "Wacky Mackey." Despite Tom's disdain for The Church of His Word's perverted founding family and con man evangelist, he was finding himself much more concerned with Mort.

In the mind of Mort Mackey, the Bible justified his belief that he, Mort, and Jesse Cope should burn for the death of Marjory Mackey, and though that sounded insane out loud, Tom could, from Mort's twisted perspective, understand it. The part Tom couldn't understand was Mort's guilt. Mort had called himself a murderer—a label people avoid even when they were, in fact, murderers. As Tom turned it over in his mind, a terrible possibility took shape, and Tom considered the prospect of Mort not being a murderer . . . yet. Perhaps Mort Mackey wasn't a murderer today, but maybe he will be tomorrow.

"That's a pretty good reason not to go back," Tom said, and decided neither he nor his mother should go to The Church of His Word in the morning, but it wasn't entirely up to him. As Tom tucked in under his blankets, he put his hands on his head and ran his fingers through his hair, wishing he could ask his father for advice. *Dad would know what to do.*

The longer he tossed and turned, awake and restless, the more he wanted to stop his mother from going back to that ticking time bomb of a church, but how could he persuade her not to go? Tom reached for his Walkman, turned his cassette over to side B, and hit play for a melodic lifeline back to normalcy, to give himself a break from predators, preachers, and promises of fire. It wasn't until the album reached its end, and Hellslayer played their final downbeat, that Tom fell sleep. But he hadn't passed from wakefulness into rest. He'd passed from restlessness into something vile.

The Wolves and the Sheep (Part Two)

Tom found himself back at The Church of His Word. A discordant hymn droned from the congregants as they stood in a queue for the pulpit, where an altar of flesh and bone waited, laden with cash and coin. The DeVilles stood in line with the congregants. Behind the altar of mammon, receiving the offerings, stood Reverend Cope. One by one, congregants stepped up to the altar, where Reverend Cope heard their prayer requests. Some asked for wealth, while others asked for health. One congregant hobbled forward and laid cash on the altar, hoping their hunched body would be free of its aching arthritis. Another stepped up and gave in faith, praying that the cancer would leave their grandchild, so that the boy could return to building pillow forts with his grandpa. Each needful soul gave whatever money they could as the "Lord" impressed upon their hearts. Reverend Cope received each offering gladly, taking their hands and praying with each one. But behind the reverend, a creature stood like a long shadow creeping up the barn wall. The shape was not like that of the reverend. The creature had a taller, more sinewy frame. Long, twig-like legs stretched up to a bulbous core, from which arms like the crooked branches of a barren tree angled outward, ending in gnarled claws. The head was heart-shaped and seemed too big for its body, reminding Thomas of a praying mantis.

Tom blinked and found himself at the front of the line, face-to-face with Reverend Cope. Looking into the reverend's eyes was like peering into spiraling, cavernous pits. The reverend took Tom by the shoulders, pulling him closer. Tom looked around for his mother but found himself alone. He cursed and struggled to pull free, but the reverend reaffirmed his grip on Tom's shoulders and said, "Be not afraid." Though the reverend's mouth moved, his voice carried none of the charismatic warmth Tom had heard on Sunday. Cope's voice came like a choir of people speaking at once. The voices were harmonious and pleasing to the ear. "You have been chosen to bring new life."

Tom tried to curse, to shout, to say anything, but his words stayed trapped in a mouth that couldn't open.

"Your mother will have all she asked for. She will be well taken care of," Reverend Cope said, his fingers pressing into Tom. "Your mother will know a comfortable life, and you will be married to a loving wife with two marvelous children of your own."

Tom tried to jerk his body free from Cope's grip, but it was like fighting underwater.

"And when I require you, I will come," Reverend Cope said. "I will consume you, and you will be like an ember added to the fire in my chest—the fire that sustains me. You have been given purpose, my son."

With that, Reverend Cope released Tom. The reverend threw his arms out wide, and a loud boom sounded. The barn walls blew apart, revealing a tenebrous void surrounding the church. Bands of deepest violet swirled in the void. Debris from the walls and the loose straw took flight, devoured by the darkness. The floorboards splintered, thumping as though they may break free and take flight.

The reverend continued, his euphonic, polyphonic voice resounding, "I give to you my mark."

The shadow creature behind Reverend Cope leaned forward, looming over Tom. The creature reached out its right hand and pressed a sable finger like a needle into Tom's chest. Tom clenched his teeth, unable to move and grunting in pain as the finger pierced into him. Hot liquid spread under his skin from the creature's finger. When the creature withdrew its finger, it left behind a red shape on Tom's aching flesh. The shape was that of a triangle with a jagged line splitting the middle.

"Now, awake," the reverend said and released Tom. At once, Tom shot upward into the cosmic void that churned above the church. The void swallowed Tom and he awoke with a gasp. A string of slurred, incoherent words tumbled out, as he found himself sitting upright in his bed. He looked around his bedroom, fearing the worst. After a moment, his pulse slowed, and he collapsed back into bed. It was then he noticed he'd sweat through his clothes, leaving his sheets damp. Remembering the creature's finger in his chest, he looked down, and there, on his chest, he saw the red mark—the creature's mark.

Cope is a devil, Tom thought, his pulse racing. Tom wondered what his mother had done—if she had really made a deal with a devil. "And why the hell do I have to pay for it?" he said aloud.

Tom began to feel like a lamb awaiting slaughter. He imagined his mother finding him dead. He wondered if Mort had found Marge, and then it dawned on him. If Marge was dead, and Cope was behind it, then someone close to her must've made a deal. Tom snatched up Mort's Bible and turned to the picture taped to the inside back cover. Looking more closely, he saw pen strokes protruding from behind the photo. Tom clawed at the edges of the tape till he could peel it away and free the picture. Setting the old photo aside, he found an inscription on the back cover.

I made a deal with an angel of light. I asked to find the love of my life. I didn't know the angel was a demon. He came for what I loved most as payment. Please forgive me, Marge. God knows I can't forgive myself.

"Mort made a deal," Tom said, his stomach churning. "Mom made a deal." He picked up the photo to see the happy couple. "Marge is dead." Tom swallowed hard, his stomach in his throat. "I'm going to die."

The sleepless night bled into the next morning. Tom found himself standing in the shower—for how long he couldn't say, but the hot water had gone lukewarm, and his chest was raw from scrubbing with a washcloth. Despite his efforts, the red mark on his chest remained. Memories from last Sunday's service mingled with scenes from his nightmare. The water washed over him as he thought back to the smothering press of hands when the congregation had prayed for his deliverance. The memory coalesced with images of claws like creeping shadows reaching for him. Tom stood expressionless, staring at the tile wall.

After the water had turned from lukewarm to cool, Tom shut off the shower and toweled dry.

Standing eye to eye with his reflection in the mirror, he looked to the mark on his chest—the mark denoting a devil owned him. Tom wondered if that was what demon possession actually was—a devil taking ownership of someone. Tom thought that made sense, seeing as Cope had branded Tom like cattle. Closing his eyes, Tom felt a knot in his throat. Tears wanted to come, but Tom didn't want them. He wanted to rewind time—to go back to when he was just a misunderstood teenager, before he became a misunderstood, possessed teenager.

There has to be a solution, Tom reasoned, desperately wanting a solution. He pulled on his favorite Hellslayer shirt and a pair of boxer briefs and made his way to the kitchen, wondering if he'd be safe from Reverend Cope if the reverend were locked up in prison. *Maybe someone would shiv him or something*, Tom thought, coming to a stop in the eerily undisturbed kitchen. The lights were off. There was no morning paper on the table, and the coffee pot sat empty. There were no signs of his mother at all. He stepped slow and quiet through the kitchen toward the hall that led to his mother's room, unsure of what he'd find. The worst possible scenarios played in his mind. *What if Cope is in there? What if they sealed the deal last night, and that's why I had the dream?* As he passed through the kitchen and neared the dark hall, the scrape of dragging footsteps approached. A hand appeared and flicked the lights on, causing Tom to jerk back. Indifferent, Dolores pushed past him, ambling like a zombie.

"You're up early," she said, tossing the Sunday paper on the table. It was still in its plastic sleeve. "Did you make coffee?"

Tom said nothing.

"Hello?"

Tom snapped to. "I don't drink coffee," he said, sinking into a seat at the kitchen table.

"Well, I don't eat chicken nuggets, but I made them for you for nine years. Wouldn't kill you to make your mother a pot of coffee once in a while."

As Dolores pulled the Folgers from the cabinet, Tom got up. "I'll get it, Mom."

"I've got it," she said, waving him off. "Grab a bowl of cereal or something and get ready."

"No!" The words leapt out of him loud and clear.

His mother spun around. Once the apparent surprise wore off, she planted a hand on her hip, and glared at Tom from beneath her wealth of sponge curlers. Her stare cut though him, piercing down to the bone.

The shock of his nightmare and the mark on his chest had pushed the Sunday service far from his mind, but seeing Dolores in her curlers brought him back to Mort's threat.

"Don't come to church," Mort had said last Sunday. "Judgment is coming."

"Look, Mom. I had a terrible dream, and there was a devil, and we were at church, and—" Tom stopped himself, certain his mother wouldn't find his rambling convincing, and started over. "Do you remember that old dude—Wacky Mackey? And — and the DeVilles?" He paused, waiting for her confirmation. Dolores motioned for him to continue to his point. "Well, Mackey has it out for Cope. Okay? And I— I just," he stopped, trying not to sound hysterical. "I don't think we should go to that church today."

It was clear his mother was unmoved and unconvinced. Tom watched her closer, and after a moment, he was sure she hadn't even blinked.

From under the weight of her silence, he continued, "Wacky Mackey gave me this Bible, and he'd marked certain verses in it—some crazy stuff."

With that, Dolores pounced. "There's nothing *crazy* about the Bible, and you *promised* Reverend Cope *and* the DeVilles *and* me that you'd come back this Sunday—today. You promised you would in front of the *whole* church and—"

"I never promised anything."

"You said before God—in *His* house—that you would

come back to church *today*, and you know what the Bible says about liars. They—"

"Mackey thinks Cope is a murderer," Tom said, a note of panic rising in his voice. "And I don't know if he's killed anybody, but Reverend Cope is evil, and Mort Mackey is *definitely* dangerous."

Tom fell silent, awaiting his mother's reply, but Dolores said nothing. She stood with her arms crossed and a single eyebrow raised.

"I can show you," he said. "When you see for yourself—"

"Tom," his mother said. "Mort Mackey is a quirky old man, but to say the reverend might be a murderer is just evil. He is a man of God."

Tom threw his head back, frustrated, knowing his clumsy words had failed him spectacularly.

"You are going to church this morning like you said you would," Dolores continued, her tone firm but restrained. "Reverend Cope is a good man. More than that, he is a godly man."

"Jesse Cope is *not* a good man," Tom said.

"Do you *really* think a murderer would be gathering people together to pray and worship?"

"Maybe. I don't know, but the whole church seems crazy."

"You know what this is?" she said, her jaw tight. She leveled a finger at Tom's shirt. "It's all that demonic music you listen to."

Tom rolled his eyes. "Mom. Seriously."

"It's a demonic influence—it's secular—it's straight from Hell."

"Mom—"

"It's not glorifying to God and—oh, wait," she said, pausing, leaving Tom to dread whatever revelation she thought she'd stumbled upon. "They're playing a concert today, aren't they? And that's why you're trying to get out of going to church."

"No."

"Do *not* lie to me. You need to ask yourself why the house of God scares you but a demonic rock concert doesn't."

Tom shrank into himself.

"You know that band made a deal with Satan. They said so themselves. It was on the news."

"That's just their image, Mom. They didn't *actually* make a deal with Satan."

"So, that doesn't bother you, but going to a church where souls are saved and the sick are healed bothers you?"

Tom looked up at his mother. "Who was healed?"

"No one yet, but we're believing for it," she snapped defensively.

"Okay, look," he said, certain she couldn't possibly deny the evidence drawn on his chest—the red mark over his heart. He pulled up his shirt and pointed to the mark on his chest. "You see this? I got this last night. I saw your Reverend Cope in a dream, and this demon-looking shadow thing came out of him and drew this on my chest. Right here!" He jabbed a finger at the mark on his chest.

Dolores looked beside herself but leaned in, squinted, and the shook her head. "There's nothing there."

"What?" Tom said, his voice cracking. "I'm looking right at it." He looked down to see the red triangle, split by a jagged line.

Dolores straightened up, a look of concern mingling with her anger. "There's nothing there."

For a moment, Tom felt as though he'd lost his mind. He looked between the mark on his chest and his mother's expression and couldn't reconcile the two. She clearly couldn't see it, and yet it was right there—blood red on his pale skin. Tom lowered his shirt and felt the weight of defeat.

If there'd been any hope of her trusting him, that hope had vanished.

Though he was Dolores's own flesh and blood, he was her rebellious son. And after throwing out accusations that her beloved man of God was a murderer and partially undressing to prove it with an invisible mark, he wasn't *just* her rebellious son. He was also her delusional, ungodly son. So, it was his word against the reputations of the DeVilles and Reverend Cope—respected Christians. Unlike Tom, they looked, sounded, and acted the part. As much as he wished his mother would believe him, he listened to the wrong kind of music and wore the wrong kind of clothes to be taken seriously.

"Look," he said, deflated. "I know I sound crazy, but I really don't feel safe there. I'm not going back, and you shouldn't, either. That's all I'm trying to say."

Dolores said nothing.

Tom avoided her gaze and pulled the newspaper from its plastic sleeve. He doubted she'd seriously considered a single thing he'd said and decided there was no more use in trying. Her mind was made up, but so was his. There was nothing that could get him through the doors of that church.

Dolores, with her eyes ablaze and jaw locked, jabbed a finger, accentuating every point, saying, "Either you go to church this morning—no—either you attend *regularly*, or I'm throwing out all of that demonic music. I mean every cassette, every poster, and every one of those damned shirts are gone."

Tom watched her storm out of the kitchen. Normally, he would shoot facts, reason, and other rubber bullets at her impenetrable armor. Instead, he sat alone in a mix of anger, hurt, and fear. His mind raced, looking for a way to keep her home, until the front page of the newspaper caught his eye.

Local celebrity comes home! Forget the tour bus or private plane. Pawkinsville native and the voice of Hellslayer, Aksel Eriksson, was spotted Saturday rolling through town in his '69

Mustang Mach 1. There was a picture of a Mustang parked outside a diner in Pawkinsville. Tom leaned in, squinting, hoping to see Aksel. *The rocker stopped at Deb's for steak and eggs, and signed a few autographs. When asked if he had any plans before the show, the Grammy-award-winning singer said he planned to look up an old acquaintance.*

The thrill of knowing *the* Aksel Eriksson was in the next town over quickly gave way to the crushing realization that there was no way he, Tom, could make it to the memorial concert. Frustrated, Tom looked down the page. Below the article on Aksel was a headline that read, *Search For Pawkinsville Killer Continues.* Beneath the headline was a picture of an older woman. She had familiar blue eyes, a round nose, and feathered gray hair. Beneath the picture was a name: *Marjorie Mackey.*

Tom's mouth fell open. "Holy shit," he said a bit too loud, drawing a reaction from his mother down the hall, which he ignored as he read on.

Authorities have released the identity of the victim of what appeared to be a ritualistic sacrifice. The victim was Pawkinsville's own Marjorie Mackey.

Mrs. Mackey leaves behind her husband, Mortimer Mackey. The two had been members of an outreach ministry led by traveling evangelist, the Reverend Jesse Cope. Reverend Cope is said to have left his congregation in Pawkinsville days before the death of Marjory Mackey and is currently wanted for questioning. Authorities are asking anyone who may have information to call the tip hotline provided below.

"Hello?" Dolores shouted from the opposite side of the kitchen table.

Tom gave a start. He looked up to find his mother, with her hands on her hips and glaring. Whatever she'd been saying, he hadn't heard a word of it.

"Are you ignoring me?" she said.

Feeling emboldened, Tom spun the paper around and planted a finger where the tip hotline was printed in bold. "Sorry. I was just distracted by your *reverend*. Maybe we should ask him why the police want him for questioning."

Dolores rolled her eyes and looked to see for herself. There was a long pause before she responded. "Well, it seems he knew the poor lady. The police always question those close to the victim. They probably had trouble finding him, as he is a fairly private man."

"That's Mort's dead wife," Tom said, pointing to the picture of Marjory Mackey. "Reverend Cope is wanted for questioning, and Mort thinks Cope did it."

"It says they want to ask him some questions. It doesn't say he's wanted for murder, but if it did, I wouldn't be surprised. The media lies and—"

"The police—not the media—say he is *wanted* for questioning," Tom cut in.

"The secular news media is anti-Christian. They target Christians all the time. Now, go get changed and put on a *nice* shirt. I don't want to hear another word of it."

Tom watched his mother march down the hall and vanish into her bedroom. *Like a lamb to slaughter*, he thought and cursed his mother's stubbornness. Knowing he couldn't let her fall victim to Cope or Mackey or whatever wolf awaited her at The Church of His Word, Tom thought through ways to keep her home. Slashing her tires could work, but then she'd just call someone from the church to pick her up, and his last hope of making the benefit concert would be lost. The idea of tying her up or locking her away for the morning seemed like the kind of thing their relationship couldn't come back from. After all, what if absolutely nothing happened at church this morning?

Tom returned to the newspaper and eyed the tip hotline. But what if the police took Cope in? Surely that would prevent Mort from pulling something at church. After a glance down the hall to be sure his mother's door was closed, Tom hurried to the corded phone on the wall and dialed the hotline.

After ringing twice, someone answered with a drowsy, "Hello?"

"I'm calling with information about Jesse Cope," Tom said.

After what felt like far too long of a pause, the voice on the other end said, "Please hold."

As Tom held the line, his mother called out from her bedroom, "We're leaving in two minutes!"

The voice came over the phone, but as Tom craned his neck to be sure his mother's door was still shut, he missed what had been said.

"Sorry," Tom said quietly, turning toward the corner of the kitchen—away from his mother's end of the trailer. "I missed that."

"I said, how may I help you?" a man said.

"I know where you can find Jesse Cope," Tom said.

"Okay," the man replied and grunted, as though shifting in his seat. He seemed unmoved by the urgency in Tom's voice. The man cleared his throat and continued, "First, let me get your name."

"Tom Dalton. Listen—Cope is staying at the DeVilles' farm. He's preaching in their barn, where a crazy old man— Mort Mackey—said he knows Cope is a murderer. They're all going to be at—"

"Whoa, whoa, whoa. Slow down," the man said. "Now, you said your name was what again?"

"Listen to me," Tom said in an urgent whisper. "Jesse Cope is at the DeVilles' barn. You need to send the cops. Someone might die if you don't—"

The line died. Tom turned to see his mother with her

finger on the receiver. His heart beat in his throat, the phone trembling in his hand.

"We are going to church," his mother said, her voice dangerously stern yet calm. "You are not chatting with your friends, and I am *not* playing games. Go get dressed, and let's go."

Tom stood stunned, slowly returning the phone to the receiver and starting for his room. His mother's voice carried a note of finality beyond anything his obstinate behavior had ever evoked before. So, he grabbed a red and black flannel button-down to cover up his Hellslayer shirt. As he buttoned up, he read the lyrics printed down the front in a font that looked like dripping blood.

Evil surrounds
But stand your ground
The battle begins
Blood and fire
Light the pyre
Don't let the devil win

Tom took a deep breath and determined that nobody—not Mackey, the DeVilles, or the reverend—would harm him or his mother without a knock-down, drag-out fight.

Dolores and Tom sat in silence for the entire drive to church. To fill the silence, Dolores had put on a sermon on cassette. An evangelist, known for her eight-hundred-dollar suits, blamed the audience for their poverty, chronic illness, depression, and any other problem they had, saying they needed to think and speak positively and simply believe. This sermon was, of course, delivered after those very people in the audience had been implored to give that it may be given back to them. Tom, who had a lot to say on the matter, bit his tongue.

"You overthink things," Dolores said out of the blue as they pulled into the empty plot of land being used as a parking lot for the church. She offered her son a patronizing look and a stick of sugar-free spearmint gum. "Don't be afraid to let go and let God."

Tom declined the gum and got out of the car. As the two approached the barn doors, his blood simmered. *If she thought for herself for even one goddamned minute, we wouldn't be in this powder keg of crazy.*

Tom and Dolores approached the open barn doors and stepped into The Church of His Word. The last time he'd been here, he'd worn his angst on his sleeve. Like sharks to chum, the church had swarmed him, so he put on a smile and even waved to a few congregants. Dolores broke off from Tom and crossed over to Reverend Cope, putting Tom's forced smile to the test. The reverend wore a gray, pinstripe suit and waited between the apple crate pulpit and the back wall, where the crosscut saw, axe, and pitchfork hung. Reverend Cope lit up at the sight of Dolores—though for a heartbeat, his eyes moved beyond Dolores to catch Tom's. Tom blinked, as he was certain the reverend's eyes, if only for a moment, had appeared completely black.

"Tom!" Mrs. DeVille called, approaching in a pantsuit of thin, white linen with a low cut, undersized blouse beneath a matching, white linen blazer. The buttons on the blouse were earning their keep, struggling to contain Mrs. DeVille's expensive endowments, between which a bejeweled, glittering cross hung from a delicate, gold chain. She took Tom's hands in hers and pulled him in closer. "We are overjoyed to have you."

A hand landed on the small of Tom's back. "My sheep know my voice and follow me," Mr. DeVille said, appearing at Tom's side. Mr. DeVille wore a tailored, sharkskin suit. He seemed to notice Tom eyeing his suit and proudly confirmed, "It's Italian," and rubbed Tom's back.

Tom shifted uneasily. Though there were only two of them, he felt surrounded.

"Come on, dear," Mrs. DeVille said, entwining her arm with Tom's. "You're sitting with us as our guest."

Tom's mouth opened and closed, searching for his voice. He glanced around, hoping his mother might see the DeVilles' paws all over him, but she was engaged in conversation with Reverend Cope. Her back was to Tom, and before he knew it, he was seated with the DeVilles in the front row. Maybe he was overwhelmed, or perhaps it was how effortlessly the DeVilles had swooped in, but Tom wondered if he'd left the determined, courageous version of himself back in his bedroom.

Mrs. DeVille prattled on about the body of Christ and how Tom was like Christ and she was like a bride or something. Tom wasn't really listening, and he didn't care. His attention was fixed on his mother. Dolores's conversation with the reverend ended with the two nodding agreeably. The reverend took her hands in his, and the pair joined in prayer. As the two concluded with a loud amen, Tom's chest burned.

Tom's hands balled into fists. Dolores turned, her countenance lifted, and waved to Tom. Tom forced a smile and patted the empty seat to his right, while Mrs. DeVille sat on his left, unnecessarily close so that her hip pressed against his.

"I talked with Reverend Cope," Dolores said, taking her seat. "He explained everything."

Tom glared back at his mother as she sat and folded her hands in her lap, content.

"And?" Tom said.

At once, his mother shushed him, and Mrs. DeVille gripped high on his thigh and squeezed, also shushing him.

Tom stiffened up, hands in his lap. He pursed his lips, so as to trap the fount of profanities percolating inside of him.

The reverend stepped up behind his makeshift lectern, gripped the edges and put on the look of a man burdened.

"Family," Reverend Cope began, "I have a confession to make."

At this, the twelve congregants in attendance fell silent, all eyes fixed on the reverend.

Reverend Cope continued, "There's a good chance you all saw this morning's paper. If you didn't, you'll hear about it one way or another. I believe the best thing to do is to face this sort of thing head-on. So, it is with a heavy heart that I confess. Yes. I was a shepherd to Mrs. Marjory Mackey, who was found dead in Pawkinsville. My heart is broken and my spirit grieves —not only for her—but also for the loved ones she left behind."

Reverend Cope paused, looking toward the back of the church. Tom wondered if the reverend was eyeing Mort and made to look over his shoulder for the old man, but Mrs. DeVille caught Tom's gaze with what she clearly meant as a smoldering look. Tom smiled uncomfortably and faced forward.

The reverend blotted his eyes with his handkerchief, though Tom hadn't seen a single tear.

"I knew her," Reverend Cope said. "I *was* her shepherd, and . . . I failed her. But to be absent from our bodies is to what, church?"

"To be present with the Lord," the church said.

The reverend continued, "Now, I have tried—*really* tried —to warn each and every one of you. That ol' devil comes to steal, to kill, and to destroy. That attack on our dear sister Marjory is a reminder of why we must remain vigilant. The Bible says to be wary of false prophets, for they come as sheep in God's flock, but really, they are ravenous wolves."

A chair scraped along the floor in the back, prompting the congregation to turn toward the sound. Looking back, Tom saw Mort rise unsteadily to his feet and hobble forward. Every eye in the place followed Mort as he made his way up the center aisle. Tension mounted as the old man approached the reverend. It appeared there'd be a confrontation of sorts, but to the apparent surprise of all, Mort Mackey didn't stop. He walked right past Reverend Cope to the wall where the tools hung. The church sat in strained silence, as the old man lifted the pitch fork off of its hooks and turned to face the congregation. Not a soul moved and hardly an eye blinked. Tom had stopped breathing, and he felt certain he wasn't the only one wondering what Wacky Mackey intended to do with the pitchfork. Reverend Cope seemed to be asking himself the same question as he stood frozen, looking between the three prongs of the pitchfork and the unsettlingly stone-faced man holding it.

Mort turned and looked at the congregation. There was no grand speech, no tears, and no plea for understanding. The old man straightened his thick, smudgy glasses, squinted at the congregation and said, "Judgment." The word percolated among the congregation in questioning whispers, as Mort passed down the aisle for the back of the barn.

"Brother Mort," the reverend began once Mort was a safe distance away. "I am heartbroken over the loss of your wife, but I ask you to stay, please. Let us lay hands on you and—"

But the reverend's words were cut short, as Mort, with a strained grunt, slammed the barn doors shut behind him, causing the congregation to flinch.

"Folks," Reverend Cope said, "would you join me in praying for Brother Mort? Let's lift him up. He needs the healing hand of the Lord now more than ever."

As heads bowed and hands raised, Tom thought he heard something like chains clinking and looked back at the doors, but whatever he'd heard had been drowned in the din of prayer. After a resounding "Amen," the reverend segued to the offering. Reverend Cope brimmed with enthusiasm as he admonished the congregation on being cheerful givers, as though a grieving member of the congregation hadn't just exited the church with a pitchfork in hand.

As congregants reached for their purses and wallets with almost Pavlovian obedience, Tom noticed a few of them seemed distracted. They were sniffing at the air, looking curious. They then turned and asked those seated around them if they smelled it, too. Tom joined in and sniffed the air. He smelled the usual blend of hay, old wood, and the headache-inducing bouquet of perfumes, but then something unmistakable wafted by.

Reverend Cope didn't seem to notice anything unusual as he continued his impassioned plea for the congregants to give a sacrificial offering, so that he could afford a proper vehicle— a vehicle worthy of God's service that would represent the Lord well. The reverend said that when he'd inquired of the Lord, the Lord had said, despite the reverend's protests, that he should have a Mercedes Benz.

As the reverend justified his "need" for such a car, he was cut short when a man in the congregation shot up to his feet and said, "Is that gasoline?"

A few more voices spoke up, agreed, and in a blink, the church found itself teetering on the edge of panic.

Reverend Cope hurried out from behind his lectern, arms spread, in an attempt to calm his flock. "Now, hold on everybody. Let's get these doors open and let some fresh air in. I'm sure everything is perfectly fine." The reverend hastened to the barn doors. Taking hold, he pushed and pulled and shook the doors, but they refused to budge. After a moment, he looked over his shoulder and motioned for Mr. DeVille to join him.

Mr. DeVille hopped up and rushed to the reverend's side.

As the congregation grew more restless, Tom leaned over to his mother and said, "It's gotta be Mort. He locked the doors."

"You don't know that," she replied.

Tom gave her a look.

"I'm sure the reverend and Mr. DeVille have it under control."

"Those guys?" Tom said, thumbing toward the pair struggling feebly with the unmoving doors.

His mother looked back, the sight bringing an apparent flicker of doubt.

"Mort?" Mr. DeVille called through the door. "Is that you?"

"Yeah, it's me!" Mort shouted back.

Tom gave his mother an 'I told you so' look that his mother stubbornly ignored.

"Did you lock the doors?" Mr. DeVille said.

"Sure did!" Mort said.

Reverend Cope and Mr. DeVille looked at each other before the reverend continued, "Well, now, Mort—"

But the reverend was cut short when an elderly woman in the front row shouted, "Sweet Jesus!" and all eyes snapped to her. "Wacky Mackey is gonna burn us alive!"

"Mort?" Reverend Cope snapped. "Did you start a fire?"

"Nope!"

"Oh, thank God," Mr. DeVille said, dropping his head in relief.

Reverend Cope turned to the congregation and raised a soothing hand. "It's all right. Mort didn't start a fire."

The congregation seemed to relax a bit.

Mort continued, "*You* told me I'd find the love of my life, but you didn't tell me what it'd cost. *You* started the fire when you killed my precious Marge!"

A flood of gasoline spilled in from under the barn doors, pooling around Mr. DeVille's and Reverend Cope's feet.

"Holy hell!" Mr. DeVille shouted as Reverend Cope shoved him aside, causing Mr. DeVille to slip and fall into the puddle of gas. Mr. DeVille cursed in pain before rolling over to plead for mercy. "Wait, Mort! Let me go. I had nothing to do with your wife."

Reverend Cope bolted through the church away from the doors. He made it to the far wall as a chest-shaking *boom* sent congregants falling to the floor. The barn doors blew apart as a fireball erupted. The fire roared in on the gas that had pooled inside the barn.

Mr. DeVille got to his feet amongst the flames, legs ablaze. Mrs. DeVille shrieked, recoiling at the sight of her husband.

"Do something, Vicky!" Mr. DeVille said, his arms flailing as he stumbled forward.

The sight of Mr. DeVille on fire ensured any hope of an orderly escape had, much like his tailored Italian slacks, gone up in smoke. One congregant, a six-foot, potbellied man in khakis and a light blue button-down, slung a folding chair, clearly aiming across the room for one of only two windows in the barn. The throw fell painfully short, and the chair bodied the elderly woman in the front row. The old lady crumpled, and the man yelled, "Move, idiots!" and let fly another folding chair. This time, his aim was true. The chair crashed through the window, letting in a rush of air and feeding the flames. Loose hay that lie gathered in the corners went up like kindling. Smoke billowed overhead, and the fire raged, lapping up the old barn walls. Tom stood, mouth slack and lost in the moment, until Reverend Cope charged in, shoved Tom to the ground, and took hold of Dolores. Tom stayed down as the air had grown hot—nearly too hot to breathe. He quickly pulled off his button down and held it up to his nose, hoping to breathe clearer.

"Dotty!" Reverend Cope said, pulling Dolores away from Tom. Tom shot out a hand and caught the reverend by his ankle. Cope twisted in place, his face flush and eyes black. He cursed and delivered a swift kick to Tom's head, sending Tom back. Writhing, head in hands, Tom attempted to shout for his mother.

Mrs. DeVille stumbled toward Tom. She looked disoriented as she tripped over him, landing face first on the floorboards. The brutal crunch was followed by a moment of silence and then a high-pitched scream. The scream joined the sound of chairs tumbling as congregants crashed about.

"Someone call the fire department!" one man howled.

"Just be calm!" a woman screamed, her voice cracking.

The elderly woman, who'd taken a folding chair to the head, struggled to her feet and pointed to the window, saying, "The window's open!"

The man who'd thrown the chairs shoved his way through the flock, charging toward the broken window, but as he reached it, a pitchfork met him head on. The man ducked aside, narrowly missing the prongs.

"No one escapes the judgment," Mort said, thrusting the pitchfork through the open window repeatedly.

The smoke grew thicker, and the flock of lost sheep churned in the chaos. Tom crawled toward the spot where he'd last seen Cope, hoping to pry his mother from his grip. Though Tom's voice was hoarse from the smoke, he made to call for her. There was no discernible reply amidst the pandemonium, and Tom found himself straining for his next breath, until what little breath he could muster burned in his chest.

Mort shouted from outside the broken window. "Murderers and liars shall have their place in the lake which burneth with eternal fire!"

Tom felt lightheaded. Mr. DeVille stood, nearly nude, having removed all of his gas-soaked clothing save for his white briefs. He limped toward Tom, stepping over Mrs. DeVille, who laid on her side with blood running from her broken nose. Mr. DeVille reached the back of the barn and braced himself on the wall, gasping for breath. His flesh was bright red, his hair singed. The congregants were on the floor, crawling about, running into each other and getting nowhere.

Tom slumped to the floor, feeling weak. His thoughts meandered, slipping from the present to thoughts of Heaven. He'd heard of streets of gold, which he'd always considered a relatively soft choice of metal for critical infrastructure. He'd been told of treasures in Heaven, and saw believers vying for bejeweled crowns to wear in their mansions. This had always led Tom to wonder why Heaven was always pitched as a gold-plated, white-washed, suburban utopia, and why sex and rock and roll had been relegated to Hell.

What exactly do people do in Heaven forever? Tom wondered. As his head swam and thoughts grew unfocused, the fiery heat swelled, joined by the rising sound of pounding drums. Maybe Heaven did have rock and roll, or maybe he was on his way to Hell? As the drums played louder, he felt more certain he was slipping into Hell. The beat was too good. The source of the music sped closer, until the thunder of a V8, followed by the sound of skidding tires, triggered Tom's fight or flight instinct, and he scrambled away from the rising sound.

The skidding sound came to an abrupt end as a car crashed through the back wall of the barn. The vehicle collided with Mr. DeVille, sending splinters of wood shrapnel flying along with the zombie-like rag doll form of Mr. DeVille. He soared through the barn, shrieking, and landed with a thud in the gas-fueled puddle of flames he'd escaped only moments ago.

Looking to the source of the crash, Tom saw smoke swirl, peeling back to reveal the chrome front end of a Mustang Mach 1. The driver's side door swung open. The music trapped inside the car was set free, and the primal howl of rock and roll invaded the church. A black, alligator skin boot hit the ground, and a man stepped out into the smoke. The man was tall and burly with long, black hair and thick mutton chops. He was shirtless, with a black leather vest covered in patches. His large, horned skull belt buckle glinted above faded, gray jeans.

Congregants started crawling toward the car, but not Tom. He sat gawking, doubting his eyes.

"Jesse!" the dark-haired man shouted over the chaos.

There was no mistaking the chesty, booming voice.

"Aksel Eriksson," Tom breathed.

"Jesse Cope!" Aksel called out. He withdrew a flask, took a swig, held the drink in his mouth, and tossed the flask aside. Noticing the axe hanging on the wall, he crossed over, took the axe, and spit his mouthful over the head of the axe. Aksel held the head up to a nearby flame and it ignited. "You remember our deal?"

Tom turned to see Jesse Cope standing amidst the smoke and flames, Dolores cradled in his arms.

"Your payment isn't due," Jesse replied in a bargaining tone. "I'm certain we can work something out if—"

"Naw," Aksel said, working his grip on the axe like a hungry batter warming up. "The situation's changed."

Reverend Cope dropped Dolores and threw up his hands up. "If you kill me, I will come back in one hundred years, and—"

"I'll be dead," Aksel said.

"Then I'll hunt your children," the reverend said, his voice twisting into a guttural snarl.

"And they'll be ready for ya," Aksel said, raising the axe over his head.

"Wait!" Jesse shouted, his words resounding in a chorus of voices.

Aksel paused. "Everyone is so scared of devils, but you're

all cowards." And with that, Aksel Eriksson brought the flaming axe down. Jesse threw his hands up defensively, but the axe cut through his hands and sank into his head. A fount of black smoke erupted from Jesse Cope's skull. Jesse's lips peeled away from his teeth, the flesh around his mouth splitting. His eyes rolled back and something like a quartet of death rattles inharmoniously poured out.

Aksel wrenched his axe free, leaving the body to collapse. He looked down at Dolores and around at the surrounding chaos. Aksel tossed the axe into the flames and gathered Dolores in his arms. Turning, he noticed Tom. He gave an approving nod to Tom's shirt and then looked to Tom and said, "Can you walk?"

Tom heard Aksel, but his mind was slow, so he sat silent with his jaw slack and eyes unblinking.

"I'll come back for ya," Aksel said, and marched out of the barn with the unconscious Dolores in his arms.

After a moment, Tom gathered his wits and turned to crawl out of the barn. Nearby, the elderly woman called out incoherently. She was flat on her back, reaching toward the exit. Tom made to crawl toward her, when a pair of snakeskin boots stepped into view. Aksel knelt down beside the woman and scooped her up. He turned to Tom and nodded toward the large opening the Mustang had made in the side of the barn. Tom nodded in reply and started crawling toward the car, but along the way, he found Aksel's discarded flask. Tom grabbed it, tucked it into his pocket, and joined the other congregants as they stumbled out of the barn into fresh air.

Once outside, Tom hobbled past the others, including Mrs. DeVille, who laid in the grass with her head in her hands, lamenting having not updated her late husband's will. Continuing forward, Tom found Aksel had laid Dolores down in a patch of green grass beneath a birch tree.

"I think everyone's out," Aksel said, approaching Tom and his mother.

"Everyone except Mr. DeVille. He was on fire, and I think you hit him with your car," Tom said.

"Damn," Aksel said. "Was he a friend?"

Tom shook his head. "He was a friend of Cope's."

"Ah," Aksel said. "Fuck 'im."

Tom nodded, taking his mother's hand.

"She'll be all right, kid," Aksel said.

"Thanks to you," Tom said, looking up at Aksel. "I was useless."

Aksel eyed Tom for a moment and then looked back at the inferno. The barn collapsed, sending plumes of ash and cinder into the air. Tom and Aksel watched for a moment before turning to each other.

"You stuck by your mom," Aksel said. "You did good."

Dolores shifted and groaned, planting a hand on her forehead.

"Mom?" Tom said. "Are you okay?"

Her eyes cracked open, squinting in the sunlight. "Where are we?"

"At church," Tom said.

"Oh," she said, sounding relieved. "Did the Lord move?"

"Something like that," Tom said.

"Why do I smell smoke?" Dolores said.

Tom began to tell her about Mort, the fire, and all that had transpired, but it seemed to be too much for her in the moment, so he thought it better to save the story for another time and summed it up with, "Basically, Mort burned down the church."

Emergency sirens sounded in the distance. Tom wondered if it was in response to the tip he'd called in earlier, or if someone had seen the smoke and dialed 9-1-1.

"Just lie still, Mom. Help is on the way," Tom said.

"And that's my cue," Aksel said, straightening up and brushing ash and soot off his jeans.

"Wait—why?" Tom said.

Aksel replied in a low voice, "The cops won't understand why I had to split the good reverend's head."

"Oh, yeah," Tom said. "Wait. Why *did* you come for Cope?"

"Jesse was the devil I made a deal with. He gave me rock and roll fame, and in return I promised to give him my first born. Thing is, I didn't plan on having kids when I made the deal, so I thought I was being pretty slick." Aksel shrugged. "But a lot changes in thirteen years."

Tom nodded.

"Turns out I'm not the eternal bachelor I thought I was. I've become a family man with one on the way—a baby girl. We're gonna name her Astrid. She's just a little peanut right now, but I'd kill for that little peanut."

Dolores popped up, looking disoriented. "Who's killing what now?"

"Nobody, Mom," Tom said.

"Okay," she said, settling back down.

"What'd Cope want with my mom?" Tom asked.

"Devils are always making deals. They have to. Whatever they get out of the deal keeps them alive and attached to our world."

"I think my mom made a deal."

"If she did, the deal's off now, or at least for a hundred years."

"Why a hundred years?"

"I don't know. It's just what the bastard said before I axed him." Aksel looked toward the main road as the chorus of emergency sirens grew louder. "Okay, kid. I really gotta go."

"Oh," Tom said and held the flask out to Aksel. "This belongs to you."

Aksel looked from the flask to Tom. "Keep it."

"Really?" Tom said.

Aksel nodded.

"What's in it?" Tom asked. "Holy water?"

Aksel shook his head. "Holy whiskey."

"You can sanctify whiskey?"

"Sure," Aksel said, starting toward his car. "If you can sanctify a sinner, you can sanctify whiskey."

Aksel climbed into his fastback Mustang. Hellslayer's latest album came on when the V8 engine ignited. As Aksel pulled away and the rumble faded from earshot, Tom thought about how Aksel's deal with Cope had been broken. He pulled at the collar of his shirt and looked down at his chest where the red mark had been. After a heartbeat, he smiled. He actually had gotten what he'd wanted, after all. That devil, Jesse Cope, was gone. The DeVilles were more or less done with. He was no longer possessed, and most importantly, his mother was safe. He no longer had to worry about his mother falling victim to some evil hiding in a church.

Dolores sat up, massaging her temples.

"Feeling any better?" Tom asked.

Dolores nodded, albeit gingerly. "You know, as I've been lying here, I've been thinking."

Tom scooted closer, putting an arm around his mother. "What've you been thinking?"

"Maybe we *should* try a more traditional church."

"Okay," Tom said, though church was the last thing he wanted to think about. "What'd you have in mind?"

Dolores looked at her son, and said, "How about St. Julian's?"